Extraordinary Acclaim for Lawrence Block's

A DROP OF THE HARD STUFF

"Good to the last drop.... A Great American Crime Novel.... The perfect introduction to Scudder's shadow-strewn world and the pleasures of Block's crisp yet brooding prose....*A Drop of the Hard Stuff* reads like it's been jolted by factory-fresh defibrillator pads, as Scudder recalls his first nerve-rattling year of sobriety. Block makes the hard work of sobriety totally gripping.... A bracing distillation of Block's powers."

—Ed Park, *Time*

"Moving....Elegiac....Satisfying....Right up there with Mr. Block's best." —Tom Nolan, *Wall Street Journal*

"Smart and cunning.... Reminds us that the really good writers can make even familiar situations seem newfound and energized." —George Meyer, *Tampa Tribune*

"For my money, no one writes a better private detective novel than Mr. Block, and his Matt Scudder books, taken as a whole, are classics. In *Drop,* a childhood friend of Scudder's tries to atone for his past sins, causing a ripple effect of violence. This new entry is a look back in the tradition of his masterpiece *When the Sacred Ginmill Closes,* and a very fine addition to Block's body of work. Put down the trendy, translated crime novel you're struggling with and pick this up to see how it's done for real. Block is the modern hard-boiled master." —George Pelecanos

"The prose, as always, is like the club soda Scudder sips in the opening pages: cool, fizzy, and completely refreshing."

—*Booklist* (starred review)

"Sometimes you open up a book and you just know: You're in the hands of a master.... In the case of Lawrence Block's latest Matthew Scudder novel, the tip-off is a brazenly simple plot premise, executed faultlessly. The story line of *A Drop of the Hard Stuff* is like that apocryphal tale of Leonardo da Vinci drawing a perfect circle freehand. There's no need for red herrings or sub-plots here. Block, who years ago was rightly anointed a Grand Master by the Mystery Writers of America, has so perfected a pared-down, hard-boiled style that this story — about good intentions that backfire, fatally — seems to tell itself."

—Maureen Corrigan, *Washington Post*

"Block is a mesmerizing raconteur, the kind who collects the stories he hears on the street and then reprises the voices of the storytellers, many of them long gone.... An elegiac note reverberates throughout the book ... a lament for all the old familiar things that are now almost lost, almost forgotten."

—Marilyn Stasio, *New York Times Book Review*

"A satisfyingly adult story, with a believable number of false starts and loose ends, as it pays tribute to the power of persistence and acceptance."   —Margaret Quamme, *Columbus Dispatch*

"An intimate look into the darker crevices of an alcoholic struggling with himself.... I always sensed that it was possible Scudder could slip off the edge at any moment, and this book dances that edge like Nureyev."

—Randy Michael Signor, *Chicago Sun-Times*

"Potent...pensive and philosophical, at times bleak, and at others surprisingly warm and human. It's written with the worldly wisdom and relaxed dexterity that remind us why Lawrence Block is truly a master novelist. I could pile on adjectives, but they'd not only fail to do justice to his accomplishments, they wouldn't befit his lean prose, which doesn't rely on a thesaurus to make its impact...as rich and rewarding as it is devastating—and I mean that in the best way possible. If you haven't read any of the Scudder books yet, this might be the perfect way to introduce yourself to one of crime fiction's most enduring characters."   —www.PulpSerenade.com

"Tense and satisfying."   —Bruce DeSilva, Associated Press

"Lonesome, wintry, and compassionate...guaranteed to get under your skin."   —*Kirkus Reviews*

"There is no one better at writing crime fiction than Block. Scudder is the best private eye of the last fifty years."
                                                        —Brian Koppelman

A DROP
OF THE
HARD STUFF

Other Novels

A Diet of Treacle • *After the First Death* • *Ariel* • *Campus Tramp*
Cinderella Sims • *Coward's Kiss* • *Deadly Honeymoon* • *The Girl with the
Long Green Heart* • *Grifter's Game* • *Killing Castro* • *Lucky at Cards*
Not Comin' Home to You • *Random Walk* • *Ronald Rabbit Is a Dirty Old
Man* • *Small Town* • *The Specialists* • *Such Men Are Dangerous*
The Triumph of Evil • *You Could Call It Murder* • *Getting
Off* (as Jill Emerson)

Collected Short Stories

Sometimes They Bite • *Like a Lamb to Slaughter* • *Some Days You Get
the Bear* • *Ehrengraf for the Defense* • *One Night Stands* • *The Lost
Cases of Ed London* • *Enough Rope*

Books for Writers

Writing the Novel: From Plot to Print • *Telling Lies for Fun and Profit*
Spider, Spin Me a Web • *Write for Your Life*

Written for Performance

Tilt (episodic television) • *How Far?* (one-act play)
My Blueberry Nights (film)

Memoir

Step by Step

Anthologies Edited

Death Cruise • *Master's Choice* • *Opening Shots* • *Master's Choice,
Volume 2* • *Speaking of Lust* • *Opening Shots, Volume 2* • *Speaking
of Greed* • *Blood on Their Hands* • *Gangsters, Swindlers, Killers,
and Thieves* • *Manhattan Noir* • *Manhattan Noir, Volume 2*

A DROP
OF THE
HARD STUFF

═══ A MATTHEW SCUDDER NOVEL ═══

LAWRENCE BLOCK

MULHOLLAND BOOKS

LITTLE, BROWN AND COMPANY

NEW YORK BOSTON LONDON

Mulholland Books / Little, Brown and Company
Hachette Book Group
237 Park Avenue, New York, NY 10017
www.hachettebookgroup.com

Originally published in hardcover by Mulholland Books / Little, Brown and Company, May 2011
First Mulholland Books paperback edition, February 2012

Mulholland Books is an imprint of Little, Brown and Company, a division of Hachette Book Group, Inc. The Mulholland Books name and logo are trademarks of Hachette Book Group, Inc.

The publisher is not responsible for websites (or their content) that are not owned by the publisher.

The Hachette Speakers Bureau provides a wide range of authors for speaking events. To find out more, go to www.hachettespeakersbureau.com or call (866) 376-6591.

Library of Congress Cataloging-in-Publication Data
Block, Lawrence.
   A drop of the hard stuff : a Matthew Scudder novel / by Lawrence Block. — 1st ed.
      p. cm.
   ISBN 978-0-316-12733-2 (hc) / 978-0-316-17804-4 (lp) / 978-0-316-12731-8 (pb)
   1. Scudder, Matt (Fictitious character) — Fiction.   2. Private investigators — Fiction.   3. Alcoholics — Fiction.   4. Murder — Investigation — Fiction.
I. Title.
   PS3552.L63D76 2011
   813'.54 — dc22   2010041792

10   9   8   7   6   5   4   3

RRD-H

Printed in the United States of America

This is for MEGAN and CRAIG

As the governor of North Carolina
said to the governor of South Carolina,
"It's a long time between drinks."

A DROP
OF THE
HARD STUFF

Late One Night...

"I've often wondered," Mick Ballou said, "how it would all have gone if I'd taken a different turn."

We were at Grogan's Open House, the Hell's Kitchen saloon he's owned and operated for years. The gentrification of the neighborhood has had its effect on Grogan's, although the bar hasn't changed much inside or out. But the local hard cases have mostly died or moved on, and the crowd these days is a gentler and more refined bunch. There's Guinness on draft, and a good selection of single-malt Scotches and other premium whiskeys. But it's the joint's raffish reputation that draws them. They get to point out the bullet holes in the walls, and tell stories about the notorious past of the bar's owner. Some of the stories are true.

They were all gone now. The barman had closed up, and the chairs were on top of the tables so they'd be out of the way when the kid came in at daybreak to sweep up and mop the floor. The door was locked, and all the lights out but the leaded-glass fixture over the *table where we sat with our Waterford tumblers. There was whiskey in Mick's, club soda in mine.*

Our late nights have grown less frequent in recent years. We're older, and if we're not quite inclined to move to Florida and order the Early Bird Special at the nearest family restaurant, neither are we much given to talking the night away and greeting the dawn wide-eyed. We're both too old for that.

He drinks less these days. A year or so back he got married, to a much younger woman named Kristin Hollander. The union astonished almost everyone—but not my wife, Elaine, who swears she saw it coming—and it could hardly fail to change him, if only because it gave him a reason to go home at the day's end. He still drinks twelve-year-old Jameson, and drinks it neat, but he doesn't drink as much of it, and there are days when he doesn't drink at all. "I still have a taste for it," he has said, "but for years I had a deep thirst, and the thirst has left me. I couldn't tell you where it's gone."

In earlier years, it was not that unusual for us to sit up all night, talking the hours away and sharing the occasional long silence, each of us drinking his chosen beverage. At dawn he'd don the blood-stained butcher's apron that had belonged to his father. He'd go to the Butchers' Mass at St. Bernard's, in the meatpacking district. Once in a while I'd keep him company.

Things change. The meatpacking district is trendy now, a yuppie bastion, and most of the firms that gave the area its name have gone out of business, their premises converted to restaurants and apartments. St. Bernard's, long an Irish parish, is the new home of Our Lady of Guadalupe.

I can't remember the last time I saw Mick wearing that apron.

This was one of our rare late nights, and I suppose we both felt the need for it, or we'd have gone home by now. And Mick had turned reflective.

"A different turn," I said. "What do you mean?"

"There are times," he said, "when it seems to me that there was nothing for it, that I was destined to follow the one particular course. I lose sight of it these days, because my business interests are all as clean as a hound's tooth. Why a hound's tooth, have you ever wondered?"

"No idea."

"I'll ask Kristin," he said, "and she'll sit down at the computer and pop up with the answer in thirty seconds. That's if I remember to ask her." He smiled at a private thought. "What I lose sight of," he said, "is that I became a career criminal. Now I was hardly a trail-blazer in that respect. I lived in a neighborhood where crime was the leading occupation. The surrounding streets were a sort of vocational high school."

"And you graduated with honors."

"I did. I might have been valedictorian, if they'd had such a thing on offer for young thieves and hoodlums. But, you know, not every boy on our block wound up leading a life of villainy. My father was respectable. He was—well, I'll honor his memory enough not to say what he was, but I've told you about him."

"You have."

"All the same, he was a respectable man. He got up every morning and went to work. And the road my brothers took was a higher one than mine. One a priest—well, that didn't last, but only because he lost his faith. And John, a great success in business and a pillar of his community. And Dennis, the poor lad, who died in Vietnam. I told you how I went down to Washington just to see his name on that memorial."

"Yes."

"I'd have made a terrible priest. I wouldn't even find a welcome diversion in molesting altar boys. And I can't imagine myself kissing asses and counting dollars like my brother John. But can you guess the thought I've had? That I might have taken the road you took."

"And become a cop?"

"Is the notion that outlandish?"

"No."

"When I was a little boy," he said, "it seemed to me that a cop was a wonderful thing for a man to be. Standing there in a handsome uniform, directing traffic, helping children cross the street safely. Protecting us all from the bad guys." He grinned. "The bad guys indeed. Little did I know. But there were lads on our block who did put on the blue uniform. One of them, Timothy Lunney was his name, he wasn't so different from the rest of us. You wouldn't have found it remarkable to hear he'd taken to robbing banks, or making collections for the shylocks."

We talked some about what might have been, and just how much choice a person had. That last was something to think about, and we both took a few minutes to think about it, and let the silence stretch. Then he said, "And how about yourself?"

"Me?"

"You didn't grow up knowing you'd become a cop."

"No, not at all. I never really planned it. Then I took the entrance exam, which back then I'd have had to be a moron to fail, and then I was in the Academy, and, well, there I was."

"Could you have gone the other way?"

"And drifted instead into a life of crime?" I thought about it. "I can't point to any innate nobility of character that would have ruled it out," I said. "But I have to say I never felt any pull in that direction."

"No."

"There was a boy I grew up with in the Bronx," I remembered, "and we lost track of each other completely when my family moved away. And then I ran into him a couple of times years later."

"And he'd taken the other path."

"He had," I said. "He was no great success at it, but that's where his life led him. I saw him once through a one-way mirror in a sta-

tion house, and then lost track of him again. And then we caught up with each other some years later. It was before you and I got to know each other."

"Were you still drinking?"

"No, but I wasn't away from it long. Less than a year. Interesting, really, the things that happened to him."

"Well," he said, "don't stop now."

I

I COULDN'T TELL YOU the first time I saw Jack Ellery, but it would have to have been during the couple of years I spent in the Bronx. We were a class apart at the same grammar school, so I'd have seen him in the halls or outside at recess, or playing stickball or stoopball after school let out. We got to know each other well enough to call each other by our last names, in the curious manner of boys. If you'd asked me then about Jack Ellery, I'd have said he was all right, and I suppose he'd have said the same about me. But that's as much as either of us would have been likely to say, because that's as well as we knew each other.

Then my father's business tailed off and he closed the store and we moved, and I didn't see Jack Ellery again for more than twenty years. I thought he looked familiar, but I couldn't place him right away. I don't know whether he would have recognized me, because he didn't get to see me. I was looking at him through one-way glass.

This would have been in 1970 or '71. I'd had my gold shield for a couple of years, and I was a detective assigned to the Sixth Precinct in Greenwich Village when the prewar building on Charles Street still served as the station house. It wasn't long after that they moved us to new quarters on West Tenth, and some enterprising fellow bought our old house and turned it into a co-op or condo, and tipped his hat to history by calling it Le Gendarme.

Years later, when One Police Plaza went up, they did essentially the same thing with the old police headquarters on Centre Street.

But this was on the second floor at the old place on Charles Street, where Jack Ellery was wearing number four in a lineup of five male Caucasians in their late thirties and early forties. They ranged between five-nine and six-one, were dressed alike in jeans and open-necked sport shirts, and stood waiting for a woman they couldn't see to pick out the one who had held her at gunpoint while his partner emptied the cash register.

She was a stout woman, maybe fifty, and she was badly miscast as the co-owner of a mom-and-pop housewares store. If she'd taught school, all her pupils would have been terrified of her. I was there as a casual spectator, because it wasn't my case. A plainclothes cop named Lonergan was the arresting officer, and I was standing next to him. There was an assistant DA in the room, next to the woman, and there was a tall skinny kid in a bad suit who pretty much had to be the Legal Aid lawyer.

When I was wearing a uniform in Brooklyn, they had me partnered with an older man named Vince Mahaffey, and one of the few hundred things he taught me was to catch a lineup any time I had the chance. It was, he told me, a much better way to familiarize yourself with the local bad guys than going through books of mug shots. You got to watch their faces and their body language, you got a sense of them that would stick in your mind. Besides, he said, it was a free show, so why not enjoy it?

So I got in the habit of viewing lineups at the Sixth, and this particular afternoon I studied the men in turn while the ADA told the woman to take her time. "No, I know who it is," she said, and Lonergan looked happy. "It's Number Three."

The ADA asked her if she was positive, in a voice that suggested she might want to rethink the whole thing, and the Legal Aid kid cleared his throat, as if preparing to offer an objection.

No need. "I'm a hundred percent positive," she said. "That's the son of a bitch who robbed me, and I'll say so in front of you and God and everybody."

Lonergan had stopped looking happy as soon as she'd announced her choice. He and I stayed in the room while the others filed out. I asked him what he knew about Number Three.

"He's an assistant manager at the market on Hudson," he said. "Hell of a nice guy, always glad to do us a favor, but I've got to stop using him in lineups. This is the third time somebody's picked him out, and he's the kind of guy, he finds a dime in a pay phone, he puts it back."

"He's got a kind of a crooked look to him," I said.

"I think it's that bend in his lip. You barely notice it, but it makes his face the least bit asymmetrical, which never inspires confidence. Whatever it is, he's been in his last lineup."

"As long as he stays out of trouble," I said. "So who were you hoping she'd pick?"

"No, you tell me. Who were you leaning toward?"

"Number Four."

"On the nose. I shoulda had you for my witness, Matt. Is that cop instinct talking, or did you recognize him?"

"I think it was the expression on his face after she made her call. I know they can't hear anything in there, but he picked up something and knew he was off the hook."

"I missed that."

"But I think I'd have picked him anyway. He looked familiar to me, and I can't think why."

"Well, he's got a yellow sheet. Maybe you saw his handsome face in a book of mug shots. High-Low Jack, they call him. Ring a bell?"

It didn't. I asked his last name, and then repeated it myself—"Jack Ellery, Jack Ellery"—and then something clicked.

"I knew him back when I was a kid," I said. "Jesus, I haven't seen him since grade school."

"Well," Lonergan said, "I'd say the two of you took different career paths."

The next time I saw him was years later. In the meantime I had left the NYPD and moved from a split-level house in Syosset to a hotel room just west of Columbus Circle. I didn't look for a job, but jobs found me, and I wound up functioning as a sort of unlicensed private eye. I didn't keep track of expenses and I didn't furnish written reports, and the people who hired me paid me in cash. Some of the cash paid for my hotel room, and a larger portion covered my tab at the bar around the corner, where I took most of my meals, met most of my clients, and spent most of my time. And if there was anything left over, I bought a money order and sent it to Syosset.

Then, after too many blackouts and too many hangovers, after a couple of trips to detox and at least one seizure, the day came when I left a drink untouched on top of a bar and found my way to an AA meeting. I'd been to meetings before, and I'd tried to stay sober, but I guess I hadn't been ready, and I guess this time I was. "My name's Matt," I told a roomful of people, "and I'm an alcoholic."

I hadn't said that before, not the whole sentence, and saying it is no guarantee of sobriety. Sobriety's never guaranteed, it always hangs by a thread, but I left that meeting feeling that something had shifted. I didn't have a drink that day, or the day after, or the day after that, and I kept going to meetings and stringing the days together, and I must have been somewhere in the middle of my third month of sobriety when I next encountered Jack Ellery. I'd had my last drink on the thirteenth of November, so it would have been the last week of January or the first week of February, something like that.

I know I couldn't have had three full months yet, because I remember that I raised my hand and gave my day count, and you only do that for the first ninety days. "My name's Matt," you say, "and I'm an alcoholic, and today is Day Seventy-seven." And everybody says, "Hi, Matt," and then it's somebody else's turn.

This was at a three-speaker meeting on East Nineteenth Street, and after the second speaker they had a secretary's break, when they made announcements and passed the basket. People with anniversaries announced them, and drew applause, and the newbies shared their day counts, and then the third speaker told his story and wrapped it all up by ten o'clock so we could all go home.

I was on my way out the door when I turned at the sound of my name and there was Jack Ellery. My seat was in the front, so I hadn't noticed him earlier. But I knew him at a glance. He looked older than he had on the other side of the one-way glass, and there was more in his face than the years alone could account for. There's no charge for the seats in an AA room, but that's because you pay for them in advance.

"You don't recognize me," he said.

"Sure I do. You're Jack Ellery."

"Jesus, you've got some memory. What were we, twelve, thirteen years old?"

"I think I was twelve and you were thirteen."

"Your dad had the shoe store," he said. "And you were a class behind me, and one day I realized I hadn't seen you in a while, and nobody knew where you went. And the next time I passed the shoe store, it was gone."

"Like most of his business ventures."

"He was a nice man, though. I remember that. Mr. Scudder. He impressed the hell out of my mother one time. He had that machine, you stood with your feet in the opening and it gave you some sort of X-ray picture of them. She was all set to spring for a new pair of shoes, and your dad said my feet hadn't grown enough to need 'em. 'That's an honest man, Jackie,' she said on the way home. 'He could have taken advantage and he didn't.' "

"One of the secrets of his success."

"Well, it made an impression. Jesus, old times in the Bronx. And now we're both of us sober. You got time for a cup of coffee, Matt?"

II

WE SAT ACROSS from each other in a booth in a diner on Twenty-third Street. He took his coffee with a lot of cream and sugar. Mine was black. The only thing I ever put in it was bourbon, and I didn't do that anymore.

He remarked again on my having recognized him, and I said it worked both ways, he'd recognized me. "Well, you said your name," he said. "When you gave your day count. You'll be coming up on ninety pretty soon."

Ninety days is a sort of probationary period. When you've been clean and dry for ninety days, you're allowed to tell your story at a meeting, and to hold various group offices and service positions. And you can stop raising your hand and telling the world how many days you've got.

He'd been sober sixteen months. "That year," he said. "I had a year the last day of September. I never thought I'd make that year."

"They say it's tough right before an anniversary."

"Oh, it wasn't any more difficult then. But, see, I more or less took it for granted that a year of sobriety was an impossible accomplishment. That nobody stayed sober that long. Now my sponsor's sober almost six years, and there's enough people in my home group with ten, fifteen, twenty years, and it's not like I pegged them as liars. I just thought I was a different kind of animal, and for me it had to be impossible. Did your old man drink?"

"That was the other secret of his success."

"Mine too. In fact he died of it. It was just a couple of years ago, and what gets me is he died alone. His liver went on him. My ma was gone already, she had cancer, so he was alone in the world, and I couldn't be at his bedside where I belonged because I was upstate. So he died in a bed all by himself. Man, that's gonna be one tough amends to make, you know?"

I didn't want to think about the amends I'd have to make. *Just put that on the shelf,* Jim Faber told me more than once. *You've got two things to do today, and one is go to a meeting and the other is don't drink. Get both of those things right and all the rest will come along when it's supposed to.*

"You went on the cops, Matt. Or am I mixing you up with somebody else?"

"No, you got it right. That ended a few years ago, though."

He lifted a hand, mimed knocking back a drink, and I nodded. He said, "I don't know if you would have heard, but I went the other way."

"I may have heard something."

"When I say I was upstate, it was as a guest of the governor. I was at Green Haven. It wasn't exactly up there with the Brinks Job and the Great Train Robbery. What I did, I picked up a gun and walked into a liquor store. And it's not like it was the first time."

I didn't have a response to that, but he didn't seem to require one. "I had a decent lawyer," he said, "and he fixed it so I took a plea to one charge and they dropped the others. You know what was the hardest part? You got to do what they call allocute. You familiar with the term?"

"You have to stand up in court and say what you did."

"And I hated the idea. Just flat-out hated it. I was looking for a way around it. 'Can't I just say *guilty* and let it go at that?' But my guy tells me no, you do it the way they want, you say what you did. Well, it's that or I blow the plea deal, so I'm not completely crazy and I do what I'm supposed to do. And you want to know something? The minute it's out, I got this rush of relief."

"Because it was over."

He shook his head. "Because it was out there. Because I said it, I copped to it. There's the Fifth Step in a nutshell, Matt. You own up in front of God and everybody and it's a load off your mind. Oh, it wasn't the last load, it was just one small part of it, but when the program came along and they told me what I was gonna have to do, it made sense to me right from the jump. I could see how it would work."

AA's twelve steps, Jim Faber had told me, weren't there to keep you sober. Not drinking was what kept you sober. The steps were to make sobriety comfortable enough so that you didn't feel the need to drink your way out of it, and I'd get to them in due course. So far I had admitted that I was powerless over alcohol, that it made my life unmanageable, and that was the First Step, and I could stay on that one as long as I had to.

And I was in no great rush to get past it. They began most of the meetings I went to with a reading of the steps, and even if they didn't there'd be a list of them hanging on the wall where you couldn't help reading it. The Fourth Step was a detailed personal inventory, and you sat down and wrote it out. The Fifth Step was confessional — you shared all that shit with another human being, most likely your sponsor.

Some people, Jim said, stayed sober for decades without ever doing the steps.

I thought about the steps and missed a few beats of what Jack was saying, but when I tuned in he was talking about Green Haven, saying it was probably the best thing that ever happened to him. It had introduced him to the program.

"I went to meetings because it was a chance to sit in a chair and zone out for an hour," he said. "And it was easier to stay dry inside than it was to drink the awful shit cons brew up for themselves, or buy pills that the screws smuggled in. And, you know, I can't say I blame alcohol for the turn my life took, because I chose it myself, but going to meetings it began to dawn on me that every time I got my ass in trouble, I was always high. I mean, like, invariably. It was me making the choice to do the crime, and it was me making the choice to take the drink or smoke the joint, but the two went together, you know, and I was seeing it for the first time."

So he stayed sober in prison. Then they let him out and he came home to New York and got a room in an SRO hotel a couple of blocks from Penn Station, and by the third night he was drinking blended whiskey around the corner in a place called the Terminal Lounge.

"So called because of its location," he said, "but the name would have fit the place even if it had been in the middle of Jackson Heights. Fucking joint was the end of the line."

Except of course it wasn't. The line ran its zigzag course for another couple of years, during which time he stayed out of trouble with the law but couldn't stay out of the bars. He'd go to meetings and begin to put a little time together, and then he'd have one of those oh-what-the-hell moments, and the next thing he knew he'd be in a bar, or taking a long pull on a bottle. He hit a few detoxes, and his blackouts started lasting longer, and he knew what the future held and didn't see how he could avoid it.

"You know, Matt," he said, "when I was a kid, I decided what I was going to be when I grew up. Can you guess what it was? You give up? A cop. I was gonna be a cop. Wear the blue uniform, keep the public safe from crime." He picked up his coffee but his cup was empty. "I guess you were dreaming the same dream, but you went and did it."

I shook my head. "I fell into it," I said. "What I wanted to be was Joe DiMaggio. And, but for a complete lack of athletic ability, I might have made that dream come true."

"Well, my handicap was a complete lack of moral fiber, and you know what I fell into."

He kept drinking, because he couldn't seem to help it, and he kept coming back to AA, because where the hell else was there for him to go? And then one day after a meeting an unlikely person took him aside and told him some home truths.

"A gay guy, Matt, and I mean gay as a jay. Obvious about it, you know? Grew up in a lah-de-dah suburb, went to an Ivy League college, and now he designs jewelry. Plus he's more than ten years younger'n I am, and he looks like a wind of more than twenty miles an hour could pick him up and whisk him off to Oz. Just the type I'm gonna turn to for advice, right?

"Well, he sat me down and told me I was using the program like a revolving door, and I'd just keep going out and keep coming back again, only each time I came back I'd have a little less of myself left. And the only way I was ever gonna break the pattern was if I read the Big Book every morning and the Twelve & Twelve every night, and got really serious with the steps. So I looked at him, this wispy little queen, this guy I got less in common with than a fucking Martian, and I asked him something I never asked anybody before. I asked him to be my sponsor. You know what he said?"

"I'd guess he said yes."

" 'I'm willing to sponsor you,' he said, 'but I don't know if you'll be able to stand it.' Well, fuck, man. Come right down to it, what choice did I have?"

So he went to a meeting every day, and sometimes two, and a three-meeting day wasn't unheard of. And he called his sponsor every morning and every night, and the first thing he did when he got out of bed was hit his knees and ask God for one more sober day, and the last thing he did at night was get on his knees again and thank God for keeping him sober. And he read the Big Book and the Twelve & Twelve, and he worked his way through the steps with his sponsor, and he made ninety days, not for the first time, but he'd never made six months before, and nine months, and, incredibly, a year.

For his Fourth Step, his sponsor made him write down every wrong thing he'd ever done in his life, and if he didn't want to include something, that meant it had damn well better be there. "It was like allocuting," he said, "to every goddamn thing I ever did."

Then the two of them sat down together and he read aloud what he'd written, with his sponsor interrupting now and then to comment, or ask for amplification. "And when we were done he asked me how I felt, and it's not exactly an elegant way to put it, but what I told him was that I felt as though I'd just taken the biggest shit in the history of the world."

And now he had sixteen months, and it was time to start working on the amends. He'd made his Eighth Step list of the people he'd harmed, he'd become willing to take steps to set things right, but now it was Ninth Step time, which meant actually making the amends, and that wasn't so easy.

"But what choice do I have?" he said. And he shook his head and said, "Jesus, look at the time. You just heard my entire qualification. You sat through three speakers and now you had to listen to me, and I went on almost as long as all three of them put together. But I guess it did something for me, talking to somebody from the old neighborhood. It's gone, you know. The old neighborhood. They went and ran a fucking expressway through there."

"I know."

"It probably means more to me. The neighborhood, I mean. You were there what, two years?"

"Something like that."

"For me it was my whole childhood. I used to be able to work up a pretty good drunk out of it. 'Poor me, the house I grew up in is gone, the streets where I played stickball are gone, di dah di dah di dah.' But my childhood wasn't about the house and the streets. And it's not gone. I'm still carrying it around, and I've still got to deal with it." He picked up the check. "And that's enough out of me, and I'm paying for this, and you can call it amends for talking your ear off."

When I got home I called Jim Faber, and we agreed that Jack's sponsor sounded like a real Step Nazi, but that seemed to be just what Jack needed.

Before we parted, Jack had given me his phone number, and I felt obliged to give him mine. I wasn't much on picking up the phone, and Jim was the only person I called on a fairly regular basis. There was a woman in Tribeca, a sculptor named Jan Keane, with whom I generally spent Saturday night and Sunday morning, and one of us would call the other two or three times a week. Aside from that, I didn't make many calls, and most of the ones I got were wrong numbers.

I copied Jack Ellery's number in my book, and figured I'd run into him somewhere down the line. Or not.

III

T HE NEXT TIME I saw Jack Ellery was several months later, when I ran into him at a meeting. By then we'd spoken a couple of times on the phone. The first time was a few days after I made my ninety days. I spoke that night at my home group in the basement at St. Paul the Apostle. The church was at Columbus and Sixtieth, a few short blocks from my hotel, and I'd gone there in my drinking days to light votive candles for the dead and, while I was there, enjoy a few moments of quiet. Back then I hadn't even known there were AA meetings downstairs.

So I sat at the table in front and told my story, or twenty minutes' worth of it anyway, and everybody congratulated me, and afterward a bunch of us went for coffee at the Flame, and I went home and called Jan, and she congratulated me herself and then reminded me what comes after ninety days. Day Ninety-one.

It must have been Day Ninety-three or -four when Jack Ellery called to offer his own congratulations. "I was a little anxious about calling," he said, "because I figured you'd make it, but you never know, do you? And how would you feel if you had a slip and here's this asshole calling to congratulate you on ninety days that you haven't got? And I said this to my sponsor, and he reminded me I'm not the center of the universe, which never fails to be news to me. And that, if God forbid you did pick up a drink, you'd have more to be upset about than some guy on the other end of the telephone line."

He called again a week or so later, but it was Saturday and I was downtown at Jan's loft on Lispenard Street. The following morning we caught an early meeting in SoHo, a favorite of hers. Afterward we went out for brunch, then walked through some galleries on West Broadway, and I had my standing Sunday dinner date with Jim. We always had Chinese food on those evenings, though not always at the same restaurant, and afterward we'd fit in a meeting. So it was late by the time I got back to my hotel and collected my message, and I didn't return Jack's call until the following day, and when I called he was out and there was no way to leave a message.

We played telephone tag for a few more days, and then one of us reached the other, and it was one of those awkward calls where neither party has a great deal to say.

I remember he talked again about the problem of making amends. "For instance," he said, "there was this buddy I ran with. We knocked off a couple of stores together, then hunkered down with a fifth of Johnnie Black and told each other what heroes we were. Then one time, we did this little store in the Village, pots and pans and household shit. I mean, what were we thinking? How much cash were they gonna have, you know?"

I remembered the woman at the lineup.

"And I guess he got drunk and ran his mouth in front of the wrong person, or maybe I did, because who remembers that shit? But I got picked up, and the woman blew the ID, picked out the poor mope standing next to me. And when they went to pick up Arnie, Jesus, he went for his gun, the crazy son of a bitch, and they shot him full of holes, and he was DOA at Beth Israel. Now I didn't lead him into a life of crime, and I didn't rat him out, but he wound up dead and I didn't have to do any time, I didn't even have to give back the money, and what do I owe him for that? And how do I make it even?"

There was another call later on, and he left a message. He'd be speaking at a meeting on the Upper West Side, and if I wanted to come hear his story maybe we could grab a cup of coffee afterward. I thought about it, but the day came and went. I liked him okay and wished him well, but I wasn't sure I wanted the two of us to become best friends. The Bronx was a long time ago, and we'd taken very different paths since then, even if we'd managed to wind up in the same place. There wasn't much chance I'd ever be a cop again, although I sometimes thought about it, but I couldn't be as sure about Jack. If he stayed sober he'd be all right, but if he didn't, well, pretty much anything could happen, and I didn't want to be that close to him if it did.

The next time I saw him was at a meeting of the Sober Today group on Second Avenue and Eighty-seventh Street. I'd never been there before, and went because someone had booked Jan to speak. I had never heard her tell her drinking story, although I'd been around for some of it while it was going on, so we arranged to meet there and go out for dinner afterward. I found the place, got myself a cup of coffee, and on the other side of the room I saw Jack Ellery in conversation with a studious-looking man in his twenties.

I had to look a second time to make sure it was Jack, because he was a mess. He was dressed well enough, in pressed khakis and a long-sleeved sport shirt, but his face was swollen on one side, and he had a black eye. There was a conclusion available, and I went ahead and jumped to it. People who stay sober generally don't get to look like that unless they're overmatched prizefighters, and I figured all his focus on the steps hadn't kept him from tripping over the first one.

It was a shame if he'd had a slip, but that sort of thing happened, and the good news was he was at a meeting now. Still, I was in no rush to go over and talk to him, and purposely chose a seat where he'd be less likely to get a look at me. And then the meeting started.

The format featured a single speaker, followed by a general discussion. First, though, they read "How It Works" and the steps and the traditions and a few other selections from the wisdom of the ages, and I let my mind wander until they were doing day counts and anniversaries. Somewhere along the way I shifted in my seat so that I could get a look at Jack, and sure enough, his hand was raised.

No surprise there, I thought, and waited for him to get called on so he could tell us how many days he had this time around. But they were done with the day counters, they were on anniversaries, as I found out when he said, "My name is Jack, and the day before yesterday by the grace of God and the fellowship of AA, I was able to celebrate two years."

They applauded, of course, and I joined in as soon as it all registered, beating my hands together and feeling like an idiot. Where did I get off looking at a man and assuming he'd been drinking?

Then the chairman introduced Jan, and she started telling her story, and I sat back and listened. But I leaned forward once or twice and caught another glimpse of Jack. He was sober, and that was all to the good, but why did he look as though someone had beaten the living crap out of him?

I caught up with him during the break. "I thought that was you," he said. "You're a long way from home, aren't you? I don't think I've ever seen you here before."

"The speaker's a friend of mine," I said, "and this is the first chance I've had to hear her qualify."

"Well, that's worth a trip, isn't it? I enjoyed hearing her myself, and all I had to do was walk a couple of blocks."

"We've got a dinner date afterward," I said, and wondered as I said the words why I felt compelled to share that information with him. On the way back to my seat I figured it out. I was cutting him off at the pass, letting him know we wouldn't be available for coffee.

I hadn't asked about his face, not feeling it was for me to raise the subject, and he hadn't chosen to bring it up. I couldn't avoid wondering about it, though, and thought I'd get my curiosity satisfied when I saw his hand go up during the discussion. It took her a while to call on him, despite my efforts to influence her by force of will, but eventually she did, and he thanked her for her qualification and found something in it to identify with, some common element in their blackouts or hangovers, something that ordinary. Nothing to explain the lumps and bumps he'd taken as he reached the two-year mark in his sobriety.

After we'd closed the meeting with the Serenity Prayer, he and the fellow who'd been sitting next to him were among the ten or a dozen people who went up to shake Jan's hand and thank her for sharing her story. I hung back, helping with the chairs, and I was still doing that when he and his friend headed for the door.

But he stopped in midstride and came over to me. "Now's not

the time for it," he said, "but there's something I'd really like to talk to you about. What's a good time to call you?"

Jan and I would be having dinner, probably at a German place she'd said she'd like to try. Then I'd see her home, and I'd most likely stay the night on Lispenard Street. She'd want to work in the morning, so I'd clear out after breakfast, and then what would I do? Catch the subway back to my hotel, unless I decided to take my time and walk home, maybe stopping en route at a noon meeting. There'd be one at the Workshop on Perry Street, or I could keep walking and go to the bookshop meeting at St. Francis of Assisi, on Thirtieth Street.

I thought of something, and I guess it showed on my face, because Jack asked me what was so funny.

"I was just thinking," I said. "Something I've heard people say. How the literature tells us sobriety is a bridge back to life, but sometimes it's just a tunnel to another meeting."

"Greg says that," he said, and his friend approached at the sound of his name, and Jack introduced us. I wasn't surprised to learn that this was Jack's sponsor. He was wearing an earring, and I'd already decided he had designed it himself.

"Ah, Matt from the Old Neighborhood," Greg said. "Now long since leveled and paved over, and far better in nostalgic recollection than ever it was in reality. I wish someone would run a highway through my own old neighborhood. Or divert a river through it."

"Somebody did that," I seemed to remember, and he said it was Hercules, as a way of cleaning the Augean stables.

"He had Twelve Labors, we have Twelve Steps," he said. "Who ever said staying sober was easy?"

Jan was heading over, and I was ready to grab her and get out of there. I suggested to Jack that it might be simpler if I called him, but he said he'd probably be out most of the day. I told him

I'd probably be back at my hotel in the late morning, and if he missed me then he could try me around two.

New York's Little Germany was on the Lower East Side until the *General Slocum* disaster of 1904, when a ship by that name burned and sank on the East River, with thirteen hundred of the neighborhood's residents on board for an annual excursion. Over a thousand of them died, and that took the heart out of Little Germany. It was the end of the neighborhood, as surely as if you'd run an expressway through it. Or diverted a river.

The residents moved out of Little Germany, and most of them wound up in Yorkville, in the blocks centering around Eighty-sixth and Third. It wasn't just German, there were Czechs and Hungarians as well, but they'd all begun moving on in recent years, and the rents these days were too high for new immigrants. Yorkville was losing its ethnic character.

You wouldn't have known that inside Maxl's, where Jan took a long look at the menu and ordered sauerbraten and red cabbage and potato dumplings, which she called by their German name. The waiter, who looked pretty silly in his lederhosen, approved her choice or her pronunciation, or perhaps both, and beamed when I said I'd have the same. His face registered shock and dismay, though, when he asked what kind of beer we wanted and we said we'd be fine with coffee. Later we'd have coffee, he suggested. Now we would want good German beer to go with good German food.

I had a sudden sense memory of good German beer, Beck's or St. Pauli Girl or Löwenbräu, strong and rich and full-bodied. I wasn't going to order it, I didn't even want it, but the memory was there. I blinked it away, while Jan made it clear that he wasn't going to sell us any beer that evening.

The ambience was touristy, but the food was good enough to

take your mind off it, and we had more coffee afterward and shared a gooey dessert. "I could do this every night," Jan said, "if I didn't mind weighing three hundred pounds. That fellow who looked like he took a beating, I think he said his name was Jack?"

"What about him?"

"You were talking to him."

"I've mentioned him."

"From when you lived in the Bronx. And then you wound up arresting him years later."

"That's close," I said. "I didn't make the collar, I was just there to view the lineup, and when he went away it was for something else. I never told him about that lineup, incidentally."

"I asked him what happened to his face. I wouldn't have said anything, but he brought it up, said he didn't always look this handsome. You know, making a joke of it, to clear the air."

"I met George Shearing once," I recalled.

"The jazz pianist?"

I nodded. "Somebody introduced us, I forget the occasion. And right off the bat he reeled off three or four blind jokes. They weren't terribly funny, but that wasn't the point. You meet a blind man and you're overly aware of his blindness, and he'd learned to get that out of the way by calling attention to it."

"Well, that's what Jack was doing, so I went ahead and asked what had happened."

"And?"

"He said he blamed the whole thing on the steps. He slipped on one of them and landed flat on his face. I guess this meant something to his friend, because he rolled his eyes. I would have asked him which step, but before I could say anything he was thanking me again and making room for the next person in line."

"Nine," I said.

"As in Step Nine? Or is that German for *no?*"

"He's been making amends. Or trying to."

"When I did," she said, "what I mostly got was hugs and for-giveness. Along with a couple of blank stares from people who couldn't figure out why I was apologizing."

"Well," I said, "you and Jack probably associated with a differ-ent class of people, and had different things to make amends for."

"I threw up all over a guy once."

"And he didn't punch you in the mouth?"

"He didn't even *remember*. At least that's what he said, but I think he must have been being polite. I mean, how do you forget something like that?"

I reached for the check, as I generally do, but she insisted we split it. Outside she said she was exhausted, and would I be heart-broken if she went home alone? I said it was probably a good idea, that I was tired myself. It was Thursday, so I'd be seeing her in two days. I hailed a cab, and when I held the door for her she said she'd drop me at my hotel, that it was practically on her way. I said I felt like walking off that dessert.

I watched her taxi head south on Second Avenue and tried to remember the last time I'd had German beer. Jimmy Armstrong had Prior Dark on tap, and I found myself remembering the taste of it.

I forced myself to walk two blocks, then caught a cab of my own.

Back in my room, I got out of my clothes and took a shower. I called Jim Faber and said, "What the hell's the matter with me? She said she was tired, and I was going to be seeing her Saturday."

"You thought you'd be going home with her tonight. More or less took it for granted."

"And she asked if I was all right with it, and I said sure, that was fine."

"But that's not how you felt."

"I felt like telling her to forget about Saturday, while she was at it. That way she could get plenty of rest. All the fucking rest she wanted."

"Nice."

"And thank you very much, lady, but I'll get my own cab. But what I said was I felt like walking."

"Uh-huh. And how do you feel now?"

"Tired. And a little silly."

"Both appropriate, I'd say. Did you drink?"

"Of course not."

"Did you want to?"

"No," I said, and thought about it. "Not consciously. But I probably wanted to, on some level."

"But you didn't drink."

"No."

"Then you're okay," he said. "Go to sleep."

Not counting our Bronx boyhood, that was the third time I saw Jack Ellery—once through one-way glass, and twice at meetings.

The next time I saw him he was dead.

IV

I WENT OUT for breakfast at the Morning Star Friday morning, and went straight from there to the Donnell Library on West Fifty-third. In the restaurant the night before we'd talked some about the *General Slocum* disaster, but I'd been uncertain exactly when it had occurred and how many lives had been lost. I found a book that would answer all my questions, including some that hadn't come to mind until I started reading about it. Just about everyone involved had been grossly negligent, from the owners and line management on down, but the only one who went to jail was the captain, and his sentence struck me as awfully light for the enormity of his actions.

As far as I could tell, nobody bothered to bring a civil suit, and I thought how the world had changed in three-quarters of a century. Nowadays people filed a lawsuit at the drop of a hat, even if it was somebody else's hat and it hadn't been dropped within half a block of them. I tried to decide whether the country was better or worse for all that relentless litigation, and I chose to postpone my decision, because something I'd read was leading me to another book on another subject.

That took care of the morning, and I went straight from the Donnell reading room to the Sixty-third Street Y, getting there just in time for the 12:30 meeting. It broke at 1:30, and I stopped at a pizza stand for a slice and a Coke, which would do me fine for lunch, although I didn't suppose it would bring a smile of delight to the face of a board-certified nutritionist. It was around 2:15 when I got home, and there were two slips in my message box. The first call had come at 10:45, and I'd missed the second one by less than ten minutes. They were both from Jack, and both times he'd said he would try again later.

I went upstairs and called his number on the off chance that he was home now, or that he'd acquired an answering machine. He wasn't and he hadn't.

I stayed in the room until it was time to go out to dinner. I had no reason to go anywhere and I had a book to read, so I wasn't there specifically to wait for his call, but that was probably a factor. The only time the phone rang it was Jan, confirming that we were still on for Saturday night. Then she asked if I'd walked all the way home the previous night, and I took a breath before I answered. "I walked two blocks," I said, "and then I said the hell with it and flagged a cab."

We established when and where we'd meet, and I hung up and wondered at my first impulse, which had been to say yes, that I'd walked all the way home from Yorkville. And what else? That my feet were sore and my calves ached? That I'd been mugged and pistol-whipped en route and it was all her fault?

But instead I'd paused for breath and told her the unremarkable truth, and she'd passed up the chance to remind me I could have saved a couple of bucks by sharing her cab. I suppose you could say we were both making progress.

Friday night I went to St. Paul's. I saw Jim there but he complained of a headache and went home at the break. I joined a few others for coffee afterward, where the chief topic of conversation was a member who'd just come out as a lesbian. "I knew Pegeen was gay," a man named Marty said. "I figured it out about ten minutes after I met her. I was just hoping I could get lucky before *she* figured it out."

"While visions of threesomes danced in your head," somebody said.

"No, I'm an uncomplicated guy. I just wanted to nail her a couple of times before she turned into a pumpkin."

"But your Higher Power had other ideas."

"My Higher Power," Marty said, "was clueless. My Higher Power was asleep at the fucking switch."

There was a message waiting for me at the hotel desk, the same message: Jack had called and would call again later. It didn't say to call him, and I decided not to because it was late. Then I changed my mind and called him after all, and there was no answer.

Saturday started out cold and rainy. I skipped breakfast and wound up ordering an early lunch from the deli down the block. The kid who delivered it bore an unsettling resemblance to a drowned rat, and it earned him a bigger tip than usual.

I spent the afternoon in front of the TV, switching back and forth between a couple of college football games. I didn't pay much attention to what I was looking at, but it was better than being out in the rain, and I figured I'd be in one place long enough for Jack to get hold of me.

But the phone never rang. I picked it up myself a couple of

times and tried his number. No answer. It was frustrating in a curious way, because I didn't really have a burning desire to talk to him, but neither did I want to be haunted by an endless stream of message slips.

So I sat there in my room, and when I wasn't looking at the TV I was looking out the window at the rain.

Jan and I had arranged to meet at a restaurant at Mulberry and Hester, in Little Italy. We'd been there a couple of times together and liked the food and the atmosphere. I was a few minutes early, and they couldn't find our reservation but had a table for us, and Jan showed up ten minutes late. The food was fine, the service was fine, and I could have flavored the conversation by pointing out a stocky gentleman at the bar whom I'd arrested ten or a dozen years earlier.

We might have walked around after dinner, but it was still drizzling and there was a chill in the air, so we went straight to Lispenard Street and she made a pot of coffee and put some records on — Sarah Vaughan, Ella, Eydie Gormé. It should have been just the ticket for a rainy October night, domestic and romantic at the same time, but there'd been a stiffness at dinner, a distance between us, and it didn't go away.

I thought, Is this it? Is this how I'll spend every Saturday night for the rest of my life?

We went to bed sometime after midnight, with an all-night jazz station on the radio, and lying together in the dark, we did each other some good. And afterward I felt something lurking in the shadows out there on the edge of thought. I turned away from it, and sleep descended like a fast curtain.

Some months ago I had taken to keeping some clothes at Jan's place. She'd turned over one of the dresser drawers to me, along with a couple of hangers in the closet. So I had clean socks and underwear to put on after my morning shower, and a clean shirt, and I left what I'd been wearing for her to wash.

"You're coming up on a year," she said at breakfast. "What is it, a month away?"

"Five, six weeks. Somewhere in there."

I thought she'd have more to say about that, but if she did she decided to leave it unsaid.

That night I met Jim Faber at a Chinese restaurant on Ninth Avenue. Neither of us had been there before, and we decided it was all right, but nothing special. I told him about my evening with Jan, and he took it in and thought about it, and then he reminded me that I was coming up on a year sober.

"She said the same thing," I said. "What's that got to do with anything?"

He shrugged, waiting for me to answer my own question.

" 'Don't make any major changes in the first year.' Isn't that the conventional wisdom?"

"It's what they say."

"In other words, I've got five or six weeks, whatever the hell it is, to decide what to do about my relationship with Jan."

"No."

"No?"

"You've got five or six weeks," he said, "*not* to decide."

"Oh."

"You get the distinction?"

"I think so."

"You don't have to make a change when the year's up. You don't have to come to a decision. You're under no obligation to do anything. The important thing is not to take any action before then."

"Got it."

"On the other hand," he said, "what we're talking about here is your agenda. She may have one of her own. You're sober a year, it's time for you to shit or get off the pot. That sound about right?"

"Maybe."

"You know," he said, "that business about waiting a year, that's just a general rule. Some people, they're best advised not to make any major changes for the first five years."

"You're kidding, right?"

"Or even ten," he said.

We took in a meeting at St. Clare's Hospital. Most of those attending were from the detox ward, and their attendance was compulsory. It was hard to get them to stay awake, and almost impossible to get them to say anything. Jim and I had been there a few times; you rarely heard anything insightful, but it served as a good object lesson.

I walked him home, and at one point he said, "Something to bear in mind. Something Buddha said, as it happens. 'It is your dissatisfaction with what is that is the source of all your unhappiness.'"

I said, "Buddha said that?"

"So I'm told, though I have to admit I wasn't there to hear him. You seem surprised."

"Well," I said, "I never thought he had that much depth to him."

"Buddha."

"That's what everybody calls him. And what he calls himself, as far as that goes. Big guy, must stand six-six, shaves his head, belly out to here. He's a regular at the midnight meeting at the Moravian church, but he turns up other places as well. I think he's a former outlaw biker, and my guess is he's done time, but—"

The look on his face stopped me. He shook his head and said,

"*The* Buddha. Sitting under the Bodhi tree? Waiting for enlightenment?"

"I thought it was an apple tree and he invented gravity."

"That was Isaac Newton."

"If it was Newton, it should have been a fig tree. Buddha, huh? Listen, it was a natural mistake. The only Buddha I know is the one at the Moravian church. Works the doors at one of those rough bars on West Street, if I'm not mistaken. You want to run that by me again? The source of all unhappiness?"

After I'd seen him home I went home myself. I'd stopped at the hotel earlier, surprised that there were no messages, and I didn't see anything in my box this time, either. I asked the fellow behind the desk and he said that there'd been one person who'd called a couple of times but hadn't given his name or left any kind of a message. All he could tell me was that the caller had been a man.

Jack, I thought, and he'd given up leaving messages because they didn't do any good. I went upstairs, and I was hanging up my jacket when the phone rang.

A voice I didn't recognize said, "Matt? This is Gregory Stillman."

"I don't think —"

"We met the other night at Sober Today. Jack Ellery introduced us."

"I remember." Jack's sponsor, the jewelry designer, with one of his creations dangling from his ear. "I don't think we got as far as last names."

"No," he said, and drew an audible breath. "Matt, I have some very bad news."

V

THE MEMORIAL SERVICE for John Joseph Ellery was held Monday afternoon in the same church basement where I'd heard Jan tell her story on Thursday evening. There was no AA meeting scheduled, but Greg had been able to make arrangements with the church for the use of the room. As far as I could tell, all of the thirty or so in attendance had known Jack in AA.

All but two, a pair of men in suits who might as well have been wearing blue uniforms. Cops, following the long-established routine of attending a service to see who showed up. I'd done that myself a few times, and couldn't remember ever learning anything useful in the process. But that didn't mean it never paid off.

The service was nonreligious, and there was no clergyman in attendance. When I arrived there was a tape playing quietly, something classical that I recognized but couldn't identify, and when it faded out Greg Stillman got up in front of the group. He was wearing a dark suit, and had left the earring home.

He introduced himself as Jack's friend and sponsor, and spoke for five minutes or so, telling a couple of stories. There was a moment when he seemed on the verge of being overcome by emotion, but he stopped talking and waited and the moment passed, and he was able to go on.

Then people stood up in turn and shared something about Jack. It was like an AA meeting except you didn't wait to be called on, you just took your turn. And all of the sharing was about Jack. Aside from the anecdotes, the gist of it was that Jack had had a rough life and a bad drinking story, but that he'd found real hope and comfort in the program, and was genuinely reborn through the twelve steps. And, by the grace of God, he'd died sober.

There's a comfort.

The service concluded with a song. An ethereal young woman with big eyes and see-through skin stood up in front of the room and said that her name was Elizabeth and that she was an alcoholic. She hadn't known Jack very well, she said, but she had sobriety in common with him, if nothing else, and Greg had asked her to sing, and she was glad to do it. She gave an a cappella rendition of "Amazing Grace," including one verse I couldn't recall having heard before. Not long before I got sober, I'd heard Judy Collins sing the song on a record they played at a whore's funeral. That would have been hard to improve on, but this version came close.

There was a coffee urn—it was, after all, an AA crowd—and people gathered around it afterward. I turned to look for the cops, thinking I could see if they wanted coffee. I figured they wouldn't take it without an invitation. But they had slipped out, and I headed for the door myself until I heard my name called.

It was Greg. He took my arm and asked me if I had a minute.

"A few minutes," he said. "There's a conversation we ought to have, and then I've got a favor to ask you."

The next time I saw Jack Ellery he was dead.

And that was at the viewing room at the morgue, where Greg and I looked for a long moment at the mortal remains of a man we'd both known. Then he said, "Yes, that's him. That's Jack Ellery." And I nodded in affirmation, and they let us out of there.

Outside he turned up his collar against the chill and wondered if we'd get more rain. I said I'd missed the forecast, and he said he never knew what the forecasts meant. "They used to tell you what it was going to do," he said, "and even if they were wrong a lot of the time, at least they gave you a clear-cut answer. Now it's all percentages. What on earth is a fifty percent chance of rain? How do you respond to that, carry half of an umbrella?"

"This way they're never wrong."

"That's it exactly. 'Well, we said only a ten percent chance of rain and it poured all day, so all that means is a long shot came in.' Just because you're a meteorologist doesn't mean you don't feel the need to cover your ass." He took a breath. "I never asked you this, but do you prefer Matt or Matthew?"

Either's fine with me, but it only confuses people to tell them that. "Matt's good," I said.

"Matt, why do they insist on a formal identification? He was in prison, he has a police record, they'd already identified him from fingerprints. Suppose there was nobody around who could do it. They'd get along without it, wouldn't they?"

"Sure."

"I really didn't want to see him like that. My father's funeral was open-casket, and there he was, like something from a road-company Madame Tussauds, and that's the image I was left with, this lifeless waxen effigy. We had our problems, God knows. I was not the son he'd had in mind, as he made all too clear. But we made it up during his last illness, and there was love and mutual respect there at the end, and then that final hideous glimpse of him eclipsed the strong and vigorous man I wanted to remember. I knew that would happen, I dreaded it, but at the same time I couldn't *not* look. Do you know what I mean?"

"How long ago was this?"

"A little over a year. Why?"

"Because time will probably change that," I said. "The earlier memory will supplant the other."

"That's already begun to happen. I didn't know whether I could trust it, whether it was real. Or just some form of wishful thinking."

"Wishful thinking may have something to do with it," I said, "but it's still real. We wind up remembering people the way they were, or at least the way we knew them. I had an aunt with Alzheimer's, she spent the last ten years of her life institutionalized, while the disease ate her mind and her personality and everything that made her human. And that's how I knew her, and how I remembered her."

"God."

"And that all faded out after she was gone, and the real Aunt Peg came back."

Over coffee he said, "I barely looked at him just now. All I really saw were the wounds."

He'd been shot in the mouth and the forehead. They'd shown the corpse with a sheet covering him from the neck down, so if there were other wounds we wouldn't have seen them.

"I hope you're right," he said. "About the image fading. It can't fade too soon for me. Thank you for that. More than that, thanks for making the trip."

I hadn't much wanted to keep him company, but it was a hard request to say no to.

"I didn't want to go at all," he said, "and I certainly didn't want to go by myself. I could have found someone else to come, some AA friend of Jack's, but you felt like the right choice. Thank you."

We'd headed north on First Avenue when we left the morgue, and stopped at a coffee shop called Mykonos just past Forty-second Street. When he ordered a grilled cheese sandwich, I realized it had been a while since I'd eaten, and said I'd have the same.

"Besides," he said, "there's something else I want to talk about."

"Oh?"

"The two men at the back of the room. They were police officers."

"Somehow I sensed as much."

"Well, I didn't need radar, because I saw their badges when they interviewed me. In fact they were the ones who asked me to make the formal ID. I asked them if they were close to solving the case, and they said something noncommittal."

"That's no surprise."

"Do you think they'll solve it?"

"It's possible they've solved it already," I said, "in the sense that they may know who did it. Of course that's not the same as having sufficient evidence to bring a case to trial."

"Could you find out?"

"Whether or not they know who did it?" He nodded. "I suppose I could ask around. An ordinary citizen wouldn't get a straight answer, but I still know a few people in the department. Why?"

"I have a reason."

One he evidently preferred to keep to himself. I let it go.

I said, "I'll see if anybody wants to tell me anything. But I can make an educated guess right now as to who killed Jack."

"You can?"

"Not by name," I said. "Maybe it's more accurate to say I can guess why he was killed. Somebody wanted to shut him up."

"He was shot in the mouth."

"At very close range. Essentially, somebody stuck the gun in his mouth and pulled the trigger, and this would have been after the forehead shot killed him. Put that together with the Ninth Step work Jack kept talking about and the message is pretty clear."

"I was afraid of that," he said.

"Oh?"

He looked at his hands, then raised his eyes to meet mine. "I got him killed," he said.

VI

Dennis redmond was a detective attached to the Nineteenth Precinct, on East Sixty-seventh Street. I reached him at his desk, and let him pick a time and a place to meet.

"I got a few calls to make," he said, "and then I can get out of here. You know the Minstrel Boy?"

"I know the song."

"On Lexington," he said, "right around the corner from us. Say two o'clock?"

The minstrel boy to the war has gone
In the ranks of death you will find him . . .

It was, not surprisingly, an Irish tavern, and I got there a few minutes early and took a booth on the side, sitting where I could see him come in. I walked over to the jukebox while I waited for the waiter to bring me my club soda. There were a lot of Irish selections, and among them was "The Minstrel Boy," the Thomas Moore song, with "The Rose of Tralee" on the flip side, both of them performed by John McCormack. I spent a quarter and listened to that great tenor voice from the past singing about a war that was before my time or his.

The record ended and I sipped my club soda and glanced now and then at my watch, and wondered how McCormack would do with "The Rose of Tralee" and thought about spending another quarter to find out, and then at 2:12 Redmond came through the door. I recognized him right away from Jack's memorial service, and he may even have been wearing the same suit. He took a moment to scan the bar and tables — there wasn't much of a crowd — and came right over.

"Dennis Redmond," he said. "And you're Matt Scudder, and you didn't happen to mention you were at the service yesterday."

"I saw you there," I said, "with another fellow —"

"That'd be Rich Bikelski."

"— but I didn't know it was you, not until you walked in just now."

"No, how would you?" He shook his head. "Been a long day. I can use something. What's that you got there, vodka tonic?"

"Club soda."

He straightened up. "I don't think I'm gonna follow your lead on that one," he said, and went over to the bar. He came back with a tall glass of pale amber liquid over ice. Whiskey and water, from the look of it, and I found myself wondering what kind of whiskey it was, and which brand.

He sat down, raised his glass to me, and took a sip. He was a bulky man with a beefy face and a whiskey drinker's ruddy complexion, but a look at his eyes let you know there was a working brain in there. "Joe Durkin called to put in a word for you," he said. "Says you're all right. You were on the job, had a gold shield. That how you came to know Joe?"

I shook my head. "We didn't meet until a little over a year ago. I was a few years off the force by then."

"Working private."

"That's right."

"But I guess the two of you got along. That what you're doing now? Working private?"

"When something comes my way," I said. "But my interest in Ellery is personal."

"Oh?" He frowned in concentration. "You were at the Six, and it seems to me he took a bust down there once. Nothing came of it, but was that your case? Years ago, that would have been."

I told him that was a good guess, that it hadn't been my case but that I'd been present as a spectator when the witness blew the ID. "We went back a little further than that," I said, and explained how I'd known Jack briefly in the Bronx.

"Boys together," he said. "One turns bad, the other goes on the cops. Years pass and they're facing each other down in a darkened alley. A shot rings out. I think I saw the movie."

"You probably did. Barry Fitzgerald played the priest."

He took a hit of his drink, and I got enough of a whiff of it to identify it as Scotch. He said, "Then you lose touch, and he goes off to the joint for something else, and he gets out and gets himself killed, and a couple dozen people from AA hold a service for him, and here you sit drinking club soda. Is it any wonder they made me a detective?"

"I'm surprised they didn't name you commissioner."

"Just a question of time," he said. "So it's the same movie, but now the cop and the crook meet up again in the same AA room, and instead of Barry Fitzgerald you've got Queen for the Day running the show. What's his name, Spellman? No, Jesus, that was the cardinal. This was the gym. *Still*man."

"He said you talked to him."

"Couple of times. Took the whole thing pretty hard, but you get the sense that he's got some toughness to him, under all the glitter. He was Ellery's sponsor, whatever that amounts to. Is that anything like having a rabbi in the department?"

"That's close."

"Somebody who pulls your coat, steers you right."

"There you go."

"You got a sponsor yourself?" I nodded. "It's not Stillman, is it?"

"No."

"And I don't suppose you're Stillman's sponsor."

"I haven't been sober long enough to start telling other people how to do it."

"How long? Or isn't that something I'm supposed to ask?"

"I don't know what anybody's supposed to do or not do. I'm coming up on a year the middle of next month."

"And Ellery—"

"Just celebrated two years."

"Just in time to get shot. You know who shot him?"

"Somebody who wanted him to keep quiet."

"Yeah, that's our thinking on the subject. 'Here's a little something for that big mouth of yours. *Bang!*' Far as who that somebody might be, I'd say your guess is as good as mine, but what I'm hoping is it's better. You got anything?"

"No."

"My position, where would you go with this, Matt? You made detective, and I understand you were good at it. Who would you look at?"

"People he ran with. Guys he jailed with."

"Uh-huh. And when that didn't go anywhere?"

"I'd probably wait for somebody who knew something to use it as a bargaining chip."

"A Get Out of Jail Free card."

"Right."

"Other words, wait for the case to clear itself. Something to be said for that. You got a high-profile case, prominent and affluent victim, that's another story. Then you have to look like you're doing something, so you take action whether or not there's much point to it. Ask you something, Matt? The vic here, you knew him way back when, and you knew him again this past year, with both of you sober."

"So?"

"I was just wondering how close you were with him."

"Close enough to show up at the funeral."

"But no closer?"

"Not really. I'm here now because someone asked me to see what I could find out."

"Somebody with an earring would be my guess. Why I ask, I don't want to say anything's gonna rub you the wrong way. But what it comes down to, nobody's gonna stay up all night sweating this one out. What do they say about speaking ill of the dead?"

"They say not to."

"Well, sometimes you can't help it. This was a low-life criminal for all but two years of his life, when he suddenly decided to get off the booze and find God. Is that what happens? You find God?"

"Some people seem to."

He thought about it, finished his drink, put down the empty glass. "More power to them," he said. "Would I like to clear this one? Of course I would. I'd like to clear all my cases and watch all the bad guys get convicted and go away. But what are the odds? Words of one syllable, your friend was a bum, and after his dry spell what's he gonna do but pick up a drink and point a gun at somebody? Happens all the time."

Not all the time, I thought. Often, though. I had to give him that. But not all the time.

"So I'd like to clear it," he said, "because it's on my plate, and my mother raised me to finish everything." He patted his stomach. "A lesson I learned all too well. But on the dinner plate of crime, my friend, Jack Ellery is the Brussels sprouts."

VII

"Most people overcook them," Greg Stillman said. "If you don't, there's nothing wrong with Brussels sprouts."

"Next time I see Redmond," I said, "I'll be sure to tell him that."

"Sautéed in coconut oil, just long enough to ensure that they're cooked through, but still crisp. And a little curry powder makes all the difference."

"I'll bet it does."

"But if you boil them into mush, of course they're awful. That's true of all the members of the cabbage family. Broccoli, cabbage, cauliflower. The smell when they're overcooked—oh, you're making a face. I take it you're no fan of the cabbage family?"

"There's a smell you get in tenements," I said. "Mice and cabbage. If poverty has a smell, I guess that's it."

"And who cooks cabbage—and cooks it to death, more often than not?"

"Poor people."

"Poor Irish people," he said. "And poor Polish people. Poor people from northern and eastern Europe. But times have changed and they've all clambered up into the middle class. So what would be the smell of poverty now, do you suppose?" He gave the matter some thought. "Wet dog with garlic," he decided.

It was Thursday night, and I'd gone back to Second Avenue and Sober Today, where the speaker was a balding fellow from the Ridgewood section of Queens who'd held the same job as a bank teller for over thirty years. He never moved out of the house he grew up in, conveniently located three blocks from his place of employment. It was a two-family house, and his parents rented out the upper flat until their son got married, at which time he and his bride moved in upstairs.

"The girl next door," Greg whispered. "Who else would he marry?"

It was as boring a story as I'd ever heard in or out of an AA meeting, and he recounted it in an affectless monotone. His father died, and then a few years later his mother died, and he and his bride and their only child moved down to the first floor, whereupon he installed a young couple as upstairs tenants.

"With such an exciting life," Greg murmured, "why would he feel the need to drink?"

The story got more interesting, to listen to if not to live through, when he started making the hospital wards and the detoxes. There was this bar he'd pass on the way home from work, and he got in the habit of stopping in every day for a beer, and sometimes two. And he'd go back a couple of evenings a week to watch sports on the big screen, and of course he'd have a couple of beers in the course of an evening. He didn't get falling-down drunk, he didn't have blackouts, and his occasional hangovers never amounted to more than a parched feeling and a slight headache; all it took to put him right was a big glass of water and an aspirin.

The progression of his alcoholism was achingly slow, but what did the man have besides time? The bank cut him loose, his wife told him to move out, and it got so he never had a day when he felt anywhere near all right. A counselor at one of the detoxes got through to him and managed to get him in an outpatient program, and he went to so many meetings that they finally started making some sense to him, and he was back with his wife again, and they were taking him back at the bank.

"A true AA success story," Greg said when the applause died down. "It's too bad Milton already used the titles."

"Milton?"

"*Paradise Lost* and *Paradise Regained*. Do you know what Samuel Johnson said of *Paradise Lost*?"

"I bet you'll tell me."

"He said no one ever wished it longer, which rather fits what we just heard, wouldn't you say?"

Afterward each of us admitted we were hoping the other would suggest leaving on the break, but neither of us took the initiative, and the meeting picked up during the second half and I got to hear some good things. We stayed through the Serenity Prayer, picked up chairs and emptied ashtrays, and headed up Second Avenue discussing something somebody said. When that ran out we walked a block or two in an easy silence.

I'd given him the gist of my conversation with Redmond over the phone, and it must have been on both our minds. He broke the silence by saying, "I guess they're not going to do anything about it," and the antecedents of the two pronouns were self-evident.

I explained that they would go on working the case, putting

the word out like a fisherman chumming the water. When you worked a case hard, I said, sometimes all you were doing was trying to push the river. And when it broke, your efforts had precious little to do with it. Some guy with a resentment dropped a dime.

"The awesome power of resentments," he said. "Who knew they could turn out to be a good thing? But you would still work the case."

"When there was something to work."

"It's all very Third Step, isn't it? Taking the action and turning over the result. I had a sponsee who couldn't get a job, the man had a real Swiss cheese résumé, holes in it you could drive a van through. I had him send in job applications at the rate of one a day, and he did that for three weeks. And he didn't get an offer from a single one of the firms he applied to."

"And?"

"And what he did get, during the fourth week, was an offer out of the blue from a firm he hadn't applied to, for a job he didn't even know about. A good one, too. Would it have come his way if he hadn't been sending out those applications? You couldn't prove it one way or the other, but my own belief is that the result wouldn't have come about without the action."

"Do you sponsor many people?"

"Just a few. I get asked with some frequency, but before I say yes or no I'll spend an hour over coffee with the person, and more often than not we'll conclude that it wouldn't really work too well. Or we decide to give it a try, and after a month or two one of us fires the other. I'm what they call a Step Nazi, and even when someone thinks that's what he wants in a sponsor, the reality's not always what he thought it would be. We keep walking past coffee shops."

"I know."

"I'm not hungry myself. Are you?"

"I filled up on cookies at the meeting."

"Precisely why I'm no longer hungry. I don't know who brings those boxes of Entenmann's chocolate chip, but I wish he'd stop. I can't stay away from them, and I may have to put them on my First Step list and cut them out altogether. And just thinking about it makes me shudder, which suggests it's something I have to do." He grinned, his face lighting up. "But not today," he said.

"Like St. Augustine."

"Exactly! 'Lord, make me chaste, but not yet.' I wonder if he actually said that. Matt, since we've established that we're not hungry, do you want to come up to my place? I've got something there that I probably ought to show you. And I promise you I make better coffee than the Greeks."

This wasn't the first time I'd heard Greg refer to himself as a Step Nazi. He'd used the term after the funeral, when he told me he'd gotten Jack killed. He'd been pushing him through the steps, working him hard, and Jack had given himself over whole-heartedly to the process, rushing headlong into the amends called for in the Ninth Step. *We made direct amends to such people wherever possible,* the step read, *except when to do so would injure them or others.*

Or oneself, I thought. But I couldn't remember any warning to that effect in the literature.

Greg's apartment was on East Ninety-ninth between First and Second, three blocks above the unofficial boundary between Yorkville and East Harlem. Irish and Italian Harlem, it used to be, but the Irish and Italians had long since moved a little closer to the American dream. There was still an Italian restaurant whose customers found it worth a special trip, and there were a few Irish bars left on Second Avenue. Well, bars with Irish names, anyway. The clientele looked to be largely Hispanic and West Indian, and it was Red Stripe and not Guinness advertised in neon in the window of the Emerald Star.

I hadn't been here in years, and I could see that the neighborhood was changing once again. Between Ninety-seventh and Ninety-eighth, we passed a couple of five-story brick buildings undergoing renovation, with Dumpsters at the curb piled high with plaster and lath and flooring. And across the street they were throwing up one of those needle high-rises, a twenty-story glass-and-steel building on the site of a tenement.

I said it wasn't what you expected to find in Harlem, and Greg reminded me that they were calling it Carnegie Hill now, the latest invention of the Realtors who'd thought up Clinton as a new name for my own part of town. Until then we'd been happy enough calling it Hell's Kitchen.

He reminded me of Thoreau's observation. "'Beware of all enterprises that require new clothes.' And of neighborhoods that feel the need to change their names."

The city kept reinventing itself, creating more and more places for its prosperous citizens. There's nothing new about this, the process has been going on for more than a century, but when I looked at the buildings getting a gut rehab, I wondered what had become of the people who lived there before somebody got rid of their walls and floors.

I told myself to think about something else. *Sure,* an inner voice said. *Forget the poor bastards. The city'll take care of them, find 'em a nice Dumpster to live in.*

What was it Jim had told me? *It is your dissatisfaction with what is that is the cause of all your unhappiness.* The wisdom of the Buddha, if not the one from the midnight meeting. Something to think about, on my way to Greg Stillman's apartment.

*　　*　　*

"Mice," he said, and sniffed the air. "But no cabbage. No wet dog with garlic either. Indeterminate cooking smells. Not too bad, all in all."

Not as bad as the stairs themselves. The building code calls for an elevator in any structure of seven or more stories, and as a result there are a lot of six-story buildings in New York. This was one of them, and he lived on the top floor.

"I don't actually mind the stairs," he said. "I've been here long enough to take them for granted. When I came to New York I had a share on Eighty-fifth and Third, but I wanted my own place, and after a few months I moved in here. I got sober in this apartment, after having spent several years getting drunk in it. When I think of navigating those stairs drunk and stoned, I remember how they say God protects drunks and fools. I qualified on both counts."

The apartment was small but well-appointed. I think it must have started life as a three-room railroad flat, but he'd removed the nonbearing walls to create one long room. He'd stripped the exterior walls to the brick, which he'd rendered glossy with some sort of lacquer. He'd painted the mortar black, and here and there among the red bricks was one he'd painted white or blue or yellow. There weren't that many of those, just enough to provide an accent.

The chairs and tables were different styles, but somehow went together. Except for a couple of thrift-shop finds, he said with some pride, everything had been salvaged from the streets. In New York, he said, you found finer goods and furnishings out on the curb for trash pickup than other cities displayed in their shops.

An abstract painting, all vivid colors and sharp angles, hung on one wall. It was the gift of the artist, a friend he'd lost touch with. Another oil, a pastoral scene of barefoot nymphs and satyrs in an elaborate carved frame, he'd acquired by trading jewelry he'd made.

By the time he'd finished pointing things out, the coffee was ready, and it was as perfectly done as his apartment, even better than what Jan made on Lispenard Street. I wasn't surprised to learn that he ground the beans himself.

He said, "Matt, I have an ethical dilemma. May I ask where you are on the steps?"

"I'm concentrating on the first one," I said. "And thinking some about the second and third."

"You haven't done a formal Fourth Step."

"My sponsor says I shouldn't be in a rush. He says there's a natural progression of a step a year, and I'm in my first year, so my focus should stay on that first step."

"That's one school of thought," he said. "And there's something to the step-a-year principle, in that it takes a year for a step to really sink in. But the people who started all this back in the thirties and forties, they'd haul prospects out of hospital beds and get them on their knees, proclaiming their powerlessness over alcohol and their faith in a Higher Power and all the rest of it. They didn't even wait for the poor sons of bitches to stop shaking. They were the original Step Nazis, decades before anybody came up with the term."

"So you're not the first."

"I'm afraid not. And, as I've said, I'm not the sponsor everybody's looking for. But I wouldn't have made it in this program if I didn't have a sponsor who was every bit the hard-liner I've turned into. He made me write everything out, which I hated, and he made me pray on my knees, which I considered demeaning, and likely to interfere with the buddy relationship I'd been hoping to have with God. Two reasonable men, you know, working things out on an even footing. Lord, what an arrogant little prick I was!"

He shook his head at the memory.

"Up until the day he died," he went on, "I'd have told you I was the right sponsor for Jack. We had next to nothing in common—he was almost twenty years older, he had a much rougher life, he was straight and even a little homophobic. But he wanted what I had and he liked the message I carried, and I could tell that the only way he was going to stay sober was if he was forced to do the program the way they laid it out. Prayer every morning, prayer every night, a minimum of a meeting a day, and you do the steps in order and in writing. Can you see my dilemma?"

"He wrote it all down."

"Everything he told me, and everything he wrote out, was in strictest confidence. I'm not a priest and the seal of the confessional wouldn't protect me in a courtroom, but that's how I'd regard it, irrespective of the law. But now..."

"Now he's dead."

"Now he's dead, and what he wrote might point the police in the right direction. So where does my responsibility lie? Does his death release me from the obligation to keep silent? I know it's generally considered okay to identify a deceased person as a member of Alcoholics Anonymous. To paraphrase a syrupy book and film, death means never having to maintain your anonymity. But this is a little different, wouldn't you say?"

"In some ways."

"And not in others?" He sighed. "You know what I miss about drinking? The many opportunities it gave you to just say, 'Oh, what the hell.' Sometimes it's a pain in the ass to think things through."

"I know what you mean."

"Jack has a lot of people on his Eighth Step list. He didn't just write down the names of the people he'd harmed during his drinking years. He wrote a paragraph about each person, what he'd done and what effect it had had and what action he could possibly take to make things right. Some of the people on the list had died, and it bothered him that there was no way to make amends to a dead person."

"He told me about his father."

"How he hadn't been there when the old man died. I suggested some things he could do. He could go someplace quiet — a church sanctuary, a park. The old neighborhood in the Bronx might have been a good choice if they hadn't run an expressway through it. The venue's not important. He could go there and think about his father and talk to him."

"Talk to him?"

"And tell him all the things he wished he'd been able to tell him on his deathbed. And let the old man know he was sober now, and what that meant to him, and — well, you know, I wasn't going to compose a speech for him. He'd think of plenty of things to say."

"And who's to say if the message would get through?"

"For all I know," he said, "the old fellow's off on a cloud somewhere, and he's got ears that can hear a dog whistle." He frowned. "I mean one of those whistles only dogs can hear."

"I knew what you meant."

"It could have meant, you know, a dog whistling. Not even the dead can hear that."

"So far as we know."

He gave me a look. "There's more coffee," he said. "Can I get you another cup?"

VIII

Jack was sitting in your chair when he took the Fifth Step. He'd written out his Fourth Step, spent several weeks on it, making sure he got it all down. Then he sat there, and I sat where I am now, and he read it out loud. His voice broke a few times. It was hard going."

I could imagine.

"I would stop him now and then, you know. For amplification. But mostly he read and I took it in, or tried to. It wasn't easy."

"Heavy going?"

"Very much so. Matt, my own Fourth Step had no end of things of which I was deeply ashamed. And in program terms what matters is how your deeds weigh on your conscience, not how far down they rank on some consensus of morality. But I felt like a lightweight sinner, a positive dilettante of turpitude. My only crimes were jaywalking and cheating on my taxes. Oh, and sneaking under subway turnstiles a couple of times. You won't report me, will you?"

"I'll let it go this time."

"Don't worry, it won't happen again. I did things that weren't crimes, but that were morally reprehensible, and that I don't feel the need to mention now. But, you know, I never robbed anyone, I never hit anyone with a club. I never, Christ, I never killed anyone."

"And Jack did?"

His silence was answer enough.

After a long moment he said, "I don't feel comfortable sharing what he told me. And his character defects and his resentments didn't get him killed, and neither did his bad actions, so my feeling is they can go to the grave with him."

"That seems reasonable."

"Except there won't be a grave to go to. I've made arrangements to have him cremated, as soon as they're able to release the body. My thought is to scatter the ashes at sea. There are people who'll take you out in a boat, and you just empty the container of remains overboard." He rolled his eyes. "Or cremains, as the insiders would say. If I had a copy of his Fourth Step inventory it could go to the oven with him, if not the grave. And into the water, and—"

He'd been speaking almost cheerfully, and then it all caught up with him and choked him up. I watched him set his jaw and blink back the tears, and when he resumed speaking, his voice was steady and strong.

"My dilemma," he said, "is with his Eighth Step. I think I said it was detailed."

"A paragraph about each person."

"And some of them were long paragraphs. I would think that the person who killed him would almost have to be on that list."

"And you have a copy."

"Did I already mention that?"

"No, but you wouldn't have much of a dilemma without it. You've got his Eighth Step list and you have to decide what to do with it."

"If the police had leads, if they knew who did it whether or not they could make a case, then I wouldn't have a problem. I'd destroy his list and that would be the end of it. But they don't, and they very likely won't, and won't try very hard. So I'm in possession of information that might help them, and it's my duty as a citizen to make it available to them."

"But?"

"But there are around two dozen names on that list, Matt! That doesn't mean there are that many suspects, because he's got his dead father on the list, and a couple of other dead folks, and he's got a high school girlfriend whose pants he lied his way into, and other people who'd be unlikely to respond with a couple of bullets if he turned up and said he was sorry. But that still leaves a third or more with mean lives and criminal histories, and only one of them could have killed him, and how can I chance getting all the others in trouble?"

"And if his purpose all along was to make it up to these individuals—"

"Exactly! One minute he turns up and says he's sorry, it was the drink that made him do it, and here's that ten bucks I never paid you, or a new lamp to replace the one I knocked off the table. And the next minute he's dead, and the cops are knocking on the door."

"And the men on the list aren't the sort who welcome the attention of men in blue uniforms."

"Or Robert Hall suits. Although Mr. Redmond was quite nicely dressed, as a matter of fact."

"He's a detective."

"Oh, do they dress better than the others? I never knew that."

Two days after I got my gold shield, Eddie Koehler took me to a Fifth Avenue men's shop called Finchley's. The building's facade looked like a Norman castle, and I walked out feeling like a lord, having just bought a suit for three times what I normally spent.

I'd bought the suit to impress the public, because I'd been assured that I was a detective now, and had an image to protect. But there were other benefits; my wife had admired that suit, and so had my girlfriend.

There had been other suits, of course, but that was the one I remembered — two-button, single-breasted, the medium-blue glen-plaid fabric almost silky to the touch. ("A nice hand," the salesman had said.) Uncuffed pants. ("I don't believe we want cuffs, do we?")

I wonder what happened to that suit. Far as that goes, I wonder what happened to Finchley's. The last time I happened to look, it was gone. The crenellated building had a new tenant, with a window full of fake ivory and Orientalia for the tourist trade.

Something's there and then it's not.

Greg's problem was clear enough. If he turned Jack's Eighth Step list over to the surprisingly well-dressed Dennis Redmond, he'd be making trouble for people who'd had nothing to do with the murder. If he didn't, he'd be helping a killer go free.

I asked him if he'd talked it over with his sponsor.

"I wish I could," he said. "Do you know about the gay cancer? Kaposi's sarcoma, it's called, although I may be mispronouncing it. It's extremely rare, or at least it used to be, but now every gay man starts the day checking himself for purple blotches. Adrian

got very sick, and we were afraid he was going to die of it, because
there's no cure. But what actually killed him was pneumonia. A
very rare form of pneumonia, except it's not that rare anymore
either, not if you're a homosexual male."

I'd heard a little about it. There'd been a death in my home
group at St. Paul's, and another member had been hospitalized
several times with persistent fevers that they didn't know how to
treat.

"No one knows what causes it," he said. "A friend of mine
thinks it has something to do with the synergistic effect of leather
and quiche. We may all die of it, Matt, but we'll have some laughs
along the way."

His sponsor, Adrian, had died just over a month ago, and he
hadn't picked a replacement. "I've been holding silent auditions,"
he said, "trying people out without letting them know about it.
It'll have to be someone older than I, and with longer sobriety,
but someone who still goes to meetings on a daily basis, or close
to it. I don't want a gay man because I don't want to go through
this again, and I don't want a straight man because I just don't.
Lately I've been thinking I should get a female sponsor, but do I
want a straight woman or a lesbian?"

"Another dilemma," I said.

He nodded. "And one that will solve itself in the fullness of
time. As opposed to my other dilemma, which requires action.
Matt, you were a policeman. Are you likely to go back to that?"

"Get reinstated?" I'd thought about it early on, talked it over
with Jim Faber. "No," I said. "That's not going to happen."

"So now you're a private detective."

"Not exactly. Private investigators are licensed. After I left the
department, I started working privately for people, but in a very
unofficial off-the-books kind of way. I would be doing favors,
and they'd be giving me money as an expression of gratitude."

"And now?"

"I'm looking for a job the way you're looking for a sponsor," I said. "Someone suggested a free program, EPRA, I forget what the initials stand for —"

"Employment Program for Recovering Alcoholics. Jack started going, but he wasn't able to stick with it. He got by delivering lunches for a deli. Not exactly a career, but a pretty good get-sober job."

"Well, my get-sober job seems to be the one I had when I came in. In the past eleven months I've had enough work come my way so that the rent keeps getting paid and I don't miss any meals."

"You do favors for people, and they show their gratitude."

"Right."

"Well," he said, "I'd like you to do me a favor."

IX

I T WAS WELL past midnight by the time I got home. There were no messages waiting for me, just the usual run of junk mail. I tossed it when I got to my room, but I kept the 9x12 manila envelope addressed to Gregory Stillman, with the hand-stamped return address of a firm in Wichita, Kansas. It had once held a catalog of jewelers' supplies, but now it contained Jack Ellery's Eighth Step, the list of people he had allegedly harmed, among whose number one might well expect to find the name of his killer.

I'd glanced at the first page of the list, just to make sure I'd be able to read Jack's handwriting, and had then watched Greg slip it into the envelope and fasten the metal clasp. Now I put it on my dresser unopened and got out of my clothes and under the shower.

The envelope was still there when I got out of the shower. I opened it and drew out a sheaf of unruled pages held together by a paper clip. The pages were numbered, and there were nine of them, all covered with Jack's compact but legible handwriting, dark blue ink on white paper.

The first name at the top of the first page was Raymond Ellery, who turned out to be Jack's late father. I read a couple of sentences and felt a wave of tiredness wash over me. This could wait, all of it. I put the pages back in the envelope, refastened the clasp, and got into bed.

I remembered that I hadn't prayed. I didn't see the point of it, it wasn't really my style, but I'd spent almost a year now doing things that weren't my style and that I only occasionally saw the point of. So I kept it simple, starting the day by asking for another day of sobriety, ending it with thanks for another sober day.

But only when I remembered. I remembered now, but I was in bed with the light out, and I didn't really feel like getting out of bed and down on my knees — which wasn't really my style either.

"Thank you," I said to whatever might be listening. And let it go at that.

"He gave me a thousand dollars," I told Jim. "Ten hundred-dollar bills. He didn't have to count them, he had them set aside in his wallet, so I don't guess he was making things up as he went along."

"I trust you remembered your police training."

"I put it in my pocket."

Another thing Vince Mahaffey had told me, years ago in Brooklyn. That's what you did when somebody handed you money.

"You don't sound happy," Jim said, "for somebody with a thousand dollars in his pocket."

"Most of it's gone. I paid the next month's rent, and I sent Anita a money order. I put a couple of bucks in the bank, and what's left is in my wallet."

"All of it? Or did you give up a tenth of your crop as a burnt offering to the gods?"

"Well," I said.

Some years ago I'd gotten in the habit of tithing, slipping ten percent of what money I received into the first church collection box I came to. Jim found this an amusing eccentricity, and one he assumed would fade away in sobriety. Meanwhile the Catholics got most of my money, if only because their sanctuaries were more likely to be open, and on my way home I'd detoured to pay my respects to the poor box at St. Paul the Apostle. And while I was there I lit a couple of candles, one of them for Jack Ellery.

"You're still a few dollars ahead of where you were yesterday," Jim pointed out, "and you still don't sound very happy."

"I took the money," I said. "Now I have to earn it."

"By finding out who killed your friend."

"By finding out if there's a name here I feel comfortable passing on to Redmond. I suppose that amounts to the same thing."

"Can't you just eliminate the ones who couldn't have done it and give him whoever's left?"

"Stillman could have done that himself," I said. "The idea is to avoid creating a problem for someone who's innocent of Jack's murder, even though he may not be innocent of much else."

"Some nasty people on that list?"

"I don't know who's on it," I said, "except for Jack's father, and he's been dead for a few years now."

"Which would constitute exculpatory evidence, wouldn't it? You haven't read the list?"

"I was too tired last night, and this morning I found other things to do. I guess I'll go read it now."

"That's probably a good idea," my sponsor said.

But it still wasn't something I wanted to do, and I went back to the room entertaining the fantasy that the manila envelope would have disappeared during my absence. The maid—whose weekly visit was a day away—would have come early, changing my sheets and emptying my wastebasket and consigning Jack's Eighth Step to the incinerator. Or a burglar would have broken in and, annoyed at having found nothing worth stealing, would have walked off with it. Or spontaneous combustion, or a flash flood, or—

It was there. I sat down and read it.

By the time I was done I'd skipped lunch, and the sun was down. I went out and had something to eat before my regular Friday night step meeting at St. Paul's. I had the urge to leave at the break but made myself stay for the whole meeting.

"I'm going to pass on coffee tonight," I told Jim. "I think I'll go to a bar instead."

"You know, there's been many a time I've had that thought myself."

"I read that fucking list," I said, "and it took forever, because I kept stopping and staring out the window."

"At the liquor store across the street?"

"At the Trade Center towers, I suppose, but I wasn't really looking at anything. Just gazing off into the distance. It was hard going, Jim. I got more of a peek than I wanted into the guy's heart and soul."

"So what else would you want to do but go to a bar?"

I gave him a look. "I've got a slip of paper with five names on it, and there's a guy I want to run them past."

"And the bar's where you have to meet him."

"It's where he'll be. The Top Knot or Poogan's Pub. He switches back and forth."

"A man wouldn't want to get stuck in a rut," he said. "You think it might be a good idea to take someone with you?"

"I'm not going to drink."

"No," he said, "you're not, but you might be more comfortable with a sober friend along."

I thought about it, weighed that against the inhibiting effect of a stranger at the table. "Not this time," I said. "I'll be fine."

"Whichever bar you'll find him in, I'm sure they'll have a pay phone. And you've got plenty of quarters, don't you?"

"Quarters and subway tokens. Although I won't need a token. I'll be on West Seventy-second, I'll walk there and back."

"That's fine," he said. "The exercise'll do you good."

I walked up to the corner of Seventy-second and Columbus. Poogan's was half a block one way and the Top Knot was about as far in the other direction, and I felt like the donkey standing midway between two bales of hay. Either you made an arbitrary choice or you starved to death. I flipped a mental coin and went to the Top Knot, and of course he was at Poogan's, sitting at a table with an iced bottle of Stoli in a wood-grained plastic bucket.

The man at the table was holding a Rubik's Cube, not manipulating it, just frowning at it. I walked over and said, "Hello, Danny Boy," and without raising his eyes he said, "Matthew, have you ever seen one of these things?"

"I've seen them. I've never actually played with one of them."

"Somebody gave this to me," he said. "The idea is to wind up with solid colors on all six sides, though why anyone would want to go to the trouble is beyond me. Do you want this?"

"No, but thanks."

He put the device on the table, looked up at me, smiled broadly. "Sit down," he said. "It's good to see you. Maybe I'll leave this toy for the waitress. I get the feeling she's easily amused. You're looking well, Matthew. Something to drink?"

"Maybe a Coke," I said, "but there's no hurry. We can wait until she shows up to collect her Rubik's Cube."

"*That's* what it's called. I was thinking Kubek, but I knew that was wrong. Remember Tony Kubek?"

The Yankee infielder, and I did indeed remember him, and we talked baseball for a few minutes. Then the waitress came by and I ordered a Coke, and Danny Boy took a drink of vodka and let her top up his glass.

Danny Boy Bell is a diminutive albino Negro, always superbly dressed by the boys' departments at Saks and Paul Stuart. His albinism has made him a creature of the night, but I think he'd keep vampire's hours regardless of his skin's sensitivity to sunlight. The world needs two things, I've heard him say, a dimmer switch and a volume control, both of them dialed way down. Dark rooms and soft music are his natural preference, all washed down with vodka, with the occasional company of some pretty young woman unburdened by much in the way of brainpower.

When I was working out of the Sixth, Danny Boy was my best snitch, and one of only a few whose company didn't make me feel like I needed a shower. He wasn't looking to beat a criminal charge, or even a score, or feel important. He was in fact not so much a snitch as a broker in information, and every night he put in his hours at Poogan's or the Knot, and people on every side of the law pulled up a chair at his table to ask him things or tell him things or both. He lived within a few blocks of both of his hangouts, and he rarely went anywhere else unless it was to watch a fight at the Garden or catch a set at a jazz club. Mostly he sat in his chair and drank his vodka, and it might have been water for all the visible effect it had on him.

My Coke came, and I took a sip and wondered what visible effect it had on me.

I said, "There's a fellow who got himself killed a week ago. Lived in a furnished room in the East Nineties, made ends meet by delivering lunches for a delicatessen in the neighborhood."

"The ends couldn't have been too far apart," he said, "if that brought in enough to make them meet. What was his name?"

"John Joseph Ellery, but everyone called him Jack."

He shook his head. "Didn't hear about the murder, and I can't say the name rings a bell. What did he do before he decided to give UPS some competition?"

"A little of this and a little of that."

"Ah, a useful trade. And was he still doing a little of both when he wasn't helping them out at the deli?"

"He went straight," I said, and brandished my glass of Coke. "And found a new way of life."

"A drier path, so to speak. A path I see you're still pursuing yourself, Matthew. It's been a while now, hasn't it?"

"A year next month."

"That's great," he said, and it was clear he meant it, which pleased me. Not everyone I used to drink with was all that enthusiastic about the road I'd taken, and Jim said their reaction said more about them and their own drinking than it did about me and my sobriety. Some felt threatened, he said, while others assumed I'd disapprove of them and wanted to beat me to the punch.

All the subject of drinking did for Danny Boy was remind him that he had a full glass in front of him, and in response he drank some of it. He said, "John Ellery, better known as Jack. Jack Ellery. Where'd he get killed?"

"At home."

"In his furnished room. How?"

"Two bullets. One in the forehead, one in the mouth."

" 'Keep your mouth shut'?"

"Most likely."

"As opposed to 'You shoulda kept your mouth shut, you fucking rat bastard,' with the penis severed and stuffed into the mouth, or sometimes halfway down the throat. Are the Italians the only ones who employ that particular calling card, Matthew, or is it in wider use?"

I had no idea.

"A little of this, and a little of that. I hate to press for details, but—"

"Armed robbery, mostly. That's what he went away for. Liquor stores, mom-and-pop groceries, walk in, show a gun, walk out with what he could grab out of the register. It's not surprising if you never heard of him, because he was very small-time, and it's no surprise you didn't hear about the homicide. If there was anything in the papers, I didn't see it myself."

He was frowning in concentration. "Jack, Jack, Jack. Did he have a sobriquet?"

"Come again?"

"A nickname, for Christ's sake. And don't tell me you didn't know the word."

"I knew it," I said. "I've come across it in print, but I'm not sure I ever heard anyone say it before. I certainly never heard anyone say it in Poogan's."

"It's a perfectly fine word. And it's not exactly the same as a nickname. Take Charles Lindbergh. His nickname was Lindy—"

"As in hop," I suggested.

"—and his sobriquet was the Lone Eagle. George Herman Ruth, nickname was Babe, sobriquet was the Sultan of Swat. Al Capone—"

"I get the idea."

"I just wanted to keep on saying it, Matthew. Sobriquet. I know it from reading, and *I* don't think I ever heard it before, and I know for certain I never *said* it before. I wonder if I'm pronouncing it correctly."

"I'm the wrong person to ask."

"I'll look it up," he said, and he picked up his glass and put it down without drinking. "High-Low Jack," he said. "Wasn't that his fucking sobriquet? Isn't that what they called him?"

X

HIGH-LOW JACK," Greg Stillman said.

"They didn't call him that in the rooms?"

"They just called him Jack, which is what he called himself. Oh, and Jailhouse Jack or Jack the Jailbird, but not to his face."

One result of anonymity is that we mostly know each other by our first names, so we come up with handles to distinguish one Jack from another. At St. Paul's, we've got Tall Jim and Jim the Runner and my own sponsor, Army Jacket Jim, because of the beat-up garment he's rarely seen without.

If I've got a nickname — or a sobriquet, if you prefer — I don't know what it might be. Matt the Cop? Gumshoe Matt? I'm the only Matt at St. Paul's, so they probably haven't needed to come up with a name for me.

"There was no insult implied," Greg added. "Jack's prison experience figured in a lot of his shares. How he got what he deserved, and how he'd never have wound up in prison if he hadn't been drinking. So if you were looking for something to call him, it was a logical choice. But High-Low Jack. What does it even mean?"

"I don't know. I heard the phrase from a cop at the Sixth when I was on the job myself, and I never heard it since until this evening."

"From—?"

"A source," I said, and wondered if *Danny Boy* was a nickname or a sobriquet. I'd never heard him called anything else, and for all I knew you'd find *Danny Boy Bell* right there on his birth certificate.

"And this source knew Jack?"

"Never met him, and didn't know very much about him."

"But he knew what people called him, or used to call him, which is more than I knew. It wasn't in his Fourth Step, and I think I'd remember the phrase if I'd ever heard it before."

"Was he a gambler? A cardplayer?"

"Jack? I don't think so. He did mention a day he'd spent at a racetrack some years ago, but more in the context of drinking than gambling. Something about how he couldn't ever seem to get to the window in time to get his bet down, because he'd hang around at the bar and have one more drink."

"In other words, drinking saved him money."

"So it wasn't all bad."

They did have a pay phone in Poogan's Pub, and I know it was in working order because I'd seen people talking on it while I sat watching Danny Boy drink enough Stolichnaya vodka to restore the Soviet economy. It was free when I was ready to leave, but instead I walked to the corner. The first phone I tried was out of order, but there was a working one across the street, and the first call I made was to my sponsor.

"No, it's not too late," he assured me. "I hear the squeal of brakes, not the cries of the inebriated, so my guess is you're calling me from the street."

"You're the one who should have been a detective. What do the words *High-Low Jack* mean to you?"

"There's a card game," he said, "the name of which is Spit in the Ocean, if I remember correctly. Or just Spit for short. I forget how you play it, but there are four things you get points for — high, low, jack, and the game. That's the phrase, as I recall. 'High, Low, Jack, and the Game.' That help?"

"I don't know."

"I can't see how it would," he said. "High-Low Jack. High-low in poker is what you call it when the best and worst hands split the pot. I don't know how Jack enters into the equation."

"Jacks or better," I suggested.

"Which brings to mind another game, a form of draw poker. You need a pair of jacks to open —"

"Right."

"— but if nobody has jacks or better, then the hand turns into lowball, and the low hand takes the pot. That would be five-four-three-deuce-ace, or six-four-three-deuce-ace, or even seven-five-four-three-deuce, depending on the house rules."

"I didn't know you were a poker player."

"Just buck-limit games, mostly printers, we played in the back room of a shop on Hudson Street. I lost my enthusiasm for the pastime when I came out of a blackout in the middle of a hand with no idea why I'd been betting it so hard. Jacks and Back, that's what we called that particular variant. But that can't be any help either. It go all right this evening?"

"It went okay," I said. "It was good to see Danny Boy, and I put some things in motion."

"And you didn't pick up a drink."

"No, I didn't. When I left, Danny had just given the waitress a Rubik's Cube and you'd have thought it was the Hope Diamond."

"Isn't that the one with the curse?"

"Well, unless *she's* the one with the curse, I'd say he's going to get lucky tonight."

"I teed that one up for you, didn't I? You can thank me another time. High-Low Jack. You hit 'em high and I'll hit 'em low. Or is it the other way around?"

After he'd agreed to sponsor me, one of the first things Jim did was give me a little red leather change purse as a present. There was a quarter in it, and a subway token.

"That's a starter," he'd said. "Make sure you've always got a dozen quarters in there, and half a dozen tokens. So you can always make a phone call and you can always hop on a bus or a subway home."

"Like a mob guy," I said, and explained that every wiseguy we brought in always had a ten-dollar roll of quarters in his pocket. They'd learned to avoid wiretaps by making all their calls from pay phones, and a roll of quarters came in handy other times as well; wrap your fist around it, and you could punch a whole lot harder.

I hadn't felt the need to hit anybody since I got sober, nor was I worried that someone was tapping my phone. But I never left my room without my supply of quarters and tokens, and I spent a second quarter on a call to my client, and learned as little from him as he did from me. He seemed pleased that I was working the case and putting things in motion, but I got the sense that he wasn't hugely concerned about how my investigation was going.

Walking home, I figured out why. He'd had a dilemma— what to do?—and he'd resolved it by passing the ball to me.

What happened now didn't matter all that much to him. He'd done what he needed to do, and now he could turn it over.

It was very much in the spirit of the Third Step: *We made a decision to turn our will and our lives over to the care of God, as we understood Him.*

I'd heard the words no end of times—in specific discussions of the step, and in "How It Works," the Big Book selection read at the beginning of most meetings. I liked the idea of it, but I didn't have a clue how to do it. There was something in the literature about using the key of willingness, and sooner or later it would open the lock; that was nicely poetic, but I still didn't know what the hell they were talking about.

The Third Step doesn't mean God will do the laundry and walk the dog. That was another of the things I'd heard people say. In other words, what? Turn it over and do it all yourself? That didn't sound right.

Don't drink, Jim told me. Don't drink, and go to meetings. That's all you need to know for now.

There was a message from Jan at the desk. Call anytime before midnight, it said, but it was well past the hour. We hadn't confirmed our standing date, and I'd have to remember to do that in the morning. Or I could invent a reason to skip it this week, but wasn't it too late to do that? It seemed to me that Saturday morning was too late to break a Saturday night date, and I'm sure it's all explained logically in the Big Book and the Twelve & Twelve, with the proverbial key of willingness playing a starring role.

I remembered, for a change, and hit my knees before I got into bed. "Thank you for another sober day," I said, feeling righteous and stupid at the same time. It's remarkable how often the two feelings coincide.

XI

I READ THE *TIMES* with my breakfast, then went back to my room and called Jan. We agreed we'd go to the SoHo meeting at St. Anthony's, and I said I'd rather have dinner after than before, if that was all right with her. She said that was fine, she'd have a late lunch.

"I'd have called last night," I said, "but it was too late by the time I got home. I had to see a fellow, a dedicated night-owl type."

"It sounds like you're working."

"I am," I said. "I'm not sure there's much point to it, but I'm getting paid."

"Isn't that point enough?"

"It may have to be. There are some people I want to see, and I don't know if I'll be able to, but I'm going to spend the day trying. That's why I'd like to wait and have dinner afterward."

Why was I explaining? Why did I always feel I had to explain everything? We weren't married, for Christ's sake, and even if we were—

"So I'll see you at SoHo," she said, cheerfully oblivious to the silent argument we were having, "and afterward we can go to one of those Eyetie places on Thompson Street, and you can tell me all about your case."

Besides Jack Ellery's, I'd had five names to try on Danny Boy. He'd scanned the list, then tapped one name with his forefinger. "Alan MacLeish," he said. "Or Piper MacLeish, as I've heard him called."

"Because he's Scottish?"

"That may have been a factor, but I think it had less to do with bagpipes than the kind you hit people over the head with."

"That was his weapon of choice?"

"So far as I know," Danny Boy said, "he only used it once, but he did time for it, and the name stuck. You know the story about poor Pierre the Bridge Builder."

"Sure."

"'Ah, monsieur, I, Pierre, built zat bridge. I have built dozens of bridges. But do zey call me Pierre ze Bridge Builder? Zey do not.'"

"That's the one."

"'But suck one cock.' Jesus, the old jokes are the best jokes. That's why they lasted." He picked up the Rubik's Cube, gave it a look, put it down again. "I'm pretty sure Piper's back inside. He was middlemanning a heroin transaction and the Rockefeller drug laws got him a long sentence. That was a few years ago, but I'd be surprised if he got out yet."

The next two names didn't register at all. "Crosby Hart. I don't recall ever hearing about anybody with Crosby for a first name. Seems to me I'd remember if I had. On the other hand, this next one goes to the other extreme. Robert Williams? How many folks do you suppose answer to that one?"

"I'm not even sure he was a crook," I said. "He was a friend of Jack's, and Jack screwed his wife, and thought he might have fathered a child."

"In other words, start looking for a Robert Williams with a wife who fucks around. Narrows it down."

There were two more names, and Danny Boy recognized them but didn't know what they'd been up to or where to find them. "There was a Sattenstein, an uptown fellow. Cabrini Boulevard? Somewhere up there. A small-time fence, if I've got the right person, and then he fell off the radar. Frankie Dukes, now there's a name I know, though I can't think why. Is Dukes a surname or did they call him that because he was handy with his fists?"

Not too handy, I thought. *Gave him a bad beating,* Jack had noted on his list. *Broke his nose and two ribs.*

"Well, somebody will probably know something," Danny Boy said, "or they'll know somebody who does. You know how it works."

I knew how it worked. In my hotel room I looked at my list of names and crossed off Alan MacLeish. *Got him in trouble,* Jack had noted after his name, and if he'd been responsible for getting him sent away, I'd have to call that an understatement. But he'd also noted the difficulty in making things right with the man, and a closer reading showed that the Piper was indeed behind stone walls, and that Jack had known as much. *Have to be on visitors' list, have to be approved correspondent. How?*

How indeed?

That left Crosby Hart, Mark Sattenstein, Frankie Dukes, and the cuckolded Robert Williams. I opened the Manhattan phone book and let my fingers do the walking. There were Harts but no Crosby, Dukeses but no Frank. There was a single Mark Sattenstein, with an address on East Seventeenth Street.

Easy choice. I dialed the listed number. It rang four times, and then an answering machine picked up and a male voice invited me to leave a message, sounding as though he didn't much care if I did or not.

I hung up and copied down Sattenstein's address and phone number. Then I let my feet do the walking as far as Columbus Circle, where I caught the subway downtown.

Up until recently I'd have made another phone call, one to Eddie Koehler, who'd been my rabbi in the NYPD and had a lot to do with my assignment to the Sixth, where he headed the detectives squad. He'd have helped me out over the phone, thus saving me a trip downtown, and while he was at it he'd go through the motions and urge me to apply for reinstatement as a cop.

I put in my papers not long after a stray bullet of mine killed a young girl in Washington Heights. That incident didn't cause my resignation from the department any more than it caused the end of my marriage, but it would be accurate to say it precipitated both of those events, and left me with something to spend the next several years drinking about.

As far as the NYPD was concerned, it was a righteous shooting. I'd been chasing two holdup men who'd already killed a bartender, and my bullets killed one of them and brought down the other, which is pretty good when it's night and your targets are moving. The bullet that struck the child did so on the hop, ricocheting wildly and to chilling effect. Her death was a tragedy, but I didn't get a reprimand because I hadn't done anything wrong. What I got was a commendation.

I never felt it was justified. I discharged my service revolver and a child died, and it's not as though the two phenomena were unconnected. When I write out my own Eighth Step list, Estrellita Rivera's name will be up there near the top, though what I can ever do in the way of amends is beyond me.

But all that is beside the point. When I got sober, Jim and I had one of those talks about the future, and one question that came up was what I was going to do to earn a living. Resuming my career as a cop was one option we discussed, and I talked about it with Jan as well, and then Eddie Koehler, who'd already stayed in harness a couple of years past retirement age, put in his papers, and sold his house and moved to Florida.

I suppose I still had the option of applying for reinstatement, but a day at a time I left that road untaken, and it began to seem less and less realistic. I'd been away long enough so that some strings would have to be pulled to get me back in, and Eddie wasn't around to pull them, and what friends I had in the department didn't have his clout.

And, on occasions like this one, I had to use the subway instead of the phone.

I could picture the cop with whom I'd watched Jack Ellery's lineup, saw the high forehead and the bright blue eyes and the bulldog jaw, but I couldn't remember his name. I got to within a block of the station house on West Tenth before it came to me. Lonergan—but I still couldn't come up with his first name. I asked the desk sergeant for Detective Lonergan, and his face clouded.

"That'd be Bill Lonergan," he said, and told me he'd retired back in March or April. He gave me a phone number, and I was heading for the door when he called me back and told me I could use the phone. "Save you the price of a call," he said, "and the six-block hike looking for one that actually works."

I made the call and a woman answered on the second ring. She put him on the line, and I recognized the voice. I told him who I was and he repeated my name and said he couldn't place me. I told him I was looking into the death of Jack Ellery, and that name didn't seem to ring much of a bell, either.

"It was a case of yours," I said, "but this was some years ago."

"It'll come to me," he said. "Listen, why don't you come out here? I'll remember you once I get a look at you, and this Ellery too, most likely."

"High-Low Jack, you called him."

"Now that's familiar," he allowed. "Time you get here, I'll see if I can't get my memory working."

He lived in the Woodside section of Queens, in one of a row of small single-family houses with tiny front lawns and asphalt siding. The ride took the better part of an hour, I had to take two trains to get there, and on the way I considered the fact that he couldn't have been more than a few years older than I, which made him young for retirement. And I remembered how the desk sergeant's face had darkened when I mentioned Lonergan's name.

I put that in the hopper, along with the sergeant's quickness to supply a phone number and even to provide a phone, and I tossed in Lonergan's willingness, even eagerness, to have me visit. There was really only one way all those elements added up, and so I wasn't much surprised when Mrs. Lonergan opened the door to my knock and led me in to meet her husband. He was wearing a robe and pajamas, and he was sitting in an easy chair watching a TV with the sound turned off, and his face was gaunt and his complexion jaundiced, and he was dying.

Because I was prepared, I don't think my face showed much in the way of shock, but Lonergan was a detective, so he probably got a reading. But all he said was "Yeah, sure, Matt Scudder. Came to me the minute I got off the phone. I don't recall that we ever worked a case together, but there was a time or two we went out and had a few. What was that joint on Sheridan Square? Not the Lion's Head but the place next door to it."

"The Fifty-five."

"That's it. Jesus, that was a good place for serious drinking. You didn't go there to sip a fucking white wine spritzer. Speaking of which, what'll you have? There's Scotch and Scotch. Or, unless someone grabbed it, there's a stray can of Ballantine's Ale in the icebox."

"I think I'll pass," I said. And added, quite uncharacteristically, "I quit drinking a while back, Bill. I joined AA, went the whole way."

"Did you. When was this?"

"It's almost a year now."

"Let me look at you," he said, and did. "You look all right. I hope you stopped in time. Would you drink a ginger ale?"

"Sure, if it's no trouble."

He assured me it wasn't, called out to summon his wife. "Edna, sweetie, could you bring the two of us a couple of ginger ales? They're cold already, don't bother with ice. In fact right out of the can is fine."

But she brought in highball glasses, with a few ice cubes in each. He thanked her, and when she'd left he said, "The doc gave me the green light, said drink if I want to, that at this point it doesn't make any difference. If you were drinking I'd keep you company. But the booze doesn't sit well on my stomach these days." He held his glass to the light. "Looks enough like booze," he said. "Little dark for Scotch, but it could be bourbon and soda." He took a sip, said, "Nope, ginger ale. Isn't that a relief and a disappointment? You're too much of a gentleman to ask, so I'll tell you, and then we can put it on the shelf. It's cirrhosis, with a side order of liver cancer. So it doesn't matter if I drink but it feels better if I don't. End of story."

He said, "Jack Ellery. You say somebody killed him? You told me that a year ago, I'd have said something along the lines of good riddance. Still, your perspective changes when you're staring at it yourself. Lately I'm not so quick to wish death on anybody, you know?"

"Sure."

"But the guy was a lowlife. No way around it. You're working this on a private ticket?"

Not quite, in that I didn't have a license. But that was close enough, and I nodded.

"So you got a client. Somebody who cares enough to pay money to find out who put him away."

"A friend of his."

He thought about it. "He's a guy who could have a friend or two," he allowed, "though he wouldn't hang on to them for long. Kind of guy who'd be a friend of his, assuming he'd want to know who killed him, is he gonna go to an ex-cop to find out?"

He was still a pretty good detective. "The friend's straight," I said, wondering how long it had been since anyone had applied that adjective to Gregory Stillman.

"It's not a girlfriend, or you'd have said so." He looked at me. "AA."

"Good catch, Bill."

"I never thought of Ellery as a drunk," he said. "I mean, he drank, but who the hell didn't? You drank, I drank——" He broke off, shook his head. "Well, there you go, huh? Look at us now. Anyway, I can't say I ever got to know the son of a bitch.

All I wanted to do was put him away, and the case fell apart, and at that point I lost interest."

"The two of you never bellied up to the bar at the Fifty-five."

He shook his head. "You ever drink with him yourself?"

"When I knew him in the Bronx, we were both drinking chocolate milk. By the time I met him again we were both sober."

"He actually quit drinking?"

"He was sober two years when he died."

I told him a little more about Jack's death—how he'd shown the effects of a beating, then took two bullets not long afterward. I ran my five names past him and explained where they came from.

He said, "Making amends, did you call it? All of your crowd does that?"

"It's recommended."

He shook his head. "Maybe it's just as well I never tried that route. A list like that, Christ, I wouldn't know where to start."

XII

WHEN I WAS ready to leave, Lonergan insisted on walking out onto the front stoop with me. "This neighborhood was all Irish," he said. "Now you've got South Americans moving in. Colombians and Venezuelans mostly, and I forget what else. Maybe Ecuador. Some of the old joints have closed. Houlihan's, used to be on the corner, now it's a travel agency for the new arrivals." He shrugged. "I guess they're all right, the new people. They can't be that much worse than we were."

I stopped at one of the new places a block before the subway entrance. It was a luncheonette, and I took a stool at the counter and ordered a café con leche. They used evaporated milk from a can, and it was sweet and not bad, but I didn't like it enough to order it again.

I thought about Bill Lonergan, and decided I hadn't known him well enough to tell how the prospect of death had changed him. We'd gotten all the conversational mileage we could out of

Jack Ellery, which wasn't much. He didn't recognize any of the names on Jack's Eighth Step list, but one of them reminded him of someone else entirely, and that sent the conversation off on a diverting tangent. We told our war stories, and talked about colleagues from the Sixth, and I stayed longer than I would have because he seemed to want the company.

The lunch counter had a pay phone, and I used it to call Mark Sattenstein. I got the answering machine, and that was response enough to keep the phone from returning my quarter.

No problem. I had a change purse full of them.

The train I caught in Woodside was headed for Times Square, but at Grand Central I transferred to the Lexington line. I got off at Fourteenth Street and tried another quarter in another phone, but this time I rang off the instant the machine picked up, and the phone gave me back my quarter. I seemed to be getting the hang of it.

I walked three blocks up and two blocks east until I came to a five-story redbrick building on the uptown side of the street, a fire escape centered on the facade. The house number was the one I'd written down for Sattenstein, and in the vestibule I found his name on the buzzer for Apartment 3-A.

I positioned my forefinger over the button, then drew it back. There were four apartments to a floor, and the A line was likely to be in front, and on the left. That wasn't carved in stone, a building's owner could number his apartments as he preferred, even as he could call his building whatever struck his fancy. The original owner of this particular structure had called it the Guinevere, and I knew this because it was indeed carved in stone, just above the front door.

Outside, I stood on the sidewalk and found what ought to be 3-A's front window. There was a light on inside, but even if it was the right apartment it didn't necessarily prove anything. I returned to the vestibule and buzzed him, and I'd given up and started for the door when the intercom cleared its mechanical throat. I stayed put, and whatever somebody said in 3-A was completely garbled by the time it worked its way downstairs. I couldn't make out a word of it.

I answered in kind, making some noises that weren't designed to be understood, and there was a long silence. Then, with what I could only assume was some reluctance, he buzzed me in.

I guess the neighborhood hadn't changed too much, because I picked up the scent of mice and cabbage in the stairwell. Three-A was where I'd thought it would be, and I approached the door quietly and was standing well to the side when I knocked. I didn't really expect him to shoot through the door, but Jack probably hadn't expected to catch two bullets in the head either.

I heard footsteps not much louder than my own, and the sound of a peephole being drawn back. A judas, they sometimes call it, though I've never known why. Betrayal? Thirty pieces of silver?

I was standing where I couldn't be shot, and hence couldn't be seen either. I had my wallet out, open to an old card proclaiming my membership in the Fraternal Order of Police. Its only use, as far as I know, is to induce an impressionable officer to cut an errant motorist some slack. I said my name, Matthew Scudder, and held the card to the peephole. "Like to talk to you about Jack Ellery," I said, and I had my wallet back in my pocket well before he'd managed to get the door open.

He was tall, six-two or six-three, big in the shoulders, small in the waist and hips. He had a rough-hewn face, but the big brown eyes could have belonged to Bambi; he looked not so much like a knockaround guy as like an actor who kept getting cast in that kind of role. He was holding the door with his left hand, and a look at his elaborately bandaged right hand explained why it had taken him so long to open it.

He looked at once frightened and relieved, and that fit his opening words: "I've been expecting you."

But how? I hadn't left a message. I said something to that effect, and he said, "Well, you or someone like you. A police officer."

He waited for me to say something, and I didn't, and he said, "Ever since I heard about Jack."

I looked at him, his face, his bandaged hand, and I got it. I said, "You're the guy who beat him up."

XIII

BEFORE HE COULD tell me any more, I undid the work of the FOP card I'd flashed at him. I'd never said I was a cop, and there were times when I was willing to let someone retain that impression, but we were past the point where I felt comfortable sailing under the blue flag. I told him I was a former police officer now working privately, that I'd known Jack Ellery when we were boys together in the Bronx. "So you're under no obligation to talk to me," I said.

That last would have been just as true if I'd been the commissioner himself. And it was safe to say, because I could tell he was ready to talk. Eager, even.

First, though, he wanted me to come in and make myself comfortable. His apartment was the *before* version of Greg Stillman's place in Carnegie Hill — before the exterior wall was taken down to the bare brick, before the floor was stripped and sanded and refinished, before the three small rooms were combined into one. Instead they remained coupled together like railroad cars. The door led into the little kitchen, with the living room at one end overlooking East Seventeenth Street, and the bedroom at the other. The furniture could have been gathered from thrift shops and the street, but the mismatched pieces didn't clash enough to be labeled eclectic.

He took me to the living room and pointed me toward an upholstered chair. He was going to make himself a cup of tea, he said, and would that suit me? Or there was beer, if I'd prefer that. I said tea would be fine.

There were two posters on the wall, both from shows at the Whitney, both artists even I could recognize — Mark Rothko and Edward Hopper. I studied them in turn, and I was still going back and forth between them when he put a cup of tea on the table beside me. He said it was Earl Grey and I said that was fine. The posters, he said, belonged to a woman who'd lived with him for just about two years.

"Then out of the blue she decided she was a lesbian. I mean, she was no kid. Younger'n me, but well up in her thirties, you know? How can you get to be that old and all along you're a lesbian and you haven't got a clue? How does that happen?"

"I gather it happens a lot."

"Does it happen to guys?"

"I think everything happens to everybody," I said, "but it seems to happen more often with women."

He thought about it, shrugged. "Well, she left the posters here," he said. "'I'm done with 'em, Mark. You don't want 'em, toss 'em.' Why would I do that? They look okay. I'm used to them. That tea okay?"

"It's fine."

"You ever bust your hand? Just about everything you do becomes complicated. I still can't tie my shoes. Thank God for loafers, huh?"

"Where did it happen, Mark?"

"Right here. He called me on the phone, said he's got something to tell me, can he come over? I tried to get him to tell me over the phone, because it's like he's from a past life, you know? And I don't remember him or that life with a whole lot of affection, so I'd just as soon hear whatever he's got to say and be done with him. But no, this has to be face-to-face. I tell him I'm busy and he says okay, pick a time that works, just about any time at all will work for him. And I'm this close to telling him fuck off, leave me alone, whatever it is I don't want to hear about it. This close."

"But you told him to come over."

"There was something made me think he'd be harder to shake than a summer cold, and I'm better off seeing him and getting it over and done with. And after I got off the phone with him I'm thinking, Hey, we used to be friends, and just because I'm living a different life these days, and there's probably no place in it for a guy like High-Low Jack, that doesn't mean I can't be civil to him."

High-Low Jack.

"So he comes in, and there's something different about him, some light in his eyes. Makes me a little uneasy. But it's been years, you know? Come in, good to see you, take a load off, have a beer. Of course he wouldn't have a beer. You know about that?"

"He'd stopped drinking," I said.

"Said he was an alcoholic, which I could believe, the way he used to put it away. But then we all did back then, you know? We were kids, we partied hard, we got in trouble. Crazy shit. You grow up and it changes." He considered. "Or you don't and it doesn't. Whatever. So okay, you don't want a beer, how about a cup of tea? But he doesn't want anything, he just wants to get down to business. To make things right, except there was another word he kept using."

"Amends."

"Right, amends. I don't think I ever heard anybody use that word outside of the context of, you know, an amendment to the Constitution. Amends. You know what he did? You know what this was all about?"

"Something about a burglary," I said. "He sold something to you and stole it back again, something along those lines."

He was silent for a moment, thinking about it. Then he said, "What I was, I was a receiver. I never went away for it, I never even got arrested for it. You needed to sell something, I'd buy it for cash. You were looking to buy something, if I had it you'd be getting a bargain. But cash, no receipts, and don't ask where it came from. Like, you know, stolen goods."

"Not usually a young man's business."

"Well, I had someone to teach me the ropes. You ever know a man named Selig Wolf? My uncle, my mother's younger brother. Uncle Selig had a new car every year, always dressed nice, money in his pocket. Used to slip me a couple of bucks whenever he saw me. 'Here, Marky, you don't want to walk around with empty pockets.' I'm out of school, I'm drifting from one dead-end job to another, and I team up with Jack and we do a snatch-and-grab at this credit jeweler's on Queens Boulevard. Now what do we do with this shit we stole? So I take it to Uncle Selig, and first he gives me hell, and then he gives me a decent price for what I brought him, and finally he gives me advice. 'Marky, you can kick in doors or hold people up, and have empty pockets most of the time, and sooner or later you get shot or do time, and what kind of life is that for my sister's boy?' Or I could buy and sell, the way he did, and he sat me down and showed me how."

"And that's what you did."

"And that's what I did, and I was no genius, but I did all right at it. I had this three-bedroom river-view apartment on Haven Avenue up in Washington Heights, and two of the bedrooms were my store. And the word got around. Next time I run into Jack, I tell him I'm in a different part of the business. So a couple of times he brings me stuff, and I take it off his hands. And another time he shows up, and have I got a nice fur? Because there's a girl who let him know that's what she wants. It happens I do, and he buys it from me.

"And then I come home one night, I've been out celebrating one thing or another, and I'm cleaned out. No damage to the locks, so I always figured somebody had copies of my keys. And I was right, because when he was making his whatchacallit, his fucking amends, he told me right off. He swiped a set of my keys, had copies made, then got my keys back where I kept them. And waited until he knew I was out, and came back with a partner, and cleaned me out. Even knew where I kept my cash."

"And you suspected Jack?"

"I had a feeling. A couple of names came to mind, and he was on the top of the list. I went to him, not to confront him but just to see, you know? And he was full of plans, what I got to do to get the stuff back. There's this saying about junkies, that first they steal your wallet and then they help you look for it. It was like that with him. He stole my wallet, and now he was helping me look for it."

"So you were out a lot of money."

"I was out of the business, man, and for a while there I was out of town, because I'd just bought a ton of jewelry and financed the deal by borrowing money from the shies. They don't know from excuses. 'Sorry for your troubles, it's a hell of a world, and by the way you owe us money.' And it's not like I can call my insurance agent, put in a claim. Everything's gone and I'm on the hook for it." He shook his head at the memory. "Uncle Selig helped me work it out. Pointed me in another direction, said I was good with numbers, had me learn bookkeeping. Been doing it ever since. A couple of clients, I keep two sets of books for them, and if that ever came to light I could probably get in trouble. But aside from that I've been completely legit for years."

"So Jack showed up—"

"And copped to what he'd done. 'You were my friend and I stole from you.' And this rage came over me. Like, not just how could you do such a thing, but how can you stand here and tell me about it? And smile while you do it?"

"So you hit him?"

"'Mark, tell me what I can do to make it right with you.' I said I ought to punch his lights out. 'Mark, go ahead, if that's what you want.' And he stands in front of me with his face hanging out, like he's fucking daring me to throw a punch at him. You ever hit anybody in the face?"

"Not recently."

"First time for me. Oh, kids on a playground, you know. I gave somebody a bloody nose once, got one myself a time or two. Nine, ten years old. Never since then, until I hit Jack."

His face darkened at the memory. "He just stood there," he said. "Maybe took a half step back but that's all. I split his lip and there was a little trickle of blood, but it didn't stop the crazy bastard from smiling. I asked him if that was what he wanted, words to that effect, and he said I could keep going. 'All you want, Mark. Whatever it takes to make it right.'

"And I fucking lost it. I hauled off and hit him again, and he kept standing there and I kept swinging. I don't know how many times I hit him." He looked at his bandaged hand. "Each time with the right hand. Three, four, five times? I don't know. I beat the shit out of my hand but I never felt a thing at the time. Later on, Jesus, whole other story."

He stopped, and I might have spoken if I could have thought of something to say. I heard a clock ticking. I hadn't noticed it before.

He said, "The last time I hit him he came close to falling down. His knees buckled anyway. I looked at him and there was something different in his face, and all I could think was he looked like Jesus Christ. I'm Jewish, so what the hell do I know about Jesus? Crazy what goes through your mind.

"And he looks at me with these fucking Jesus eyes and says, 'Mark, I'm sorry.' Just that. And his face is all bloody and I'm thinking, Shit, what am I doing? What have I done? And I just—this is hard to talk about."

I didn't say anything.

"I just started crying, okay? And then we're both crying, and we're standing in the middle of the room hugging each other like brothers and crying like fucking babies. And I can't stand to look at him and see what I've done to him, because his face is a mess. It probably looked worse later, with swelling and discoloration and all. But it was pretty bad then.

"He wouldn't let me take him to the hospital. Insisted he'd be all right, and he'd take care of it himself. And he wanted to know how much it had cost me, what he'd done. How much money I was out, so he could start reimbursing me, so many dollars a month, whatever he could afford for as long as it took. I told him he didn't owe me anything, it was all money I never should have had in the first place. And if I hadn't lost it I'd have had no reason to get out of the business, and eventually I'd have gone away for it, which happened a couple of times to Uncle Selig, who was smarter and better at it than I'd ever be. So you could say he did me a favor, which is something I never thought of before then and probably never would have, if I hadn't just spent ten minutes smashing my hand against this man's face.

"Did I mention he wouldn't let me take him to the hospital? A couple of hours later I went myself, walked over to Cabrini and had my hand looked at. It took that long before I realized how badly I'd hurt myself. I didn't tell Jack, for fear that he'd decide he owed me another amends. I didn't figure either of us could stand another amends."

"You saw him again?"

"No. He called once, I think it was the next day or the day after. Just making sure everything was okay, and I was positive I didn't want any of the money back. I never heard from him again, and then I found out he was dead. Shot to death, I think it was."

"That's right."

He nodded to himself. "When I had the business uptown," he said, "I owned a gun. It came to me as part of a deal, and I kept it because a person in that line of work needs protection, right? It disappeared in the burglary along with everything else. I never had a gun in my hands before or since. Never fired one in my life."

I started to say something but he held up the unbandaged hand to stop me. "If," he said. "If I'd still had that gun, or any gun, when Jack came in with his amends, I wouldn't have thought twice. Pick it up, point it, pull the trigger. I guess that's what somebody else did."

"It was at his apartment."

"Jack's apartment?"

"Someone came to his place," I said, "and brought a gun along. He was shot twice at close range, once in the forehead and once in the mouth."

"I didn't know that. It sounds cold."

"And purposeful," I said. " 'You talk too much.' "

"Maybe." He looked at me with Bambi's big soft eyes. "He was just trying to make things right with everybody, and it doesn't make any more sense to me now than it did then. What's done is done, you know? Leave the past alone. But the point is he was trying to accomplish something, and all it did was get him killed."

XIV

THERE WAS A message in my box at the Northwestern, a call logged an hour earlier from Greg Stillman. I called him from my room, and he said he thought I might have been trying to reach him. His answering machine had been able to tell him that there had been several calls from someone who hadn't left a message.

"So who else could it be?"

"You know," he said, "I think there's a country song along those lines. 'If nobody answers, it's me.' It wasn't you, though, was it?"

"I did hang up on an answering machine," I said. "A couple of times. But it wasn't your machine." And I filled him in on my meeting with Mark Sattenstein.

"So you found out who gave Jack the beating. But he didn't shoot him."

"No."

"You don't think he could be lying about it?"

"Not a chance."

"It's funny," he said. "I'd more or less assumed that one person was responsible for both the beating and the shooting. 'Oh, that's not enough to get rid of you? All right, in that case *bang*. And while we're on the subject, *bang* again.'"

"By the time Sattenstein finished hitting him, there was no anger left."

"And his take now is that our Jack rescued him from a life of crime. It's a shame he didn't show up at the service. He could have told that story and had everybody in tears."

"He referred to him once as High-Low Jack," I said. "I didn't want to interrupt him at the time, and then I forgot. I was halfway out the door before I asked him about it."

"And?"

"And he didn't even remember that he'd used the sobriquet, but—"

"He said *sobriquet*?"

"No, of course not. Nickname, he must have said. He didn't recall using it today, but he could have, because he'd been familiar with it in the days when the two of them did business together. But he had no idea how Jack came by the name, or what it meant."

"That's helpful, isn't it?"

"Not terribly," I agreed, "but somehow I don't think Jack's sobriquet—"

"You just like using the word, don't you?"

"—is going to point the way to his killer."

"Will anything?"

"I don't know. If you're losing heart for this—"

"No, not at all! I think it's remarkable that we're seeing results already. You've told me two things just now, and they're both

important. We know who beat him up, and we know that someone else shot him. I can see right now I was right to enlist your
help."

"Oh?"

"If I'd gone to the police, they'd have been the ones to show up
on Mark Sattenstein's doorstep. Somehow I think he's better off
for its having been you instead."

"They'd have given him a hassle," I said.

"That may be an understatement."

"It might. They'd like him for the murder. Once you've got a
suspect in hand, you don't want to knock yourself out looking
for another one. I don't think they'd have made any kind of a
case against him, but he'd still be the worse off for having
attracted their attention."

We talked some more, and then he said, "You know, it scarcely
matters if we find out who did the shooting. We're taking the
appropriate action, and it will work out the way it's supposed to."

"It will?"

"Of course," he said. "Everything always does."

Did everything always work out the way it was supposed to? I
had that to think about, and I kept turning it around in my mind
through most of the evening meeting. SoHo group meets at St.
Anthony of Padua's, a big redbrick church on the corner of
Houston and Sullivan with a predominantly Italian congrega-
tion. I was a few minutes late getting there, and the first thing I
saw upon entering was Jan, looking my way and waving an arm
to indicate she'd saved me a seat.

I immediately wished she hadn't. There were plenty of empty
seats, as there always were in that oversized room. I could have
been trusted to find a seat of my own. We'd be going out for din-

ner, and then spending the night together, so why did we have to sit side by side while somebody with a beatific smile on his broad face told us how he used to pee in empty bottles and pour them out the window because he couldn't be bothered to walk all the way down the hall to the bathroom? Couldn't we share that experience just as well sitting ten or twenty yards apart?

I kept this to myself, and sat down next to her, right where I was supposed to, and within a few minutes realized I'd have resented it at least as much if she *hadn't* saved a seat for me. That gave me something else to think about, along with everything working out the way it's supposed to.

That particular meeting had a format I hadn't yet encountered elsewhere. After the speaker's qualification and the secretary's break, the group broke up into mini-groups of eight to ten, seated at round tables. Someone at each table would suggest a topic, and the ensuing round-robin discussion would fill the remaining half hour. Jan and I automatically headed for different tables, and the topic where I wound up turned out to be acceptance. I found myself wishing it was something else, and then realizing how ironically appropriate that was.

And the topic hardly mattered, because this was Downtown AA, and when it was your turn you said whatever you pleased. I would have happily passed, but there were only eight of us and it was easy enough for me to find something to say. I just tossed out Jim's line — well, Buddha's, I guess — about dissatisfaction being the cause of unhappiness. Then it was somebody else's turn.

The restaurant on Thompson Street was old-fashioned Greenwich Village Italian — red checkered tablecloths, straw-covered Chianti bottles as candleholders, a Sinatra record for background music. The waiter remembered us, approved our appetizer and entrée choices, and didn't try to coax us into ordering wine. The food was good, and we took our time over the meal, and I talked about Jack Ellery and my attempts to find out who'd killed him.

"Or who didn't," I said, "which is turning out to be my real mission here. If I can clear the names on his Eighth Step list, his sponsor can let it go with a clear conscience. No need to share anything with the cops if you're sure what you've got isn't worth sharing."

"Is that what it says in the penal code?"

"You're joking, but as far as the law's concerned, he doesn't have to report it even if he knows for a fact who did the shooting. He's not an officer of the court. He's a private citizen. That doesn't give him the right to lie to a police officer, but he can keep things to himself."

"So all you have to do is clear the rest of the names on the list. That's simpler than finding a killer, isn't it?"

"Well, not if the killer's on the list. In that case it'll be tricky to clear him."

We batted that around a little, and she asked how I'd feel about walking away from the case once I'd cleared them all. I said I'd feel as though I'd earned a thousand dollars.

"Would you, Matt? Oh, I'm not suggesting you wouldn't have earned your money. But wouldn't you feel as though you'd left part of the job undone?"

"Why?"

"Because Jack's killer would be walking around free."

"He'd hardly lack for company."

"What do you mean?"

"I mean there are a lot of killers walking around free. It used to make me crazy when we brought in a perpetrator and watched the case fall apart. Either the DA's office fucked it up or the evidence just wasn't there or twelve dimwits on a jury couldn't bring themselves to do the right thing, and all our work was for nothing. I'm not sure I ever got over it completely, because it's natural to have an emotional investment in a case. But you get used to it."

We moved on to some stray observations on the meeting. "I can see peeing in empty bottles," I said. "You're in a rooming house and the bathroom's at the end of the hall and somebody's probably using it anyway. And here's an empty bottle, and if you're a guy you've got something to aim with —"

"Which is probably good for nothing else at that point."

"— so you make use of what you've been given. Just cap it afterward so you don't spill it all over the floor."

"Gross."

"But what I don't get," I said, "is why it would strike him as a good idea to pour the bottles out the window. Just set them aside until you can get it together to empty them in the toilet. What's so hard about that?"

"I can see one advantage in pouring your pee out the window."

"Entertainment?"

"Well, I suppose, but that's more of a fringe benefit. The main thing is, then you don't have to worry about drinking it by mistake. Ha! Got you with that one, didn't I? The little lady wins the gross-out contest."

We both agreed it was nice enough to walk the half mile home, and she took my arm crossing Houston Street and didn't let go when we reached the curb. We'd finished the meal with espresso, and the waiter had come over with a pair of cordial glasses, the house's standard lagniappe for customers they hoped to see again. As he reached our table he remembered we were the ones who'd passed on the wine. "You no want," he said tentatively, and we agreed that we didn't, and walking home Jan wondered what we'd turned down.

"Probably anisette," I said, "or something anise-flavored."

"Not Sambuca?"

"It could have been Sambuca."

"They wouldn't pass it out," she said, "because most people can't stand the taste of it, but you know what I used to like? Fernet-Branca."

"You liked that stuff?"

"It's pretty horrible," she admitted, "but nothing beat it on a bad morning. The bitter taste, I think it did something for your stomach."

"All it ever did for mine," I said, "was turn it. The only cordial I developed a fondness for was Strega."

"Oh, Jesus, Strega! I haven't even thought of that in years. I hope that's not what he had for us."

"What difference does it make? Since we didn't drink it anyway—"

"It was definitely anisette," she said. "Some cheapo anisette with a nasty perfumy taste."

"I'm sure you're right."

"You know what *Strega* means? In Italian?"

"*Witch,* isn't it?"

"That's right. Witch." We walked along in a pensive silence, and then she said, "You know, here I am remembering the taste, and if they perfected some kind of faux Strega, exactly the same but with no alcohol in it—"

"You wouldn't want it."

"Wouldn't touch it with a stick." She gave my arm a squeeze. "Don't let this get around," she confided, "but I just might be an alcoholic."

By the time we got close to Canal Street, the acknowledged boundary between SoHo and Tribeca, I could scarcely remember how I'd felt earlier — resenting her for presuming to save me a seat, chafing under the obligation of having to spend yet another Saturday night in her company. Why on earth would I want to spend the night differently?

For a moment it seemed to me that I'd been given a glimpse of the future. We'd go on like this, growing ever closer to one another, and sometime after my one-year anniversary I'd spend all my nights on Lispenard Street. I might keep the room at the Northwestern as an office, at least for a while, but it wasn't really a place to meet clients, and what other need did I have for an office?

So we'd live together, and after a year of that, or less if it felt right, I'd put a ring on her finger.

Would she want kids? I had two sons, and sooner or later Jan would have to meet them, and I figured they'd all get along as well as they had to. But she was two years younger than I, and had been sober two years longer, and she was still young enough to have children, although that biological clock was ticking away. So how would she feel on the subject? For that matter, how would I feel?

Stay in the moment, I told myself. It's a beautiful night and you're going home with a fine-looking woman. What more do you need to know?

XV

"I DON'T KNOW what the hell happened," I told Jim. "We were the cute little couple on top of the wedding cake, and then we crossed Canal Street and everything turned to shit."

It was Sunday night and Jim and I were in a Chinese restaurant. Hot-and-sour soup, sesame noodles, orange beef, and a chicken dish named for a Chinese general, all as ritualized in its own way as my Saturday evening.

"We got to her door," I said, "and she was fumbling in her purse, so I took out my key and unlocked the door."

"You have keys to her place."

"For months now. It's a convenience. Her building's an old factory converted to artists' lofts, and it doesn't have an intercom, although there's been some talk about putting one in. What I would have to do was phone her when I was a block or so away, and then she'd wait at the window until she saw me and throw down a set of keys, and I'd pick them up off the sidewalk and let myself in. It didn't take too long for both of us to get tired of that system."

"No, it would get old fast. So you unlocked the door and she bristled."

"Exactly."

"She say anything?"

"No."

"Did you?"

"What was I going to say? 'Hey, why give me a key if I'm not supposed to use it?'"

"So you waited for it to blow over, and it didn't."

"We went upstairs, and she made some coffee, which I don't think either of us really needed at this point. And she put the radio on, and we'd picked up the Sunday *Times* on the way home, and we each settled in with a section of the paper."

"The old folks at home," he said. "This chicken's good."

"It's always good."

"I know, but somehow it always exceeds my expectations. So, domestic bliss. Unless you had a fight over the Arts and Leisure section."

I shook my head. "But I didn't want to be there. And she didn't want me there, either. And there was no way either of us could say anything or do anything, so we were stuck with each other until morning."

"And a few minutes earlier you'd been thinking of names for your kids."

"Well, not exactly. But close enough. Still, it was quiet."

"Duke Ellington working away in the background."

"Among others. The jazz station. Except for what was going on in both our minds, everything was fine."

"Not that you knew what was going on in any mind other than your own."

"Well, I picked up vibes."

"Ah, vibes. And who was playing them? Lionel Hampton or Milt Jackson?"

"I didn't know what she was thinking," I said, "but I had a pretty good idea. And I thought, All right, the thing to do is make the best of it, and there's not really anything wrong, and it'll work itself out. And when I was done with the sports section I went to take a shower, figuring that maybe she'd like me a little better if I smelled nice when we made love."

"Which you always do on Saturday night?"

"Pretty much. And I thought, you know, that it might help things work out."

"Because sometimes sex has that effect."

"Sometimes it does."

"And even if it doesn't," he said, "at least you wind up getting laid. But somehow I gather the physical manifestation of your mutual affection wasn't a great success."

"I went to bed," I said, "and she said she'd be along in a few minutes. She went to the kitchen first, to wash the coffee cups. Usually she leaves them until morning."

"The detective speaks."

"And she was a long time in the shower, and a long time in the bathroom after the shower stopped running. And lying there waiting for her, I thought of pretending to be asleep."

"So that you wouldn't have to have sex."

"And then she came in, quiet as a mouse, and she asked me if I was awake. In a whisper, too low to rouse me if I wasn't paying attention. And I knew she was hoping I was asleep, so *she* wouldn't have to have sex."

"The cute little couple on the wedding cake, as I recall."

"So I rolled over," I said, "and made room for her beside me, and we worked our way into this slow and gentle lovemaking, and eventually she either had an orgasm or faked one, but either way I was grateful. It took me forever to fall asleep."

Sunday morning she said she didn't feel much like brunch, and I said I ought to skip the morning meeting and see if I could get some work done. She made coffee and we each had a cup and accompanied it with sections of the paper we hadn't gotten to the night before. Then we kissed good-bye and I got out of there.

I wound up walking all the way uptown to my hotel. I kept thinking I'd catch a meeting or a subway, but I just kept on walking, stopping once for coffee and another time for a sausage roll. By the time I got home I was ready to lie down, and I napped for an hour until it was time to watch the Giants lose to the Packers. There was snow on the field in Green Bay, which surprised me. It was still sport jacket weather in New York, except on those days when the wind had an edge to it.

The phone never rang. I had some calls to make, but first I watched the game through to the bitter end, and then I pulled my chair over to the window and watched the sky darken. When I finally picked up the phone it was to call Jim, so he could decide where we'd have our sesame noodles.

Now he said, "You're coming up on a year."

"No kidding."

"Generally a tense time, immediately before and after an anniversary."

"So they tell me."

"Not that the rest of the time's a piece of cake, but anniversaries seem to polarize things for us. You know, you got involved way too soon."

"I know."

"But maybe you didn't have much choice."

I'd known Jan before I ever saw the inside of an AA room.

There'd been a string of murders, a guy using an ice pick on women, and a few years after I left the force they got the guy. Except there was one killing he wouldn't cop to, and it turned out he couldn't have done it, he was inside at the time. It was an ice-cold case as far as the police department was concerned, and they certainly weren't going to waste time on it, so a cop who knew me steered the victim's father in my direction, and he hired me.

The investigation led me to Jan's loft on Lispenard Street, among other places, and we liked each other's looks enough to get drunk and go to bed together.

That worked out pretty well, and it looked as though I had a girlfriend, and a drinking buddy in the bargain. And I did, until she started going to meetings. That meant she was no longer a drinking buddy, and the people she met in church basements convinced her that she couldn't be a girlfriend either, not of a man with a powerful thirst. I wished her the very best of luck and went off to get something to drink.

And some time went by, and she got sober and stayed that way, and I went on living my life. Then, when it got bad enough, I started going to meetings myself. I was in and out, I'd stay sober for a while and then I wouldn't. Jim began to take an interest in me, and talked to me when he saw me, or tried to anyway. Pretty much everybody else left me alone. *My name's Matt. I'll pass.* Right.

Over the months I'd called Jan once in a while, when I was drunk enough to think it was a good idea. She was always polite, but knew better than to spend time talking to a drunk. Then I called her when I was trying to stay sober. I had to talk to someone and I couldn't think of anybody else to call.

And we started keeping company of a sort. And one day I ordered a drink I didn't really want, which was nothing new, and left it untouched on a bar, which was. And since then I'd been sober, and we were a couple. More or less.

Jim said he'd have to pass on St. Clare's. There was something on PBS Beverly wanted to watch, and he'd agreed to keep her company. Did I want to join the two of them? I knew I didn't, and headed for the meeting instead. I left at the break and went home.

No calls. I went to bed.

XVI

THAT WAS SUNDAY. A week and a half later, on Wednesday, I cleared the last suspect. I didn't put in long hours and I can't say I made any brilliant deductions, but I used the phone and the subway to good avail, and that turned out to be enough. By the time I was done I still didn't know who'd killed Jack Ellery, but I knew five people who hadn't, and that was all I'd signed on for.

I'd spent Monday renewing my acquaintance with some cops I'd known over the years. There was a guy I'd worked with a long time back in Brooklyn, and just a few blocks from me at Midtown North there was Joe Durkin; we'd had dealings right around the time I first started trying to get sober, and since then he'd earned a couple of extralegal dollars by steering a case or two my way.

Neither of them had anything for me, but they made a few

phone calls and set up other cops for me to see. A guy from a downtown precinct knew the name Crosby Hart. He wasn't a hood, he was a Wall Street guy, but he'd developed a fondness for cocaine that led him to embezzle from his employers. Which added up: *Screwed him on a coke deal* was next to his name on Jack's Eighth Step list.

"Skinny guy in a suit, skinny tie, all the time tapping his long bony fingers, bobbing his head. Could not sit still. Cocaine, the miracle drug. We hauled him in, airtight case, but the firm changed their mind, insisted on dropping the charges. Restitution, treatment, never do it again, di dah di dah di dah. Which is fine, because once the coke's out of the picture you've got a respectable guy leading a respectable life. Isn't he better off with the wife and kids in Dobbs Ferry than a few miles further up the river in Ossining?"

"Is that where he lived? Dobbs Ferry?"

"Someplace like that. He was a commuter, took the train in from Westchester every morning. Of course when he was on a coke run he might not make it home that night. Dobbs Ferry, Hastings, Tuckahoe—one of those places. And Crosby's his middle name, if you're looking for him in the phone book." And what was his first name? "He just used the initial. H. Crosby Hart, and everybody called him Crosby. Far as what the *H* stood for, I have to admit I got no fucking idea. I must have known at one time, because it would have been on his sheet. You book a guy, his first name gets written out. Unless he's F. Scott Fitzgerald."

"Or E. Howard Hunt?"

"Howard," he said. "That's it. Sonofabitch, how'd you manage that? Howard Crosby Hart. That's his name."

Except it wasn't. It was Harold, not Howard, as I learned from Sheila Hart, who had not yet gotten around to changing the listing in the phone book for Lower Westchester County. He no longer lived there, and his current residence had an unlisted number. I sensed that she had it, but wasn't about to give it out. I could try him at his place of business, she told me.

And where was that? She turned suspicious, and questioned my need to know. She hadn't caught my name, and wondered just what sort of business I had with her former husband.

I gave my name, and said I was with Calder, Jennings & Skoog, reeling off the name as if it were one she ought to recognize and not one I'd invented on the spot. I said I understood her husband to be a nephew of the recently deceased Kelton Hart of Fort Myers, Florida, and—

Who was she to stand in the way of a legacy, especially if some of it might find its way to her? She told me what I needed to know, and I reached him at his desk a couple of hours later. I said my name but left out the imaginary Mr. Calder and his partners and said I'd like to meet with him. He didn't even ask what it was about, which suggested he'd heard my name before, and not all that long ago.

He offered to meet me after work at the Cattle Baron, at the corner of William and Platt, just around the corner from his Wall Street firm. Say 5:30? I said 5:30 was fine, and put on a suit jacket and a tie before I left my hotel room. I was done playing the part of a lawyer hunting missing heirs, but he didn't know that, and was expecting a lawyer to show up. So I figured I might as well look like one.

I don't know that I did. I tend to look like a cop irrespective of what I wear.

The Cattle Baron was new to me, but pretty much what the name and location had led me to expect. It was a steak house, all dark wood and red leather and polished brass, with Bass Ale and three German beers on tap and a good selection of single-malt Scotch on the back bar. The clientele were all men and they all wore suits, and most of them spoke in loud voices. I stood in the doorway looking for a skinny guy with a skinny tie, and my eyes kept passing over one fellow until it registered that he was looking right at me.

I approached him, and he said, "Mr. Scudder? Hal Hart. If you weren't with a law firm I'd guess you might be with the investment house. Very reputable line of mutual funds. But I don't suppose there's any connection."

"Nor with the Scudder Falls Bridge."

"Well, I'd be more worried that you might try to sell me mutual funds. I've already bought my quota of bridges."

His tie had narrow diagonal stripes of red and navy, and it wasn't skinny, and neither was anything else about him. He'd replaced the cocaine with food and drink — beef and beer, by the look of him, and plenty of both. His face was round and red, and there was a Rorschach of broken capillaries in both cheeks.

I sat at his invitation, and when the waiter appeared I ordered club soda. Hart's glass stein was still half full of dark beer, but he tapped it with a forefinger and gave the waiter a nod. "Dos Equis," he told me. "Best legal substance ever to come out of Mexico. Sure you won't have one?"

"Not right now," I said.

I could have crossed him off the list then and there, because there was no way this hearty stockbroker had put two holes in Jack Ellery. But that was the subject at hand, and I might as well get to it. The room was noisy, and the place smelled of booze and cigars and avarice, and I didn't want to stay in it any longer than I had to.

We talked sports until the drinks came. He too had watched the Giants lose to Green Bay, and had stronger feelings than I about the coaching. He was draining his glass just as the waiter arrived with a replacement, along with my club soda in a matching glass stein of its own. Hart beamed at both our drinks, picked up his, and said, "Mr. Scudder, I hope I'm wrong, but if I ever had an Uncle Kelvin this is the first I heard of him."

"I think I said Kelton," I said, "but it doesn't matter, because he never existed. And I'm not an attorney."

"Oh?"

"I'm an investigator," I said, "looking into a recent homicide."

"Well, Jesus Christ. Who got killed, if it wasn't my long-lost uncle Kelvin?"

"A man named Jack Ellery."

He was slightly pop-eyed, but I hadn't really noticed it until I said the name. "Well, I'll be damned," he said. "You can just go ahead and fuck me with a stick. Why in the hell would anybody kill Jack Ellery?"

"Uh—"

"If that crazy bastard doesn't wind up giving me a stroke," he said, "it's not for lack of trying. He's surprised the shit out of me twice in the past month. First by turning up alive, and then by turning up dead. How'd he die?"

"He was shot to death."

"And they ruled out suicide?"

"Two bullets," I said. "One in the forehead, the other in the mouth."

"If that's suicide," he said, "it shows remarkably strong will. Jesus Christ." He drank some beer. "I never expected him to turn up. Never gave him a thought in God knows how many years. Then one night I get home from the office and my doorman points to a guy sitting in the lobby, says he's waiting for me. I turn and look, and he stands up and says, 'Crosby?'

"So it has to be somebody from way back when, because it's that long since anybody called me Crosby. That's my middle name. I never liked Harold, which is what everybody called me all through high school, and as for Harry, well, forget it. So when I got to Colgate I met my freshman roommate and stuck out my hand. 'H. Crosby Hart,' I announced, 'and everybody calls me Crosby.' And from then on, everybody did." His eyes sought mine. "Until I got into a little trouble. You know about that, right?"

I nodded.

"I was lucky enough to get out of it," he said, "because I had a clean record, and because I was a white middle-class guy with a house in the suburbs. I got a fresh start, and I decided I ought to have a new name to go with it, and what's funny is I already had one, because my wife had been calling me Hal all along. You know, Prince Hal? Shakespeare?" He shook his head. "These days it's Harold, as in Harold-you're-late-with-the-child-support."

"But this guy in the lobby called you Crosby."

He grinned. "Bringing me back on track, aren't you? Very nicely done, and I can see why they named that bridge after you. Across the Delaware, isn't it?"

"I believe so."

"Guy in my lobby, and he calls me by a name I never hear anymore. I can't place him right away. He looks vaguely familiar, and he also looks, you know, a little bit seedy, a little bit down on his luck. Somebody I used to know who maybe didn't do so good for himself in the years since. He's dead, huh?"

"Yes."

"That's a shame," he said, and took a moment to think about it. "So he tells me his name, which doesn't register at all, not right away. And he'd like to talk to me, and could we maybe go somewhere private?

"So here's a guy, clean shirt but the collar's frayed, his shoes are polished but they're down at the heels and scuffed under the

polish, he shaved that morning but he's overdue for a haircut —
you get the picture?"

"Respectable but broke."

"Exactly. So this has to be a touch, right? Old time's sake,
gotta be good for a couple of bucks. I figure fifty, maybe a hundred, and then he'll stay away from me until he's in a position to
pay it back, which means forever, and you'd have to call it a bargain. Fine, but I don't need him inside my apartment. Right
here's private enough, I tell him, and I take him over to the corner, where there's two sofas at right angles to each other. And we
sit down, and I find out it's not a touch after all, because what he
says is he owes me an apology. And maybe something more than
that, he says."

He tilted his head, looked me over. "You know about this,
right? You're an investigator, which I guess means private, and
you're looking into his death, and you're sitting there drinking
club soda. I can't help connecting the dots."

"You're not a bad investigator yourself."

"Well, two plus two, you know? He owes me an apology, he
wants to make amends. He used to be an alcoholic, but he's not
drinking anymore, and part of staying sober is what he's doing
now. There was an expression he used, something about cleaning up the mess he made —"

"The wreckage of the past."

"That's it." He drank some beer. "The hell, I know a little
about addiction. Fucking blow took me down big-time. And
right about this time I place the guy. If I ever knew his last name
I long since forgot it, but I'm listening to him and he's talking
about a coke deal, how he beat me for a couple of grand, and of
course, Jesus, he's High-Low Jack."

"That's what you used to call him?"

"Well, I don't know that I ever called him that. I called him

Jack. Or man, we all called each other man all the time. *Hey, man. Where's it at, man?* But if somebody wanted to know which Jack I was talking about—"

"High-Low Jack."

"Right. And I remembered the deal. Not the numbers, whether it was two grand or five or whatever it was, but I was making this quantity buy and I was no rube, I checked it out first, laid out a line and had a taste, and it was very good and righteous coke."

"And you got it home and it wasn't."

"It magically turned into baby laxative," he said, "somewhere between Googie's men's room and my apartment. Not the first time I got burned, and not the last, either. I was mad as hell, believe it, but at the same time I had to admire how slick he'd been. And now here he is, parked in my lobby, perched on the edge of this sectional sofa, asking if I remember the amount because he wants to make arrangements to pay me back. Just so much a month, but for as long as it takes to make it right."

I hadn't seen him signal the waiter, who appeared magically with another Dos Equis. I had barely touched my soda.

He said, "Cheers," and took a sip. "You can probably guess what I told him. I said he didn't owe me a thing. Whatever he beat me out of would have gone straight up my nose. And the money wasn't mine in the first place. It was my firm's, and it was a drop in the bucket I siphoned out of that place. I had to make restitution, and I did, but you never pay back everything you took, because they didn't know just how bad I hurt them and neither did I. Whatever my debt was, they'd marked it paid in full, and that's how I felt about whatever Jack thought he owed me."

"And that's what you told him."

"Yes, and I had to spell it out, because he didn't want to get off the hook that easily. What I didn't say, but I have to admit it was going through my mind, was what did I want with a guy in a thrift-shop overcoat showing up once a week to slip me a ten-dollar bill? Makes you feel better, I said, find a charity you like and give them a few bucks. But as far as you and I are concerned, I said, we're square."

"And he accepted that."

"Finally. He said he guessed he could cross me off his list. I guess I wasn't the only person he burned."

"One way or another," I said, "there were quite a few people he felt he needed to make amends to."

"And everybody in your crowd goes through something like that?" He didn't wait for an answer, brandished his stein of beer. "Might find out for myself," he said. "One of these days."

I didn't say anything.

"Except I pretty much stick to beer these days. Cocaine was my problem, you know. I got one noseful of blow, and nothing was ever gonna be the same. But I stopped, and I never had a taste since. And I got to tell you it's all over the place. There's a guy at the bar, I'm not gonna point him out, but all I'd have to do is tip him a wink and go to the can, and he'd follow me there and sell me whatever I want. And he's here all the time, and wherever you go there's somebody just like him.

"So these days just about the only thing I allow myself from south of the border is this here, and maybe a small glass of brandy after a big meal. Can't turn into an alcoholic that way, can you?"

"It's not what you drink," I said, as I'd heard others say. "It's what it does to you."

"That the party line on the subject? Well, who knows where I'll end up. But that doesn't mean I'm asking you to save me a seat."

Lord, make me sober. But not yet.

XVII

FRANCIS PAUL DUKACS was easy to find, once I had that name to work with. By then I'd called every Dukes in the Manhattan book, and every Duke, too; there weren't all that many of either, and it seemed reasonable that one of them might be related to Frankie Dukes, or at least know of him. But plural or singular, nobody could help me out.

Then I got home from St. Paul's one night and there was a message to call Mr. Bell. I dialed the number on the slip and they answered at the Top Knot and called Danny Boy to the phone. "You could stop by," he said, "and I was going to suggest that, but it's easier to pass this on over the phone. Unless you feel the need to compare the Top Knot's Coca-Cola with Poogan's, in which case I'd welcome your company."

I told him I was just about ready to call it a night.

"Then write this down, Matthew. Francis Paul Doo-kosh, except that's not how it's spelled." He spelled it out for me. "It's

Hungarian, I think, or maybe Czech. One of those countries that get in the papers whenever the Russians send in their tanks."

"Frankie Dukes."

"The man himself. And that is all I know about him, though I could probably find out more. But that may be all you need to track him down."

And indeed it was. I opened the book as soon as I got off the phone, and there he was, with a listed phone and an address all the way east on Seventy-eighth Street. That put him south and east of the furnished room where Jack had been shot to death, but not more than ten minutes away. It would have been easy enough for Jack to find him, I thought. Or for him to find Jack.

I called a couple of times the following morning and couldn't even reach an answering machine, so I took a bus across Seventy-ninth and found his address in the middle of a row of brownstones. I pushed the buzzer for Dukacs, got no answer, and a framed note on the wall led me next door, where I was able to find the super. She lived in a basement apartment, and I don't know what she had on the stove, but I wanted some. It smelled terrific.

I told her I was looking for one of her tenants, a Mr. Dukacs. I must have pronounced it correctly, because her face registered approval. In good but accented English she told me I would probably find him at his shop on First Avenue, Dukacs & Son. He was the son. Dukacs, God rest his soul, was his father. If the younger Dukacs wasn't there, he was most likely taking a break next door at Theresa's. He had all his meals there.

"Whatever he gets," I said, "I'll bet it's not as good as what you've got cooking."

"My lunch," she said levelly. "Only enough for one."

*   *   *

Theresa's would have been a standard New York coffee shop, but the specials were kielbasa and goulash instead of spanakopita and moussaka. Two women shared a booth, having either a late breakfast or a very early lunch, and an old man with a patterned cloth cap sat at the counter stirring a cup of coffee. I suppose he could have been Frankie Dukes, but the odds were against it.

The shop next door was a Korean greengrocer, but next to it was a meat market, and the sign overhead read DUKACS & SON. You could see where a final S had been long since painted out. A man my age or a little older stood at a counter, cutting a rack of lamb into individual rib chops. He was short and stout, a fireplug of a man with a full head of glossy black hair and a luxuriant mustache. There were a couple of gray hairs in the mustache, and in his abundant eyebrows. He wielded his cleaver with an efficiency that made it clear he'd done this before.

When I went in he put down the cleaver and asked what he could get for me this morning. "Beautiful chops here," he said, and held one up for me to admire. "On special, matter of fact."

"I'm afraid I'm not here as a customer."

"Oh?"

"You're Francis Dukacs?"

"Why?"

I dug out a wallet, flipped it open at random, flipped it shut. He might not be holding the cleaver, but he was standing close enough to it so that I was just as happy to have him assume I was an officer of the law.

"I have a couple of questions," I said, "about a man named Jack Ellery."

"Never heard of him."

"I believe you had a recent visit from him."

"Did he come to buy meat? That's the only people come here. Customers."

"He would have come to make amends, to offer an apology—"

"That son of a bitch!"

I took a step backward. In an instant Dukacs was transformed from a stolid shopkeeper into a wild-eyed madman.

"That fucker! That cocksucker! You know about him, that son of a bitch? You know what he did?" He didn't wait for my answer. "He walked in here, he waited until my other customers left, then he stuck a gun in my face. 'Give me all your money or I shoot you.'"

"This was some time ago."

"So? Not so goddamn long I don't remember it. You got a gun in your face, you remember."

"Then what happened?"

"I was shaking. My hands, shaking. I tried to open the register. I couldn't open the fucking thing."

"And he struck you?"

"With the gun. Back, forth. Split my head open, blood down my face like a curtain. Here, you see the scar? I woke up in the hospital. Stitches, concussion, two teeth out." He tapped an incisor. "Bridgework," he said. "All thanks to him. And you know what he got out of it? Nothing! He couldn't open the cash box either. Fucking thing was jammed. Neither one of us could open it and he gave me a beating for nothing."

"Did the police—"

He waved a hand, dismissing the question. "Nothing," he said. "They showed me books full of pictures. I got a headache looking. What did he look like? It's like I went blank, I couldn't see his face in my mind. And then I'd go to sleep and I'd see it in my dreams."

"His face?"

"Perfectly clear in the dreams. Drove me crazy, those fucking dreams. I didn't want to go to sleep because I'd have the dream, and he'd be there and I'd be trying to open the register and it wouldn't open and he'd beat me like a drum. Every night, that damn face of his, and I'd wake up, and the face would be gone. I had to go to sleep to see it, and I didn't want to see it."

Sleeping pills made it worse, and for a while he couldn't sleep without them. Then he got off the pills, and eventually the nightmares became a rare event, only returning at times of great stress. A friend's death, a relative's illness, and he'd dream of the robbery. And then one day the man who'd starred in the nightmares had the colossal nerve to walk into Dukacs & Son.

"And I'm standing here, and I don't recognize him. And he starts talking and there's something about the voice, it's a voice I recognize but I can't place it. And he says he owes me something, and he uses a word you used before, that he has to make."

"Amends."

"Yeah, that's the word. And I don't know what he's talking about, and then there's all this shit about how he used to be a drunk, he used to be a drug addict, he used to rob people, and all of a sudden the years fall away and it's him, that son of a bitch, that bastard. In my store, can you believe it? Standing in front of me, saying he wants to apologize!"

"What did you do?"

"What did I do? What do you think I did? Get the fuck out of here, I tell him. Go fuck yourself, drop dead, take your apology and shove it up your ass!"

"And he left?"

"Not right away. 'Oh, tell me what I can do to make it right. Can I pay money? Can I do anything?' Fucking cocksucker. What's he gonna do, grow me two new teeth? All I wanted was for him to get the hell out of my store. So I picked this up."

The cleaver. "And he left?"

"This he understood. 'Easy, easy,' and he backs away, and he's out the door, and I can put this down again. And then, when he's gone, the shakes come."

"And the nightmares?"

He shook his head. "No, thank God. Not so far." He looked at me. "Why?"

"Why did he come? Well, as I understand it—"

"No, what do I care why he came? He's a crazy bastard, he's a son of a bitch. He beats up a man whose fingers can't open a cash box? A fucker like that, who cares why he does what he does?"

"Then—"

"You," he said. "Why are you here? What do you want from me?"

"Ellery was killed," I said. "I'm investigating his death."

"Somebody killed him? You're standing there and telling me the son of a bitch is dead?"

"I'm afraid so, and—"

"Afraid? What's to be afraid? You couldn't bring me better news. You know what I say? I say thank God the bastard is dead!" He leaned forward, both hands on the counter. "'Mr. Dukes'—'cause of course he gets the name wrong—'Mr. Dukes, just tell me what I can do to make it right.' What can he do? I tell him what he can do is drop dead, that's what he can do. Just drop fucking dead. And he did!"

"Actually," I said, "he had help."

"Huh?"

"Somebody killed him."

"Yeah? You find him, I'll buy him a drink. How? Beat him to death, I hope?"

"He was shot."

"Shot dead."

"Yes."

"Good," he said flatly. "Good, I'm glad. A man's dead and I'm glad. Wait a minute. You don't think I did it, do you?"

"No," I said. "Somehow I don't."

XVIII

I F HE'D KILLED JACK," I told Greg Stillman, "he'd have called the cops himself and claimed full credit for it. He was so happy to hear Jack was dead I thought I was going to get some free pork chops for being the bearer of good news."

" 'Ding-dong, the witch is dead.' He must have felt like the Munchkins after Dorothy's house made that famous crash landing. And you did say he was short, didn't you?"

"I don't think you'd mistake him for a Munchkin." I'd called Greg after I left Dukacs, met him at a coffee shop a few blocks away. "And he's not the type to burst into song. But I think he felt liberated in about the same way."

"No more bad dreams."

"I guess not." I drank some coffee. "If that's what you get when you make amends, I may take my time getting to that step."

"That was Jack's reaction," he said. "I had to tell him he was mistaken."

"Oh?"

"He wasn't specific. He called me right after he got his apology thrown back in his face. He didn't tell me who the man was or any of the circumstances, just that he'd been rejected and cursed out and ordered off the premises. He regarded the whole incident as a complete and total failure, and wondered if he could cross the fellow off his list or had to find a way to take it a step further."

"And?"

"And I told him he'd done it perfectly. That the object of the action wasn't to be forgiven. That's just a fringe benefit. He got the point, but he remained troubled. Said he hadn't realized just how much damage he'd done. Or that you couldn't entirely undo it."

I was still thinking that one over when he said, "Unless I've miscounted, we've only got one name left. And it's cloaked in John Doe–style anonymity."

"Robert Williams," I said.

"Whose name is Legion, or might as well be. Robert Williams, with a cheating wife. What are the odds?"

"That I'll be able to find him? Or that he'll turn out to be the killer?"

"Either."

"Slim and slimmer," I said.

"That's as I thought. Matt, are we done?"

I looked at my cup. There was still coffee in it.

"No," he said, "I mean overall. I think you've done what I hired you to do. There were five names on the list, four after you ruled out the one in prison—"

"Piper MacLeish."

"—and you've cleared Sattenstein and Crosby Hart and now Mr. Dukacs, and the object was to see if there was a name on the list that we ought to give to the police. The only name left is Robert Williams, and to give *that* to the police—"

I nodded, and imagined the conversation with Dennis Red-mond. *Years ago he had an affair with this guy's wife, and he may have tried to find him and tell him he was sorry.* Yeah, right.

"I don't know how many hours you've put in," he said, "but it seems to me you've more than earned the thousand dollars I gave you. Did you have to pay for information?"

"A few dollars here and there."

"So you didn't even clear the thousand. Do I owe you money, Matt?"

I shook my head. "You can pay for the coffee."

"And that's all? Are you sure?"

"I made out all right," I said. "And there's still a chance I'll be able to clear Williams. I put the word out and I might hear something. You never know."

And I guess you never do, because the following night I got home a little before midnight. Jacob was behind the desk, in what I'd come to recognize as a terpin hydrate fog, and he told me I'd had a batch of calls and no messages. "All the same gem-mun," he said, "each time sayin' he'd try you later, and not once leavin' a name or a number."

I went to my room, showered, and was glad my caller hadn't left a number, because I was exhausted. I'd gone to a meeting, then over to the Flame for coffee, and the conversation had gone on longer than usual. I decided to tell Jacob to hold my calls, and the phone rang even as I was reaching for it. I picked it up, and a voice like thirty miles of bad road said, "Don't tell me I'm finally talking to Matthew Scudder."

"Who's this?"

"You don't know me, Scudder. Name's Steffens, like the muckraker. I've been trying you all night."

"I'd have called you back," I said, "if you'd left a message."

"Yeah, well, I was on the move. It's no way to gather moss, so I leave that to the north side of trees. I'm parked now, in a place I understand you know right well."

"Oh?"

"Right around the corner from you," he said, "and I thought I'd find you here, which is why I'm here myself. But the fellow behind the stick says you don't come in so much these days."

I knew where he was. But I let him tell me.

"Jimmy Armstrong's Saloon," he said, "except the guy doesn't know how to spell *saloon*. It's got a star where it oughta have an *A*."

S*loon. There was a law still on the books, a piece of inane legislation dating back before Prohibition, that made it illegal to call an establishment a saloon. The law had been designed to placate the Anti-Saloon League, the idea being that, if you couldn't keep a man from running a saloon, at least you could force him to call it something else. That was why Patrick O'Neal's joint across from Lincoln Center was called O'Neal's Baloon; he'd already ordered the signage when someone told him about the law, so he decided to change one letter and be done with it. There was, he'd been known to say, nothing illegal about misspelling *balloon*.

Jimmy had managed the Baloon before opening his own place five blocks down the avenue, and his way around the law was a star where the *A* would have been. I could have reported all of this to the mysterious Mr. Steffens, but I had a feeling he already knew it.

"He may be a lousy speller," he said, "but the son of a bitch pours a decent drink, I'll say that for him. I just wish he had a jukebox. Any luck at all, Kenny Rogers'd be there to remind me of her name."

A drunk, calling me late at night. The impulse to hang up

was strong. "I'll help anyone who's trying to stay sober," Jim Faber had told me. "Any hour, day or night. But that's if they call me before they pick up the drink. After that you're just talking to a glass of booze, and I've got no time for that."

"Lucille," he said. "How do you like that? Picked it out of the air, with no help from Mr. Kenny Rogers."

"I'm afraid you lost me."

"Mrs. Bobby Williams. Isn't that who you were looking to find? Right around the corner, Scudder, waiting for you to come buy me a drink."

XIX

W[HEN A THWARTED]{.smallcaps} holdup in Washington Heights eased me out of the police department and away from Anita and the boys, I took a room at the Northwestern and decided its Spartan confines suited me well enough, and that's where I stayed while my drinking got worse and my life went on falling apart.

But it wasn't much more than a place to sleep when I could and stare out the window when I couldn't. For a combination living room and office, I ducked around the corner to Jimmy Armstrong's joint.

I passed a lot of hours there. It was where I saw friends, where I met clients, where I took many of my meals. I had a tab there, and I drank a lot of bourbon there, some of it neat or on the rocks, some of it stirred into strong black coffee.

I was a regular at Armstrong's, and I knew the other men and women who put in long hours there. Doctors and nurses from

Roosevelt Hospital, academic types from Fordham, musicians whose lives centered on Juilliard and Lincoln Center and Carnegie Hall, and a whole mixed bag of people who just happened to live in the neighborhood. They were all drinkers, and whether some of them were drunks was not for me to say. They'd talk to me when I wanted conversation and leave me alone when I didn't, and the bartenders and waitresses would keep the drinks coming.

Once in a while I might go home with a nurse or waitress, but none of those last-call cures for loneliness ever turned into a romance. One time one of the waitresses, one I hadn't ever gone home with, took a dive out a high window, and her sister showed up and couldn't accept the official verdict of suicide. She'd hired me to look into it, because looking into things for people was what I did after I gave up the gold shield. And it turned out she was right, and her sister had had help getting out that window.

Armstrong's. When I first got sober I couldn't see why I couldn't go there anymore. Whether or not you were drinking, it was a good place to sit, a good place to eat, a good place to meet prospective clients. I heard it said at meetings that one way to avoid a slip was to stay out of slippery places, but on the other hand I kept running into bartenders who'd held on to their jobs after they sobered up. It is, after all, the drink that gets you drunk, not the place where they sell the awful stuff.

I don't remember anybody at St. Paul's coming out and telling me to stay away from the joint. I figured it out on my own. The more days I put together away from a drink, the more value I attached to this new condition called sobriety. All those days would vanish the minute I picked up a drink, and each day there was one more of them at risk.

So I found myself less and less comfortable at my old table at Jimmy's, even if all I was doing was having a hamburger and a Coke and reading the paper. And then one day I picked up my coffee and smelled bourbon. I took it back to the bar and reminded Lucian that I wasn't drinking these days.

He swore he hadn't added whiskey, even as he took the cup to the sink and poured it out. "Unless I did it without thinking," he said. "And if that's what happened, I wouldn't remember, would I? So let's start over." I watched him select a clean cup and fill it from the coffee pot, took it to my table, and smelled bourbon once again.

I knew the coffee was all right, I'd watched him pour it, but I also knew I couldn't drink it, and in the hours that followed I realized I needed to stay away from Armstrong's. It was a week or two later when I told Jim Faber about it, and he nodded and said he'd figured I'd come to that conclusion sooner or later. "I was just hoping it'd happen before you picked up a drink," he said.

I'd gone back one last time to make sure I didn't have an outstanding tab, and to leave word that anyone looking for me could try my hotel. But it had been months since I'd crossed the threshold.

At least I could walk by the entrance without a problem. At meetings I heard a woman talk about her attachment to a particular ginmill near her office. She had to pass it twice a day. She'd tried walking on the other side of the street, but that wasn't enough to keep her from feeling its magnetic pull. "So I get out of the subway and walk a block out of my way, and another block back, and I do the same thing at night. That's four blocks a day, which is what, a fifth of a mile? All to keep from getting sucked into the door at K-Dee's, which I don't honestly think is very likely to happen, but I don't care. And it burns a few extra calories, and that's all to the good, isn't it?"

I didn't burn many calories. I took the elevator to the lobby, walked out onto Fifty-seventh Street, turned right, and walked a few doors to Ninth Avenue. I turned right again, and Armstrong's was halfway up the block.

And did I feel a magnetic pull? I don't know. Maybe. I suppose I was attracted and repelled at the same time, and in about equal measure.

I opened the door, walked in, and one breath told me I was in a place where people drank beer and smoked cigarettes. Two thoughts hit me at the same time — that it smelled awful, and that it smelled like home.

There were ten or a dozen people at the bar, and I recognized most of them. Around a third of the tables were occupied. No large parties, just groups of two or three. The conversation throughout was sufficiently muted so that you could hear the music. Jimmy got rid of the jukebox shortly after he opened the joint, and kept the radio on an FM station that played nothing but classical music.

The walls at Armstrong's are a collection of incongruities, and the pick of the litter is the mounted elk's head hanging on the rear wall. Directly beneath it, looking across the room at me through a pair of Buddy Holly–style horn-rimmed glasses, was a stocky guy around my age wearing a suit and a tie and a half smile on his thin lips. He was smoking a cigarette. From the looks of the ashtray, it wasn't his first.

"'Lucille,'" he said. "You know the song, don't you? Hell, everybody knows it. She picked a fine time to leave him, with their four snot-nose brats and a crop in the field. So the singer decides not to nail her after all, because he feels sorry for the whiny-ass husband. Never happen in real life, not if she was as fine-looking as the song makes out. Sit down, for God's sake. What do you want to drink?"

The waitress was new to me, a dishwater blonde, tall and slender. She had an air about her that suggested she was easily confused, but she got the drink order right, bringing me a glass of Coca-Cola and Steffens another Scotch. He said, "Vann Steffens. You don't remember me, do you?"

"Have we met?"

"As a matter of fact," he said, "I don't know. But I recognized you the minute you walked in. Of course I was expecting you. Couple of times, you and I were in the same place at the same time. Not this place, but one that's not too far from here. Or was, until it closed. Morrissey's, the after-hours. You remember the place?"

"Of course."

"They performed a humanitarian service, the Brothers Morrissey. Made sure a man didn't die of thirst just because it was past four in the morning. I was there now and then over the years, and I saw you there at least twice and maybe more'n that. You were with a guy named Devoe, had a piece of a joint on the next block."

"Skip Devoe. His bar was Miss Kitty's."

"Another joint that's closed. And it seems to me I heard he died. Our age, wasn't he? How'd he die?"

"Acute pancreatitis," I said, and that was indeed what it said on Skip's death certificate. I always figured it was a mix of drink and sadness that took him out.

Steffens shook his head. "Hell of a world," he said. "You and me, did we ever get introduced at Morrissey's? I can't say one way or the other. I was never there before three, four in the morning, and by then I was half in the bag, so there are things happened that I don't remember, and things I remember that never happened. Anyway, when I heard your name the other day, I knew who they were talking about."

"How did that happen?"

"A fellow was talking," he said, "about how you were looking for a fellow named Robert Williams with a wife who maybe had an affair with Jack Ellery, who I understand got himself killed recently." He lit a cigarette, crumpled the now-empty pack. "You don't smoke, do you?"

"No."

"And you're in here drinking Coca-Cola. I heard you were off the booze these days. Make you uncomfortable, sitting in a joint like this?"

"No," I said. That wasn't entirely true, but I didn't see that I owed him the truth. "You said your name's the same as the muckraker."

"Joseph Lincoln Steffens, dropped the *Joseph* in his writings. Wrote *The Shame of the Cities,* about municipal corruption. Put an end to it, too, as you may have noticed." He grinned, dragged on his cigarette. "But what he's most famous for is what he wrote when he came home from a trip to the Soviet Union. 'I have seen the future and it works.' Except everyone got the line slightly wrong, because he wrote that he'd been to the future, not that he'd seen it. And he changed his mind about it anyway, decided it wasn't the future and it didn't work. Proving you'd better be careful what you say, because people are going to change the words around on you, and go on quoting them long after you stop believing them yourself."

"Interesting."

"You're being polite, Matt. I know enough about him to be a bore on the subject, but that comes of sharing a name. And no, we're not related. The family name got changed a generation or two back. It used to be Steffansson, like the polar explorer, and no, he's not a relative either."

"And your first name is Vann?"

"Evander," he said. "But I've forgiven my mother for that one, God rest her soul. I chopped it down to Van, and then I tagged an extra *N* onto it because people thought that was my last name, Van Steffens, like Van Dyke and Van Rensselaer."

"And they're not your relatives, either."

"You begin to see the pattern, huh?" He patted his breast pocket, remembered he'd just finished the pack. "I need a cigarette," he announced. "Where's the machine?"

I shook my head. "No machine. There's a little food market next door, the Pioneer. They sell cigarettes."

"And this place doesn't? Why the hell not?"

"Jimmy's against smoking."

"There's an ashtray on every table. Half the people in here are smoking."

"He's not going to prohibit it. He just doesn't want to encourage it."

"Jesus. Next door?"

"Out the door and turn left."

"Jesus. It's a good thing he's not against drinking. Place would have a tough time making ends meet."

XX

WHILE HE WAS GONE, the waitress came over and emptied the ashtray. I thought about the Morrissey Brothers and the after-hours they used to own and operate, one flight up from an Irish off-Broadway theater. I thought about Skip Devoe, and I thought about Jack Ellery, and I thought about the Scotch and melting ice cubes in Vann Steffens's glass.

There was a pay phone on the wall at the far end of the bar, and just as I looked at it a fellow with a goatee and a crew cut hung up, checked to see if his quarter had come back, and headed for the men's room.

I called my sponsor. "I'm in a bar," I said, "meeting an informant, or at least I think that's what he's going to turn out to be. I didn't want to be here but I felt I had to."

"And you're all right?"

"I've been drinking a Coke. He left the table, and his Scotch is sitting there, and I figured I'd spend a quarter and wake you up."

"I was awake. The Scotch look good to you?"

"It started fucking with my head," I said. "I'm at Armstrong's."

"Ah."

"And old times managed to get into the conversation. I never met the guy, but I guess we must have traveled in similar circles."

Through the window, I saw Steffens emerge from the market. He stopped on the sidewalk to open his pack of Luckies. "There's my guy," I told Jim. "I'll get off now. I'm okay, I just thought I ought to call."

"And you've got plenty of quarters."

"Always," I said.

"Best seat in the house," Steffens said. "You know why?"

"I bet you'll tell me."

"Anywhere else and you're staring at the fucking moose. Sit right under it and you don't have to look at it."

"I believe it's an elk."

"I stand corrected. And, while we're correcting each other, it's not the Pioneer. It's the Pio-*meer*. The idiots spelled it wrong."

"It used to be part of a chain. Then the affiliation ended, and they had to change the name."

"So they changed one letter."

"Cheaper that way, I guess. Everybody still calls it the Pioneer."

"*Pioneer* with an *M, Saloon* with no *A,* and a smoke-filled room where they won't sell you cigarettes. You okay with the cola?"

"I'm fine. You were starting to tell me about Mr. Williams and his wife."

"I was, and it won't take long, either. I already told you her name was Lucille. Fine-looking woman, and what you could call free with her favors. I got lucky myself one night, and it never happened again but that doesn't mean I don't remember her fondly. I'll say this much, I've never been worried that her old man's gonna kill me for it."

"That would be Robert Williams, but I think you called him Bobby."

"I did, but there's as many Bobby Williamses and Bob Williamses as there are Roberts, and what I and pretty much everybody else called him was Scooter."

"Scooter Williams."

"On account of he had one of those whatchacallits, like a motorcycle but dinky."

"A motor scooter."

"Well, duh, obviously, but I was going for the brand. A Vespa? I think that's it. So they could have called him Vespa Williams, but nobody did. Scooter. I don't think he kept the thing that long anyway. Rode around on it long enough to get a nickname, then sold it or it got stolen."

Scooter was an NYU dropout from somewhere in the Midwest. Got himself a cheap apartment on a bad block on the Lower East Side, met Lucille and married her, and got through the days by smoking a lot of grass and selling enough to pay for what he smoked. He worked now and then for a couple of moving companies, drove a gypsy cab now and then, and did gofer work for the neighborhood Democratic club.

"Sounds like your guy," Steffens said. "The wife, plus he knew Whatshisname."

"Jack Ellery."

"Uh-huh. Ellery worked for some of the movers now and then. Funny thing—he'd move somebody, and a week or two down the line they'd have a break-in, lose their good stuff."

"And you knew Ellery?"

"I knew who he was, knew him to say hello to. That was about it."

"And you're a newspaperman?"

"Where'd you get that idea?"

"I don't know. I must have figured you were following in the footsteps of your famous nonancestor."

"Raking muck," he said. "Hell, I'm on the other side of that one. I don't rake the muck, I make it. *The Shame of the Cities.* That's me, Matt. I'm in local politics across the river. Wipe out municipal corruption, and I'd have to get an honest job."

He took out a slim black calfskin card case, handed me a card. *Vann Steffens,* I read. *Your Friend in Jersey City.* No address, but a phone number with a 201 prefix.

"Everybody needs a friend," he said. "Especially in Jersey City. You have a card?"

My sponsor's a job printer, and I'll never lack for business cards. I dug one out for him.

"And here I thought mine was minimalist," he said. "Nothing but your name and your number, and I already had 'em both." He tucked the card away. "But I'll keep it. A man gives you his card, you keep it. Be bad manners not to. But wait a minute, give me my card back, will you?"

I did, and he uncapped a pen and printed SCOOTER WILLIAMS on the back of the card in tiny block capitals, then consulted a little memo book and added an address and phone number. The book was bound in black calf, and matched the card case.

"There you go," he said. "You see him, won't take you ten minutes to rule him out."

I thanked him, glanced at what he'd written. The address was on Ludlow Street, so Scooter still had his cheap apartment in a bad neighborhood. I looked across at Steffens, and wondered what he expected in return.

He answered the question before I could ask it. "You can pay for my drinks," he said, "and that'll do me fine. I'm a machine pol in fucking Jersey City, for Chrissake. Doing favors for people is part of my job description, right up there with pigging out at the public trough. Someday you'll do me a favor back."

"I don't know what it might be, Vann. They won't let me vote in Jersey City."

He laughed. "Oh, don't you be so sure of that, my friend. You come see me on Election Day, and I'll guarantee you get to vote at least once in every precinct. I'll tell you what. I'll have one more drink on your tab, and you can tell me why you give a damn who put the two bullets in Jack Ellery."

I told him more than I'd planned. He was a good listener, nodding in the right places, stirring the pot with a question or an observation now and then. He'd seemed like a blowhard at first, but I warmed to him over the course of the hour or so we spent together. Maybe his manner softened when he felt less need to impress me. Maybe I became more at ease in Armstrong's — which might or might not be a good thing.

I took care of the check, and on the way out I remembered something. "You know everything," I said. "Maybe you'll know this."

"If it's a state capital, forget it. I'm lousy on state capitals."

"High-Low Jack," I said. "You happen to know why they called him that?"

"I didn't even know *that* they called him that. High-Low Jack? It's a new one on me."

"Not important," I said. "I just thought you might know."

"Damn, I hate to disappoint a new friend." He snapped his fingers. "You know, I just might know after all. I bet it's because Scooter was already taken."

XXI

"HEY, MAN!" Big smile, showing teeth that hadn't seen a dentist in a while. "You're the guy who called, right? You told me your name but that doesn't mean I can remember it."

"Matthew Scudder."

"Right, right. Well, come on in, Matthew. Sorry about the place. The cleaning girl's coming first thing tomorrow morning."

Magazines were heaped on a floral-patterned armchair. He scooped them up, motioned for me to take their place. He stacked the magazines on a low table made from a door and pulled up a folding chair for himself.

"I was joking about the cleaning girl," he said. "Around here, I'm the closest I've got to household help. The good news is I don't cost much."

The apartment wasn't really that messy, and for a pot-smoker's Lower East Side premises it probably ranked within a few points of the top. As far as I could tell, it was clean enough underneath the clutter.

I'd called him the morning after my late night with Vann Steffens. Before I dialed the number I checked the white pages, and there he was, Williams, Robt P., with the same phone number and same Ludlow Street address Vann had given me. He could have saved himself all that meticulous printing and told me to look in the book, but he'd said favors were his stock-in-trade, and that one was easily performed.

The phone rang a few times, and when Williams picked up he was out of breath, as if he'd hurried to pick up before the machine could take the call. I gave my name and said I'd like to talk to him about Jack Ellery, and he repeated Jack's name a couple of times, and then he said, "Oh, fuck, I heard about that. What a terrible thing, huh? First I heard he killed himself, and that didn't make sense. I mean people do it all the time and it never makes sense, but he wasn't the type. Did you know him, man?"

"A long time ago."

"Yeah, me too. But what I heard next was someone killed him, and *that* didn't make sense either, because why in the hell would anybody want to kill Jack? Wha'd they do, shoot him?"

I said someone did just that, and he said that was what somebody had said, and it was amazing, just amazing. I asked if I could come over and talk to him, and he said sure, why not, he'd be hanging around the place all day. When did I want to come? Sometime in the afternoon?

I had breakfast first, and caught a noon meeting at Fireside, and took the F Train to its last stop in Manhattan. I'd checked a map first, and was thus able to walk directly to Ludlow Street, and by 2:30 I was sitting in that armchair. The arms showed wear and the springs were shot, but it was holding me as comfortably as it had held the magazines.

The cooking smells in the building's halls and stairwell had been a mix of Latin and Asian, but the smell in Scooter Williams's apartment was predominantly herbal. A lot of marijuana had been smoked in those three little rooms, and its aroma had seeped into the walls and floorboards, even as it had taken Scooter's life and put it permanently on Hold.

He had to be somewhere in his middle forties, but managed to look both older and younger than his years. His full head of dark brown hair was shaggy, and looked as though he might have cut it himself. He had a droopy mustache, irregularly trimmed, and hadn't shaved in a couple of days.

He wore a maroon solid-color sport shirt with long sleeves and long collar points, and over that he wore one of those khaki vests with twenty pockets. Photographers' vests, I think they call them, although how anybody could remember which pocket he'd put his film in was beyond me. His blue jeans had bell-bottoms, which you didn't see much anymore, and they were frayed at the cuffs and worn through at the knees.

He talked for a while about something he'd seen on television, some science-fiction program that impressed him from a philosophical standpoint. I didn't pay much attention, just let him ramble, then tuned in again when he said Jack's name.

"Out of the blue," he said. "Hadn't heard from him in years, hadn't *thought* of him in years, and the phone rings and it's Jack. Can he come over? Well, sure. I'm in the same place. I been here since, wow, since I ditched college. Moved in and never moved out, and can you believe it's more'n twenty years?"

"And he came over?"

"Couple hours after he phones, the bell rings and it's him. You know what I figured, don't you? Can you guess? I figured he was looking to cop."

"To buy, uh —"

"Herb," he said. "Kills me when I hear people call it a gateway drug. Man, I never got out of the gate. Started NYU in September, and before the month was done my roomie turned me on with what was probably a pretty lame joint, but I took a deep drag and you know what happened?"

"What?"

"Nothing whatsoever. I smoked the whole thing and nothing, zip, zero. But I felt the tiniest little bit hungry, you know, so I got this jar of peanut butter from my desk and started eating it off a spoon. And it was the most amazing taste, like I'm suddenly noticing all the subtleties of the peanut butter, the total mystical dimension of the taste of it, and it dawns on me that I'm stoned out of my fucking mind."

He finished the jar of peanut butter, and long before it was gone he knew what he wanted to do with his life. He wanted to spend it feeling just like that.

"For a while," he said, "you chase higher highs, but eventually you tip to the sheer futility of it. And you don't have to get higher and higher. Just high is high enough, you know?"

He never had any interest in other drugs — uppers, downers, psychedelics. He tried mushrooms once and mescaline once and acid twice, just to know what they were about, but as far as he was concerned there was nothing like good dope. He smoked every day, and he sold enough so it didn't cost him, and maybe he even came out a few dollars ahead.

"Never been busted," he said, "which is probably a record, or close to it. But I only sell to people I know, and the cops around here know me and know what I do, and they know I'm not hurting anybody, or doing any kind of volume, so I don't get hassled. I always get by, and I always stay high, and there's a song lyric hiding in there somewhere, can you dig it?"

"But Jack wasn't looking to cop," I said.

"Oh, wow. Got a ways off track, didn't we? No, he wasn't. I offered, you know, like did he want a taste? And before I could finish the sentence he's telling me how he's an alcoholic, except he doesn't drink, and that means he can't do anything. Dope, pills, anything at all; if it does anything good for your head, he can't have any part of it. I couldn't figure out why at first, but he put it so I could understand it."

" 'You can't be high and sober at the same time,' " I said.

"That's it! His words exactly, and when he put it that way I could dig it. So I didn't offer him anything except an orange soda, which I've been meaning to offer you, because I figure you and him were in the same club. I'm gonna have one, and can I bring you one?"

We drank our orange sodas out of the can. I couldn't remember the last time I'd had one, and decided I was willing to go that long before I had another.

"You're an orange soda guy, you know what he came for."

"I think so."

"Amends, he called it. He was going through his life, trying to make up for everything bad he ever did. You do that yourself?"

"Not yet."

"Man, I was never a drinker, you know? Day I graduated Pembroke High I hit all the parties and came home shit-faced drunk. Fell into bed with my clothes on, and the room started spinning. Leaned over, puked on the carpet, and passed out. Woke up and said I'm never doing that again, and I never did."

Until he got to the last four words, his story was one I'd heard more times than I could count.

"Amends," he said, in something approaching wonder. "What did he ever do to me that he's got to make amends? Me and Jack, we knew each other for a few years there. Worked a few moving jobs together, smoked a little dope together, hung out some. Only thing came to mind, he tried to get me to tip him to some people who'd be good pickings. You know, people I moved, and they had good stuff, and I'd get a cut of what he got from ripping them off."

"But you weren't interested."

"No way, man!" He shook his head. "Man, run a little scam on the Welfare Department, get a check I got no right to? Go up to Klein's, boost some socks and a shirt? Okay, why not? I'm no saint, I'm cool with shit like that. But stealing from human beings? People I met, people who paid me to take good care of their stuff, people who gave me tips? Not my scene." He took a long drink of soda. "But where's the amends come in? I, like, turned him down flat on that one. Never even tempted. Didn't judge the man, just said no, not my scene. Matter of fact—"

"What?"

"Well, just thinking about it now, maybe I was the one owed *him* an amends. 'Cause what I did, a couple of the moving companies I worked for, I sort of told them not to hire him no more. Didn't say why. Just, like, he's not the most reliable cat to work with, he don't pull his weight, he slacks off. Nothing to get him banned or give him a bad name, just enough so he's the last one hired. Here I'm his friend and I'm keeping him from getting work, so maybe..."

His voice trailed off, and I could see him running the question in his mind. He looked to be capable of devoting the next hour to its philosophical implications.

I said, "But that wasn't what was on his mind."

"Oh," he said. "No, nothing like that. It was loose."

"How's that?"

"Loosey-goosey. Luce. Lucille, man. My old lady." He looked off to the side, smiled at a memory. "Years back, this was. Not my old lady anymore. Been a few of them since her. My experience, they tend to come and go. You know what's funny?"

"What?"

"They're always around the same age. The ones that move all the way in, I mean. A chick who's in my life for, like, fifteen minutes, she could be any age. But the ones who move in and park their shoes under the bed, they're always twenty-four, twenty-five years old. When I was nineteen I had an old lady six years older'n me, and now I'm what, forty-seven? And the last old lady I had, like she moved out a year ago, and *she* was twenty years younger'n me. Man, *Picture of Dorian Gray*? Can you dig it?" He frowned. "Except not exactly Dorian Gray, but you see what I'm getting at, don't you?"

"Lucille," I said.

"Oh, right. Man, she was choice. Out of her fucking mind, but sweet. Had some fucked-up childhood." He moved a hand to wave the past away. "Jack comes here, tells me how he was balling her. Him and Lucille, going at it like, I don't know, mink? Man, he thinks he has to make amends to me for *that*?"

"You already knew about it?"

"I took it for fucking granted, man! Lucille, she was balling everybody. It didn't take us more than a couple of months to get way past the whole fidelity number. We went to a few parties where everybody just did anybody who was handy. Man, after you watch your woman getting fucked by a stranger, you either let go of jealousy or you put her clothes in a box and set it out by the curb. I told him, I said, Jack, if this is keeping you up nights, man, let go of it. 'But you were my friend and I betrayed you.' By fucking Lucille? You want to make amends for that, go get in line, and it's a long line."

"Wasn't there something about a child?"

"Oh, right. He thought he knocked her up. Well, somebody did. She was pregnant a couple of times while we were together. First time she had an abortion and the second time she waited too long and decided she'd have the baby. Then she winds up having a miscarriage, which was like good news and bad news, you know?" He looked off to the side again. "Makes you wonder."

"Oh?"

"Say she had the kid. I mean, is that gonna keep us together? She could have had triplets and we're still gonna split the blanket when the time comes. You can start thinking, Oh, we have a kid, I go to work for IBM, we get ourselves a split-level in Tarrytown, but none of that's gonna happen. If she had a kid all it woulda meant is she'd have had one more thing to carry when she took off. Or she'd have left me with the kid, and what am I gonna do? Wrap it up and leave it outside a convent?"

I had this sudden unbidden image: my sons, Mike and Andy, standing at a locked iron gate, waiting to be taken in by the Little Sisters of the Poor. I took a deep breath and blinked it away.

"I wonder where she is now," he was saying. "Last I heard she was in San Francisco. She could have a kid or two by now. Not mine, though. Not Jack's either." He had that faraway look again. "I might have a kid out there somewhere. That I had with somebody else, that I never knew about."

XXII

"T HEN IT LOOKS as though we're done," Greg Stillman said. "They're all in the clear."

"You sound disappointed."

"Not exactly. I had a problem and now it's been resolved, and I'm grateful to you for resolving it. But—"

"But it feels incomplete. Unfinished."

"Yes, of course. How do you feel, Matt? You're the one who's been out there doing the work. All I did was pick up the tab."

And all I'd done was go through the motions. I was in my hotel room with a cup of coffee from the deli downstairs, looking across the rooftops at some lighted offices all the way downtown. I'd decided I could make my final report over the phone. There was no real need to sit in another coffee shop while I told my client we were out of suspects.

"I feel all right," I said. "I'd like it better if I'd managed to crack the case, but that's not what you hired me for. That's a police matter anyway."

"But they won't do anything."

"We don't know that. It'll be an open file, and when some new information comes their way, they'll pick it up and work it. Greg, you wanted to be sure you weren't holding out on them. Well, you're not. Whoever killed your sponsee, it wasn't one of the five people on his Eighth Step list."

"The man in prison —"

"Piper MacLeish."

"Obviously he couldn't have done it. Unless they give you a weekend pass so that you can even an old score. But couldn't he pass the word to somebody outside?"

"He'd have had to get the word himself. There's nothing to indicate that Jack ever visited him, or even wrote to him. And it doesn't really add up emotionally anyway."

"What do you mean?"

"Say you're in prison, serving a long sentence for something you did. 'Hi, remember me? Say, I want to apologize because I'm the guy who ratted you out, and you wouldn't have wound up in the joint if it wasn't for me.'"

"What a marvelous Ninth Step declaration."

"Well, he might have worded it differently, but that would be the gist of it. And what's MacLeish's reaction? 'That son of a bitch, he did this to me, I'd better call in a favor and have him killed.' No, we already crossed the Piper off the list, and I think we can leave it that way."

"I'm sure you're right."

"I was a cop for a lot of years," I said, "and I wasn't the NYPD equivalent of a Step Nazi. I learned how to overlook things, and sometimes I profited financially from what I overlooked. But homicide was always different. When somebody got killed and it landed on my desk, I wanted to clear the case.

"That didn't necessarily mean that anybody wound up going away for it. That was the goal, but it didn't always work out that way. Sometimes I knew who did it but couldn't make a case that would stand up. But I'd done what I could, and the case was solved, so my work was done."

"And in this case?"

"My work's done," I said. "Even though the case isn't solved. So it feels incomplete to me, and yes, maybe a little disappointing. But that doesn't mean I can't let go of it. And I will. I pretty much already have."

He was silent for a moment. Then he said, "Maybe it's just my ego."

"Because a perfect being like you ought to be able to do something?"

"That's part of it, Matt. The other part is further confirmation that I'm not really the piece of shit the world revolves around. Remember what I told you? That I got him killed, that I pushed him into the Eighth and Ninth Steps and that's why he was murdered. But I guess that wasn't it after all. I guess I'm not the prime mover of the universe. I guess I'm just another drunk."

At the meeting that night I mentioned that I'd spent an hour or two with a fellow who'd spent the past twenty-plus years quietly stoned on marijuana. "He knew not to offer me any," I said, "and he didn't smoke while I was there, but he'd smoked before I got there and I'm sure he fired up a joint the minute I left. The apartment reeked of it."

A woman named Donna came up to me on the break. She was a semi-regular at St. Paul's, and had spoken there for her third anniversary a few months ago. Her approach was purposeful, and I assumed she had something to say about marijuana and its effects over time. I didn't recall a whole lot of pot in her story, but that didn't mean she couldn't find something there to identify with.

But it wasn't that at all. Some months ago she'd moved in with her boyfriend, another sober alcoholic. He was still an alcoholic, but he was no longer a sober one, and she wanted out.

"I'm such an idiot," she said. She had long auburn hair, and kept pushing it out of her eyes, and it kept falling back across her face. "I'd heard his story, for God's sake. I knew he went out every time he put a couple of years together. But he was sober when I met him, and he had more sober time than I did, and I thought he'd stay sober."

But he hadn't. She'd kept her rent-stabilized apartment—"What is it they say? I may be crazy but I'm not stupid"—and that's where she was staying now, but she had a whole lot of stuff at his place in Cobble Hill, and she hated to leave it but was afraid to go there by herself.

"I don't think he'd do anything," she said, "because he's a very gentle guy. At least when he's sober. But he does have a history of spousal abuse. I'm not telling tales, it's in his qualification, he mentions it every time he tells his story. And he always says it only happened when he was drunk. Well, he's drunk now, isn't he?"

"You want me to go with you."

"Would you?" She put her hand on my wrist. "Not as a favor. I mean it would be a favor, a major one, but I'd want to pay you for it. In fact I'd insist on it."

"You're a friend," I said, "and it's the sort of thing friends do for each other. I don't think—"

"No," she said firmly. "My sponsor was the one who suggested this. And she was very clear that I had to pay you."

She had the time picked—Saturday afternoon—and had arranged our transportation. Did I know Richard Lassiter? Bald Richard, gay Richard, speed freak Richard? He had a car, and everything of hers in Cobble Hill would fit easily in the trunk and backseat. He was going to pick her up at Eighty-fourth and Amsterdam at three sharp, and they could stop for me on the way to Brooklyn. I said it would be simpler if I met the two of them uptown, and that three o'clock would be fine.

"I'm paying Richard too," she said. "He put up an argument but I insisted."

"Sponsor's orders."

"Yes, but I think I'd have insisted anyway. He says he'll come upstairs with me, in case Vinnie is there. I left a message on his machine, I'm coming Saturday afternoon, please don't be there, di dah di dah di dah. But what do they call it when you take a sleeping pill and it keeps you awake?"

"A slip," I said.

"Ha! Very good. No, I remember now, they call it a paradoxical effect. Very common with alcoholics. I think my phone message could have a paradoxical effect on Vinnie. 'Stay away? The fuck I'll stay away. Whose place is it, you toxic bitch?'"

"If Vinnie's from Bensonhurst, you do a good imitation."

"He is, as a matter of fact, and thank you. But if he's there, well, Richard's a sweetheart, but his is not the world's most intimidating presence."

"For that you want a thug like me."

"An ex-cop," she said, "and a man who can take care of himself on the mean streets of New York."

"Including Brooklyn."

"Including Brooklyn." She gave my arm a squeeze. "A thug indeed," she said. "Hardly that, my dear. Hardly that."

*   *   *

After the meeting I joined the crowd at the Flame, and at one point the conversation centered on my share. "Do a lot of any substance," a fellow named Brent said, "and something happens. If you drink, sooner or later you fall down a lot, you have accidents, you pick up DUIs, you crash cars, you wreck your liver — I could go on, but you get the point. If you do enough cocaine, your septum rots away and your nose caves in, and you damage your heart and God knows what else. Shoot speed, and it finds a variety of ways to kill you. Drop enough acid, and you go on a trip and can't find your way back from it. Everything you do, it's always got a price tag on it."

Someone quoted the oil-filter commercial. " 'You can pay me now,' " she murmured, " 'or you can pay me later.' "

"With marijuana, what happens is subtler than that. What happens when you smoke enough marijuana is nothing happens. Your whole life just stays where it is, treading water."

They batted that around a bit, and I said, "Yeah, that's him, all right. The women in his life even stay the same age. His first girlfriend was twenty-five and they've all been twenty-five ever since. He's living in the same apartment —"

"Well, that's New York, Matt. Who moves out of a rent-controlled place?"

"Granted, but he's using plastic milk crates for bookcases, and I'll bet he's had them performing that service for twenty years. On the other hand..."

"What?"

"Well," I said, "I know the folly of comparing my inside to somebody else's outside. And I know people have good days and bad days, and maybe I just caught him on a good day. And God knows this isn't the life his parents had in mind for him when they paid his tuition at NYU. And if you check the dictionary you'll find his picture next to *arrested development*."

"But?"

"But I have to say the son of a bitch seems happy."

I would have called Jan when I got in, but it was late and I decided to let it go until morning. I was up early, and when I came back from breakfast I called.

"I was just about to call you," she said.

"But I beat you to it."

"You did."

"I want to confirm our date for Saturday," I said. "But with the proviso that I may be late getting to the SoHo meeting. I've got a few hours of work, doing my impersonation of a thug."

"I beg your pardon?"

I outlined my task in a couple of sentences. "So we're leaving for Brooklyn at three," I said, "and we can probably get there in half an hour, and get her things packed and loaded in the car in another hour, and a half hour to get home would put me under the shower around five o'clock. But."

"But it could take a lot longer."

"We might not even get going until three thirty or later. And Richard could easily get lost on the way to Cobble Hill, or hit heavy traffic. And there might not be a hassle with the drunken boyfriend, but if the possibility didn't exist she wouldn't need to bring me along. And the longer it all takes, the more I'll need that shower."

I waited for her to say something, and she didn't. If I hadn't heard her radio playing in the background I'd have thought we'd been disconnected.

"Well, that's what I wanted to call you about," she said.

"About Donna and Vinnie?"

"No, about Saturday night. I have to break our date."

"Oh?"

"I'm getting together with my sponsor."

"On Saturday night."

"That's right. Dinner and a meeting and a long talk that we really have to have."

"Well," I said. "I guess it's not going to matter how long it takes me to get back from Cobble Hill."

"Are you upset?"

"No," I said. "Why should I be upset? You do what you have to do."

XXIII

AROUND NOON I walked over to the Y on West Sixty-third where Fireside meets. They have two meetings going at once, and I'd generally gone to the beginners meeting. This didn't mean that it was reserved for people who were still using training wheels, but that members were encouraged to keep the discussion focused on basic topics — i.e., staying away from a drink a day at a time. This rule, such as it was, was often honored in the breach, but in the main the sharing was about alcohol, and the art of getting through the hours without it.

Sometimes I went to the other meeting, generally making my decision on the basis of which room was less crowded, or whether I felt like climbing an extra flight of stairs. On this particular day I noticed that the woman in the speaker's chair at the beginners meeting was one I'd heard elsewhere within the past week, so I went upstairs. It was Thursday, so the upstairs meeting was a step meeting, and they were on the Eighth Step. If that was a coincidence it wasn't an extraordinary one; there are only twelve of those particular pearls of wisdom, and two of them have to do with amends, so that made it, what, a five-to-one shot?

Still, it struck me as the right step at the right time. I grabbed some coffee and a couple of Nutter Butter cookies and took a seat on the right, and heard the speaker explain how his perception of the step had changed over time. The first time he made his Eighth Step list, he said, there were just a couple of names on it—the wife who'd stayed with him despite what his drinking had done to their marriage, the kids he'd neglected. Most of all he'd harmed himself through his drinking, wrecking his health and costing himself jobs, and he figured he'd make sufficient amends to himself and to his family just by staying sober.

But with time, he said, he began to see how his drinking and his alcoholism had undermined every relationship he'd ever had, and how his actions or inaction had made him an emotional loose cannon, caroming around the deck of the pitching ship that was his life, smashing into everything nearby.

I tuned out for a moment, thinking about the metaphor; until he'd explained it, I hadn't understood what was so dangerous about a loose cannon. I'd always pictured an artillery piece in France, say, during one of the wars, raining shells on the enemy position. Was the aim off if the cannon was loose? But an unmoored cannon on a warship—well, sure, I could see how that could be a problem.

You show up at these meetings to stay sober and you walk out with a fucking education.

After the meeting, I decided that the coffee and the Nutter Butter cookies covered enough of the four basic food groups to add up to lunch. I went back to my room and tried to find something on TV, but nothing held my interest. I'd already read the paper at breakfast.

So I sat down and started making a list. All the people I'd harmed. I wrote down a few names—Estrellita Rivera, obviously, and my ex-wife, obviously, and Michael and Andrew, obviously—and then I stopped.

It's not that I'd run out of names, just that I didn't feel like writing them down. Or looking at the ones I'd already written, thank you very much. I turned over the piece of paper with the four names on it, but that wasn't enough, so I tore it in half and in half again, and kept going until I'd created a small handful of confetti. If I'd had matches handy I might have burned the scraps, but I decided the wastebasket would do.

I called Jim and told him what I'd just done.

"You know," he said, "there's a reason they gave each of the steps a number. It's so that a person can do them in order."

"I know."

"Which doesn't mean that you can't think about them when they come to mind. And that's what you were doing, thinking about Step Eight. So you wrote down some names and realized you're not ready for the step yet, and that's fine."

"If you say so."

"I do," he said, "but if you'd rather see this as further evidence that you're a rank or two below pond scum on the evolutionary continuum, be my guest. The choice is yours."

"Thanks. Jan broke our date for Saturday."

"Oh?"

"She made a dinner date with her sponsor."

"So you weighed your two options of drinking and suicide, and—"

"I felt two things at the same time, and they don't go together."

"Relief was one of them, and the other was what? Betrayal?"

"Something like that. I didn't know whether I wanted to thank her or kill her."

"Probably both."

"Maybe."

He stayed on the phone with me for a few minutes more, and afterward I took my emotional temperature and decided it was close enough to normal. Another thing I decided was that I didn't feel like going to a movie, or taking a walk in the park, or reading any of the books on the shelf. So I picked up Jack Ellery's Eighth Step list and took another shot at it.

I wound up taking a walk in the park after all. Somewhere between five and six I entered Central Park at its southwest corner, at Eighth Avenue and Fifty-ninth Street, and walked where my feet led me, trying to hew to a generally northeast course. I overshot a little, emerging at Fifth Avenue and Ninetieth Street. I walked across Eighty-sixth all the way to Second Avenue, looked at my watch, and decided I ought to fit in a proper dinner before the Sober Today meeting. The first thing that popped into my mind was the smell of whatever the woman superintendent at Frankie Dukacs's apartment building had been cooking. But there was no point going there. She'd had her chance to invite me for a meal, and she passed it up.

I kept going to First Avenue and walked down to Seventy-eighth, where Theresa's held the promise of a meal along the same lines. Two doors down, Dukacs & Son had closed for the day.

I went into Theresa's, half expecting to see Dukacs at the counter, but he wasn't there. I settled into a booth and ordered a bowl of that day's soup, a hearty affair thick with mushrooms and barley, and followed it with a plate of assorted pierogi. I couldn't remember the last time I'd had the little Polish dumplings. Theresa's served them with applesauce and boiled cabbage on the side, and stuffed them variously with meat, mushrooms, potatoes, or cheese.

I cleaned my plate, which made the waitress happy. And would I like some pie? They had pecan, they had apple, they had strawberry-rhubarb. I was tempted, but I had a meeting to get to.

The guest speaker was a fellow I'd heard before at a downtown meeting. As far as I could tell, he didn't say a single thing this time that he hadn't said before.

I'd looked around for Greg Stillman while I was helping myself to coffee, and again shortly after the start of the meeting, but I didn't see him. During the break I got in line for some more coffee, and was trying to decide if I wanted a cookie. It seemed to me that it wasn't the sort of thing a person ought to have to decide, that either you took a cookie or you didn't, and while I was mulling it over there was a tap on my shoulder, and it was Greg.

"You couldn't stay away," he said. "The siren song of Sober Today pulled you all the way from Columbus Circle."

"That or the pierogi," I said.

"Pierogi?"

"Theresa's," I said. "Seventy-eighth and First."

"Oh, Lord, I haven't been there in a coon's age. Can you still say that? It's not racist, is it?" He didn't wait for an answer, which was good, because I didn't have one. "I should go there," he said. "They have the most wonderful pies."

That settled it. I passed on the cookies.

XXIV

S O THAT'S FRANKIE DUKES's butcher shop," Greg said. "And look at the sign, will you? Dukacs and Son, formerly Dukacs and Sons. There's a whole human drama lurking in that painted-out *S*."

"I was thinking that myself."

"And the most likely explanation," he said, "is that the sign painter made a mistake, possibly but not necessarily a result of the use and abuse of drugs or alcohol, and whoever finally noticed did an amateur's job of correcting it. Of course, I'd much rather think the second son decided chopping up dead animals wasn't for him, and he ran off and became a ballet dancer instead."

"And made his father proud."

"No doubt. And here's Theresa's, and let's hope they've got two pieces of strawberry-rhubarb pie left, or none at all."

"If there's just one," I said, "we could split it."

"I want a whole piece," he said, "and so do you. But we'll jump off that bridge when we come to it."

There were two pieces of the pie, and thus no bridge to jump off. I ate half of mine and said, "Hell."

"What's wrong? Did you get a bad strawberry?"

"I read Jack's Eighth Step again," I said, "and I meant to bring it along."

"Don't tell me you found something."

"Nothing new. But I thought you'd want it back."

"Whatever for?"

"I don't know."

"I only kept a copy," he said, "so I'd be able to follow along if and when he wanted to report progress on the Ninth Step. I certainly don't have any use for it now."

"So I should just throw it out?"

"That's what I did with mine. What?"

I told him I'd taken a preliminary run at the step myself, and all I'd done to obliterate my own embryonic list.

"All the king's horses," he said, "and all the king's men. It's hard to do the Eighth before you've done the Fourth."

"My sponsor said something along those lines."

"And yet most of us take a stab at it. If we don't write anything down, at the very least we run names through our minds. It's hard to be aware of the step without wondering who belongs on your own list." He took a forkful of pie, a sip of tea. "Jack kept adding to his list, writing down new names as fast as he could check off the old ones. I wonder what his most recent version looked like."

"You mean the one you gave me —"

"Isn't the last word on the subject? I'm afraid not, but that doesn't mean we missed a clue that would have pointed at his murderer. The ones he mentioned to me were all from his boy-hood days. Family, friends, neighbors, and most of them were dead and he'd long since lost track of the others." He put down his fork. "You're not letting go of this, are you?"

"I've let go of it."

"Really?"

"When I was on the job," I said, "it was said of me that I was like a dog with a bone. Just because I've let go of something doesn't mean I can keep from thinking about it."

"I suppose there are different definitions of letting go."

"What I can't stay away from," I said, "is the thought that his murder somehow ties in to the amends process. Those five names from the list are all in the clear, and when I reread the list this afternoon I couldn't find anyone who'd make a plausible suspect. But it has to be related."

"That was my original thought, Matt. That's why I got all this started."

"He was running around making amends," I said, "and one guy punched him out and wound up hugging him and weeping in his arms, and another guy told him to take his amends and shove them up his ass—"

"And one said beating me on a coke deal was doing me a favor, and the other said hey, *everybody* fucked my wife. What was her name again?"

"Lucille. And the other one's locked up, and there's no way Jack could have reached him to make amends, and even if he did, well, it doesn't matter, because he didn't. Five names and they're all clear, but that doesn't mean there's no connection. It just means we haven't found it."

"What you mean we, Kemo Sabe?"

I sighed, nodded. "Point taken, Greg. It's not on your plate, and it's not on mine either."

"But it's on your mind. Don't apologize, for God's sake. It's on my mind too. How could it not be?"

"I keep thinking of that second bullet."

"The one in the mouth."

I nodded. "To send a message, though why you'd kill a man first and then send the message is something I've often wondered. A message to whom?"

"Like killing someone to teach him a lesson. He's dead, so how can he possibly learn the lesson?"

Something was trying to get through. Greg was saying something, but I tuned him out and let the thought take form, then held up a hand to stop him in midsentence. "It wasn't retribution," I said.

"How's that?"

"The shooting. It wasn't some aggrieved person on or off his list trying to get even. It was to keep him from talking."

"Not *Don't talk to me* but *Don't talk to anybody*."

"Has to be. There was no anger in the killing."

"No anger in putting two bullets into a man?"

"There was a lot more anger in the beating Sattenstein gave him. That was anger, hitting a man in the face until you turn your own hand into hamburger. This was just quick efficient homicide."

"With a purpose."

"I'd say so, yes."

"To keep him from talking."

"It wasn't something he'd said. It was something he might say."

"And this clearly would keep him from saying it. But..."

"The Ninth Step," I said. "How does it go?"

He looked at me, puzzled. "How does it work? You take your Eighth Step list—"

"No, I know how it works, how you do it. How does it go?

The language of the step, I've heard it before every meeting, it's in the chart that's always hanging on the wall. How is it worded?"

"Watch me get a word wrong, now that I'm called upon to perform. 'Made direct amends to such people wherever possible, except when to do so would injure them or others.' I *think* that's word for word, but—"

"Who would it injure?"

"Jack's amends? Only Jack, unless you want to count Mark Sattenstein's hand. No, I understand, Matt. It's not amends to any of the people we've been looking at. If it's something else he did, it might not even be on the list we're looking at."

"Didn't you tell me he killed somebody?"

"It was during a robbery. But I think there's a special term for it. When you rob people in their own home?"

"A home invasion."

"Yes, that's right. It's a term I've only heard recently. The news stories give the impression that it's happening more lately. Part of the continuing decline of everything and everybody."

"Do you remember the details?"

"I don't think I heard them." He frowned, as if to bring the memory into sharper focus. "He wrote about it in his Fourth Step, and I learned about it and everything else when I heard his Fifth Step."

He thought about it while I signaled the waitress for more coffee. After she'd filled our cups he said, "What I heard was vague. He didn't read that part aloud. He read a sentence or two, then looked up from the page and summarized. So I just heard a condensed version."

"And?"

"The person he robbed was another criminal. A drug dealer, I think. They broke in and—"

"They?"

"Jack had a partner. The two of them went into this home, I think it was somewhere on the Upper West Side, and held the man up, and he went for his gun and they shot him."

"Jack did the shooting?"

"I can't remember. I'm not sure he told me. Matt, I didn't really want to hear this part. I wanted him to go through it, but I didn't want to take in the information. He was a sponsee, he was a friend, he was someone I was trying to help, and I didn't want to deal with the fact that he was also a killer."

"Just tell me what you remember."

"The man's death didn't bother him that much," he said. "Maybe that's why I can't say whether it was Jack or his partner who did it."

"It didn't bother him?"

"There was a woman present. The dealer's wife or girlfriend, I'm not sure which, and again I don't know that Jack was specific."

"It doesn't matter."

"No." He drew a breath. "She was there, she'd seen their faces. The partner shot her."

"Not Jack."

"He said he couldn't pull the trigger. She was begging in Spanish. He didn't understand the words but she was pleading for her life, and he had the gun in his hand and couldn't shoot her."

"So his buddy did it."

"Matt, it's strange, but I think he felt guilty twice over."

"For each victim?"

"No, I'm just talking about the woman. For not being able to pull the trigger, and for the fact that she wound up dead. And he thought it was his fault the man went for a gun, that if he'd done something differently it wouldn't have happened."

I knew how that worked. I remembered running out of that ginmill after the two holdup men, remembered emptying my gun at them. If I'd just done any of that the slightest bit differently, if I'd fired one bullet fewer, a little girl might have had a chance to grow up. Oh, I knew exactly how that worked, with the mind throwing up no end of alternate scenarios, but remaining unable to rewrite the past.

I said, "They never got arrested."

"No."

"Not him, not his partner."

"No."

"I didn't see anything about this on his Eighth Step list."

"It may have made it into a later version. Or stayed in his mind, whether or not he wrote it down, because we'd talked about how one could make amends to the dead."

Someday I'd get to have that conversation with Jim.

I said, "The partner."

"All I know about him is that he shot the woman. I'm pretty certain Jack never said his name. He went out of his way to use pronouns or just refer to him as his partner. As if he were protecting his anonymity." He looked up. "Is that who killed him? His partner?"

"For all we know," I said, "this mysterious partner is long dead, or locked up tight in a cell upstate. But it might be good to know who he is."

"Would he have a motive? After all these years?"

"There's no statute of limitations on homicide."

"So he wouldn't want Jack talking about it."

"No."

"And we know he's capable of murder. Whichever of them shot the man, it was the partner who shot the woman."

"While she was begging for her life," I said. "Because she'd seen him, and could identify him. What else did Jack have to say about this paragon of virtue?"

But if he'd said anything else, Greg couldn't remember it. I went home. There was a note in my box, and my first thought was that Jan had called to tell me our date was on after all. But the caller had been someone named Mark, who'd provided a phone number, along with an initial in lieu of a surname. An AA acquaintance, it would appear, and I wondered if it was Stuttering Mark or Motorcycle Mark.

I went upstairs, looked at the message again, then crumpled the slip and tossed it in the wastebasket. Whoever he was, it was too late to call and find out more. And by now he'd found someone else to hear his problems and tell him not to drink, and by morning he'd have forgotten why he called me in the first place.

XXV

I PICKED UP the *Times* in the morning and read it while I had
my breakfast. In Woodside, a family of Colombian immigrants had been murdered in what police believed to be a home
invasion. Three adults dead, and four children, with the bodies
mutilated. Authorities seemed uncertain as to whether the motive
was robbery or revenge, and I decided it sounded like a little of
both. Somebody in the drug world had cheated someone else, or
constituted unacceptable competition. So why not kill him? And
why not walk off with his cash and inventory while you were at
it? And, of course, kill his family, because that was the way you
did business.

The first thing I thought of was Bill Lonergan. The *Times*
story didn't provide a street address, so I didn't know how close
he lived to the scene of the crime, but Woodside isn't that large. I
wondered how closely he followed the local crime scene, and
decided he'd have trouble overlooking this one. Seven people

murdered in their home, four of them children. It'd be on the TV news, at least until the police ran out of leads and some other horror displaced it from the public consciousness.

After that, of course, I thought of Jack Ellery and his partner.

I called Greg Stillman, who began the conversation by telling me he'd been trying to remember more about the partner. "But it seems to me he was trying to avoid saying anything that would make him identifiable," he said. "I don't know if they worked together more than that one time."

"Do you know when it happened?"

"The killing? It was before he went to prison. And after he'd started committing crimes, but I guess that's pretty obvious. There were a lot of years in there, but there was nothing chronological about his Fourth Step. If I had to guess, I'd say ten or twelve years ago."

"And all you know is it was uptown?"

"And on the West Side. When I picture it I see an address on Riverside Drive, but I don't know why."

"Did he say something about looking out at the Hudson after the other guy shot the woman?"

"Not that I remember."

"Was it a house? An apartment building?"

"No idea. Matt?"

"Because I can't help being interested."

"Nice. You answered the question before I could ask it."

"Well, it's one I've been asking myself. But there's nowhere to go with this, is there? A man and a woman shot to death in their home somewhere north and west of Times Square."

"I seem to have the impression it was quite a ways uptown."

"Fine. Somewhere north and west of Central Park."

"Not much easier that way, is it?"

"I don't suppose he mentioned their names. The victims."

"No."

"Or anything to set them apart."

"Those kinds of details might have been in his Fourth Step, Matt."

"But he kept them to himself."

"Or if he told me, it sailed right by. I told you I was trying not to dwell on what I was hearing."

"Yes."

"A fine time to play Second Monkey."

"How's that?"

"You know, Hear No Evil. If I'd been paying closer attention—"

"You don't want to go there, Greg."

"No."

"It's a shame you don't have a copy of his Fourth Step."

"I never read it. I just got to hear it, or to hear the parts he read to me."

"I know. Then what did he do with it?"

"I told him to throw it out."

"Toss it in the garbage?"

"Well, tear it up first."

As I'd done with my own half-assed attempt at Step Eight.

"That's what I tell my sponsees," he was saying. " 'You got all of that out of your system, and you shared it with God and with another person—' "

"How do you share it with God?"

"I've often wondered. I guess you just assume he's listening when you share it with your sponsor. Where was I? Oh, right. 'You shared it with another person, and now it's time to let go of it.' "

"And they take it home and burn it. Or shred it, or whatever. Is that what you did with yours?"

"What else?"

Shortly before noon I decided I could stand a change from Fireside, and that it was a nice enough day for a longer walk. I went to a group called Renaissance, on Forty-eighth off Fifth Avenue. The midtown location drew a lot of commuters whose offices were nearby and who would go home to the suburbs after work. That made for more suits and better grooming than was the norm at my meetings, but there was certainly no dress code, and the unshaven guy seated next to me had the air of having spent the night sleeping in a cardboard box.

Afterward I called one of my cop friends. I told him I was looking for an unsolved home invasion, the double murder of a drug dealer and his wife or girlfriend. Both shot dead, and it would have taken place on the Upper West Side sometime in the early '70s.

He said, "My first thought is there's been hundreds, but you got two people dead, both of gunshots, and the case is still open. That narrows it down. I'll see if it rings a bell for anybody."

I had essentially the same conversation with two other old friends, and hung up fairly certain that I wasn't going to get anywhere that way. I walked a few blocks down Fifth to the main library, where I spent an hour with bound volumes of the *New York Times Index* and another couple of hours in the microfiche room, hunting for a needle in a pasture full of haystacks.

Pointless.

At St. Paul's that night a woman named Josie asked if I wasn't getting pretty close to my one-year anniversary. Pretty soon, I said. She said she was sure it would be the first of many, and advised me to remember that it was a day at a time.

Stuttering Mark wasn't there, I was more apt to run into him at Fireside, but I caught up with Motorcycle Mark at the coffee urn and asked if he'd called the night before. He said he hadn't, that he didn't even have my number. I said it must have been someone else, and he said that since I'd brought up the subject, could I let him have my number? I gave him one of my minimalist cards and he found a home for it in his shirt pocket. Then he borrowed a pen and wrote out his own name and number on a scrap of paper. It seemed only polite to thank him and tuck it away in my wallet.

Donna was there, and her clothes suggested she'd come straight from the office. Her hair was pinned back, and not falling over her eyes. She confirmed that I'd be able to show up as scheduled.

"Three tomorrow afternoon," I said. "Eighty-fourth and Amsterdam."

She reached out, gave my arm a squeeze.

Maybe it was the habit she had of touching my arm, or maybe it was more the result of how she looked in the well-tailored skirt and jacket. The last conversation I'd had with Jan may have had something to do with it, too. Whatever it was, I spent the second half of the meeting wondering if she'd join the crowd at the post-meeting meeting, which is what some people had taken to calling the gathering afterward at the Flame.

She didn't show up, which was hardly surprising. I couldn't recall that I'd ever seen her there in the past. I didn't stay long myself. I had coffee and a sandwich—I'd managed to skip dinner—and said my good-byes and went home.

No messages, but I wasn't in my room for ten minutes before

the phone rang. I thought first of Jan, then Donna, and finally Mark—Motorcycle Mark, making use of my number, or the Mark who'd called before.

I settled the matter by picking up the phone, and it was Greg.

Without preamble he said, "I gave a false impression before. I've written out several Fourth Step inventories in the course of my sobriety. I still have copies of two of them."

"You know," I said, "I think that's between you and your Higher Power." I'd almost said *sponsor,* but remembered in time that his sponsor was filling a chair in the Big Meeting in the Sky.

"That's not the point."

"Then what is? Oh."

"You see, don't you? If I didn't destroy my own Fourth Step…"

"Then who's to say that Jack didn't hang on to his?"

"My thought exactly. I'll check his room tomorrow. Or do you suppose they've sealed it with that yellow Crime Scene tape?"

"I'm sure they have," I said, "but they'll have long since unsealed it by now. Once the crime lab crew is finished, there's no real reason to maintain a seal. He had a furnished room, didn't he? Did he pay his rent weekly or by the month?"

"By the week."

"Then the odds are it's been rented by now."

"And if he left his Fourth Step behind, some other tenant's reading it even as we speak. But won't they pack up his possessions? Isn't that what they do when somebody dies?"

I said that sounded about right. "And they give it to the heirs, or the next of kin," I said. "I don't suppose Jack had a will."

"Just the sort every alcoholic has, along with a whim of iron. A Last Will and Testament? No, hardly. I don't think he had anything to pass on, or anybody to leave it to."

184 · LAWRENCE BLOCK

"My guess is the super'll wait a decent interval, then keep what he wants and throw the rest out."

"That's what I thought. So what I'm going to do is go over there tomorrow and tell them I'm his cousin and I've come to collect his effects. There shouldn't be a problem, should there?"

"I can't see why. A box of old clothes and personal papers? He'll be glad to see the last of it."

"I can give the clothes to the Goodwill or the Sally. And if there's, you know, some sort of personal item like a pocketknife, I'll take it for a keepsake." He was silent for a moment, perhaps recalling other dead friends and other souvenirs. "And if there's a Fourth Step," he said, "I'll call you."

"Good."

"Matt? You wouldn't want to keep me company, would you?"

"What time?"

"It would have to be in the afternoon."

That saved me from having to invent a reason I couldn't go. Donna had already supplied me with a perfectly good one. "I can't," I said. "I have to go to Brooklyn."

"Really? Were you a bad boy? Are you being punished?"

"It's work," I said. "I have to help a member of my group move her stuff out of her boyfriend's apartment."

"Oh, God," he said. "That takes you off the hook, but at what price? You've got a worse day ahead of you than I do. Matt, if I find anything interesting I'll call you."

Won't they pack up his possessions? Isn't that what they do when somebody dies?

Well, it depends who it is, and how and where he dies. If he's a respectable member of society, and is considerate enough to leave a detailed will, his property is apportioned as specified therein. (Of course that's after the in-home nurse pockets a few things that she just knows the deceased wanted her to have.) Then the relatives get to fight over the small stuff, and siblings get to drag out and act on every grudge and resentment left over from childhood.

If there's no will, they get to fight over the big stuff too.

But if the deceased takes his last breath in a Bowery flophouse or an SRO welfare hotel, if the cops zip him into a body bag and cart him down a couple of flights of stairs, then anything worth the taking is pretty sure to get taken. The little stash of emergency cash, the couple of bucks left over from the most recent government check, the folded ten-dollar bill in the shoe—if a relative does turn up, it will have long since disappeared. The cops take it.

I always did. I learned from a partner, who explained the ethics of the situation. The ethical thing, he told me, was to divvy up with your partner.

And so I robbed the dead. It didn't keep me up nights, or lead me to drink a drop more bourbon than I'd have had anyway. I can't imagine it amounted to much over the years. Usually it was five dollars, ten dollars, certainly well under a hundred dollars. But one time I got to share $972 with my partner du jour. I remember the amount, remember how precisely we split it down the middle, remember what a nice windfall the $486 made, and how it left me with a feeling of gratitude and respect toward the derelict who'd unintentionally bestowed it upon me. (He'd gotten drunk, fell in his bathroom, gashed his head open, and bled out before recovering consciousness. We were ready to hate him for the mess he'd created, but the money he left us changed our attitude. Of course you don't have to be on the Bowery to die like that; the actor William Holden managed it just about a year before I had my last drink.)

More names for my list, if I ever actually took the Eighth Step. How did you make amends to men whose names you had

managed to forget as soon as you'd written up the report? I
wasn't even sure I'd been wrong to take the money. If my partner and I left it, that just meant somebody else would pocket it.
And who was legally supposed to get it? The State of New York?
What the hell did some bureau in Albany need with five dollars
here and ten dollars there, or even a princely $972?

On the other hand, it wasn't my money.

A lot of John Does and Richard Roes for my list, plus a couple
of Mary Moes. Because women died too, of causes natural and
unnatural, and you had to look in their purses for ID, didn't
you? And you'd always find a couple of dollars.

I was partnered with one prince of the city who took a pair of
hoop earrings from the ears of a dead hooker. "These look like
eighteen karat," he said. "What does the poor darling need with
gold earrings in potter's field?"

I told him to keep them. Was I sure? Yes, I said, I was sure. Be
a shame to split the pair, I said.

Noble of me. Maybe that'd be enough to get me into Heaven.
*What did I ever do that was good? Well, St. Peter, one time I could
have stolen the gold from a dead whore's ears. But I restrained
myself.*

XXVI

"I ALMOST DIDN'T recognize you," I said.

Donna grinned, fluffed her hair. "Is it that different?"

The long auburn hair that had flowed down over her shoulders, and occasionally drifted into her eyes, had been cropped boyishly short and permed into a tight cap of curls. Richard, behind the wheel, said, "Isn't it fabulous? And positively transformative — or do I want to say transformational?"

Nobody offered an opinion on that one.

"Well," he said, "whichever the word is, that's it. What a metamorphosis! From Brenda Starr to Little Orphan Annie."

"I wish you hadn't told me that," she said. "I always liked Brenda Starr."

"What have you got against Annie?"

"Nothing, but I never much wanted to look like her." She was in the front of the car, next to Richard, and she had an arm hooked over her seat back so that she could look at me. "Well, Matthew S.? What's your verdict?"

"It looked nice long," I said, "and it looks nice short. One thing it does, it shows off your face better."

"It used to get lost in all that hair," Richard said. "Now it pops."

"I look like Little Orphan Annie and my face pops," she said.

"These are good things, sweetie. Trust me."

"All I know," she said, "is it's done. The boy who does my hair couldn't believe it when I went in there this morning and told him what I wanted."

"Like, 'Oooh, how can you possibly want me to do that to you?'"

"Not at all," she told him. "He's been wanting to cut my hair forever. 'I finally talked you into it!' But it wasn't his doing."

"The occasion," I guessed. "Washing that man right out of your hair."

Richard said he always loved Mary Martin. Donna said, "Sort of, but not exactly. I called him last night."

"Vinnie," I said.

"Which was probably a mistake, because I didn't want to hear his voice, or for him to hear mine. But I thought I should remind him that I was coming for my things this afternoon, and that it would help if he could contrive to be elsewhere."

"And?"

"I don't know if he was able to take in the information. He started going on and on about my hair, my beautiful long hair, and how he wanted to see it spread out on his pillow and, well, other things I'd just as soon not repeat."

"We'll use our overheated imaginations," Richard said.

"I'm sure you will. And I thought, You know, buster, if you like my hair that much, there must be something wrong with it.

And whether there is or not, you've seen it for the last time. And I got up this morning and rushed straight to the beauty parlor, and Hervé was able to fit me in, and the rest is history."

"It's not history, sweetie, it's art appreciation. Just fabulous."

"Thank you, Richard."

"But Hervé? Honestly?"

"I think it used to be Harvey."

"Ooh la la," said Richard. "How continental."

Vincent Cutrone's apartment was in a six-story brick building on a street corner in Cobble Hill. A dry cleaner and a deli shared the ground floor, with half a dozen small apartments on each of the upper floors. Richard, who'd found the place with no trouble, was able to park right in front, and the three of us entered the building together. Donna had her key out, but pushed the button for 4-C anyway, and sighed deeply when the intercom made that throat-clearing noise it makes when someone's about to respond.

"Yo," he said.

She rolled her eyes. "I'm coming up," she said. "I've got people with me."

He didn't say anything, nor did he buzz us in. She used her key, and we were getting on the elevator when we finally heard the buzzer sound.

"Yo," Donna said, and rolled her eyes again. "Why did I ever think — never mind."

He must have been waiting at the door, because it opened inward as Donna was extending the key. Vinnie loomed in the doorway, his eyes taking in all three of us, then doing a pronounced double take. "Oh, Jesus," he said. "What the fuck did you do to your hair?"

"I had it cut," she said.

"By a fuckin' butcher?" He looked past her at me and Richard. "You believe this, guys? Best thing the woman had goin' for her and she chops it off. Hell of a thing. I'm the one who drinks and she's the one who goes nuts."

She said, "I came for my things, Vincent. I thought—"

"Oh, now it's Vincent. All the time it was 'Oh, Vinnie, nobody ever made me feel like you made me feel. Oh, Vinnie, I love it when you—'"

I'd seen him before. At meetings, here and there around town. I never heard his story, never knew his name, couldn't recall ever seeing him with Donna. But I recognized the face.

He was an inch or two shorter than I, and a few pounds heavier. His hair was dark brown and shaggy, and a little longer than the new Donna's. He hadn't shaved in a couple of days, and he smelled the way you do when the alcohol is working its way out of your pores. He was wearing a soiled white undershirt, the kind that leaves the shoulders uncovered, and a pair of cutoff jeans. His feet were bare.

"You said you'd stay away from the apartment while I collected my things."

"No, Donna, you're the one who said that. But you moved out, right? It's my apartment now, right?"

"That's right."

"So it's my apartment, who's got a better right to be here? You want to kick me out of it? Hey, I wanted to, I could kick *you* out of it."

"Vinnie—"

"Ah, we're back to Vinnie. I feel all warm and fuzzy now." He reached out a hand, rubbed her hair. "You know what you look like? You look like Raggedy fuckin' Ann."

"Don't touch me."

"'Don't touch me.' A different tune these days, Donna. Hey,

don't worry. I'm not gonna kick you out of my apartment." He stood aside, motioned her in. *"Esta es su casa,"* he said. "You know what that means?"

"I know what it means."

"It's Spanish, it means this is your house. Except it's mine."

I said, "Vinnie, maybe it'd be a good idea if you gave us an hour."

He looked at me. Before, he'd regarded me as an audience, but now I had a speaking part, and he responded accordingly. "I know you," he said. "Matt, am I right? Used to be a cop before they kicked you off the force for bein' an asshole. You the new boyfriend?"

"Matt and Richard are helping me move," Donna said.

"They're just what you need," he said. "Matt can beat me up and Richard here can blow me. Between the two of 'em I got no fuckin' chance."

It was a long afternoon in Cobble Hill. Vinnie had been drinking around the clock for days now, and he got to show all his emotions in turn, from self-pity to belligerence. He said he wished that Donna hadn't cut her hair, and that he'd like to wrap it around her neck and strangle her with it. He walked out of the room, turned up the volume on the TV, came back with a beer, wandered off again.

The apartment must have been nice before he picked up a drink. Now it was all empty bottles and beer cans and pizza boxes, half-eaten containers of Chinese food, and copies of *Hustler* and *Penthouse*. There was a page torn from *Screw,* hooker ads with their photos and phone numbers, taped alongside the wall phone in the kitchen. Some of the ads were circled in Magic Marker.

"This one," he announced, pointing to one of the photos,

"could give you cards and spades, Donna. Could suck a tennis ball through a garden hose. I dunno, though. Bet you could do the same, huh, Richard?"

Nobody answered him, but this didn't seem to bother him. I'm not sure he noticed.

A long afternoon in Cobble Hill.

XXVII

WE WERE ACROSS the bridge and back in Manhattan when she said, "Raggedy Ann, for God's sake. Little Orphan Annie and Raggedy Ann."

"You are fabulously glamorous," Richard said. "So will you please stop that shit?"

"Okay."

"I meant Little Orphan Annie in the nicest possible way. And you have big eyes, the same as she does, except yours are this gorgeous light brown. And they really pop now that your hair's not falling in front of them."

"So now I'm pop-eyed? I'm sorry, I'll stop."

"And you don't look at all like Raggedy Ann," he said. "The man is a drunken imbecile."

There was a long silence. Then she said, "He's not a bad fellow, you know. When he's sober."

"He's not sober, though, is he?"

"No."

"And drunk or sober, he was never right for you. And deep down you always knew that."

"Oh, God, Richard. You're absolutely right."

"Well, of course," he said.

Her belongings filled the trunk and shared the backseat with me. When we got back where we started, Eighty-fourth and Amsterdam, Richard circled the block and couldn't find a parking spot. I told him to park next to the fire hydrant, and handed him a card to put on the dashboard.

"Detectives' Endowment Association," he read aloud. "And this means I won't get a ticket?"

"It improves the odds."

"I don't know," he said. "I'd take my chances on a ticket, but what if they tow it?"

Donna said, "Honey, you'll feel a lot more comfortable staying with the car. Matt and I can manage the stuff. We'll just make an extra trip."

She lived on the fifth floor of a brownstone. It was a fine building in excellent condition, and the only smell in the stairwell was a faint hint of furniture polish. But it was a walk-up, and it took us three trips, and by the time I'd climbed those four flights of stairs for the third time I was winded.

"Sit down," she said, "before you fall down. Those stairs keep me in shape, but they're killers if you're not used to them. Plus you were carrying three times as much as I was. Can I get you a glass of water? Or maybe a Coke?"

"A Coke would be great."

"Except it's Pepsi."

"Pepsi's fine."

"Here you go. I'll just tell Richard we're all set now."

She parked me in a Queen Anne wing chair in the living room, in front of a fireplace with a marble surround. Over it she'd hung a nineteenth-century landscape in a fancy frame, and a thick Chinese rug was centered on the dark hardwood floor. It was a very pleasing room, richer and more formal than I'd have expected, and a better match to the business attire she'd worn last night than to this afternoon's jeans and sweater.

I wondered what the apartment's other rooms looked like. The kitchen, the bedroom. I stayed where I was and imagined them, and then I heard her footsteps on the stairs.

"Now just let me catch my breath," she said upon entering, and dropped onto the medallion-back love seat. "Richard said to give you his love, and tell you to have a happy anniversary, if he doesn't see you before then. You're coming up on a year, aren't you?"

"Pretty soon."

"Another Coke? Pepsi, I mean. Can I get you another?"

"One's my limit."

"Ha! I like that. Oh, before I forget—"

She came over and passed me a pair of hundred-dollar bills. We argued about it. I told her it was too much, and she said that's what she'd given Richard and that was what she was giving me. I said I'd have been happy to do what I'd done for free, out of friendship, so at the very least why didn't we split the difference? And I handed her one of the bills, and she pushed it back at me.

"I'd have happily paid four hundred," she said, "or even more, so we're already splitting the difference. And if you'll put the money away we won't have to discuss it anymore, and won't that be a pleasure?"

I agreed that she had a point there, and put the bills in my wallet. Without planning to, I said, "Well, let me spend some of this on dinner. Will you keep me company?"

Her eyes widened. "What a lovely idea. But it's Saturday, and don't you have a standing date with — is it Jane?"

"Jan."

"I was close."

"And she decided she'd rather spend this particular Saturday having dinner with her sponsor."

"Oh."

"I guess the two of them have something they feel it's important to discuss. Me, most likely."

"Oh," she said. She was on her feet, and I stood up myself, and our eyes locked. I felt as if I were on the brink of a decision, and then I realized the decision had already been made.

She took a step forward. "You're a lovely man," she said, and put her hand on my arm.

Her bedroom was frilly and Victorian, with a canopy bed. Afterward I lay there beside her and listened to my heart. I found myself wondering, not for the first time, just how many beats it had left.

Beside me, Donna lay on her back. She raised her hands over her head and stretched, then touched her armpit with one hand and brought her fingers to her face.

"Oh, dear," she said. "I stink."

"I know. It was all I could do to bring myself to touch you."

She had a good laugh, rich and just the least bit naughty. "I noticed," she said, "how much trouble you had overcoming your natural repugnance." She laid a hand on my thigh. "But I could have had a shower."

"I thought of having one myself," I said, "but we'd have had to wait."

"And that might have given one of us time to think things through."

"In which case we might not have wound up here."

"Oh, we'd have wound up here," she said. "Sooner or later."

"Written in the stars?"

"Written on the subway walls," she said, "and tenement halls. I love that song."

"I haven't heard it in ages."

"Hang on," she said, and slipped out of bed. I must have drifted off for a moment, because the next thing I knew she was curled up at my side while Simon & Garfunkel crooned softly in close harmony.

"In my fantasies," she said, "I never imagined we'd be all sweaty."

"You had fantasies?"

"You bet. And in all of them I came to you fresh out of the shower, with a little dab of perfume here and there —"

"Where and where?"

"Stop that. You're distracting me. Where was I?"

"Here and there," I said.

"You have the gentlest touch, Matthew S. Oh, my. Fresh out of the shower, subtly scented, with my long hair flowing. Well, the scent's none too subtle, and the long hair's no more than a memory."

"In *my* fantasies," I said, "the long hair didn't really enter into it."

"Hang on," she said. "You had fantasies? About me?"

"That surprises you?"

"I never got any kind of vibe from you," she said. "That's one thing that made it so safe to have fantasies about you. You weren't interested in me, and you were already taken."

"I guess I started getting ideas when you put your hand on my arm."

"You mean like this?"

198 · LAWRENCE BLOCK

"Uh-huh."

"That was just, you know, friendship."

"I see."

"I did it unconsciously."

"Okay."

"Maybe it wasn't entirely unconscious," she said, and thought it over. "Maybe it was just the tiniest bit sexual."

"Well, don't apologize for it, Donna."

"I wouldn't dream of it. What kind of fantasies did you have, that my hair wasn't a part of?"

"Well, what we just did."

"Oh."

"And a couple of other things," I said, "that we haven't done yet."

"None of them involving long hair."

"Look, I always admired your hair."

"And you wish I hadn't cut it."

"No," I said. "I actually think I like it better now. But I liked it fine before."

"Men all think they like long hair," she said, "but it's a pain in the ass to take care of, and you know what else?"

"What?"

"It gets in your mouth when you fuck. Those things we haven't done yet. Should we shower first?"

I showered later, once I'd returned to my hotel. After our second session she'd announced that she was too tired to go anywhere, but that we ought to eat something, and what if she made us some sandwiches? I said that sounded fine, and she came back with a couple of sandwiches, liverwurst on dark rye, and a bag of corn chips made from organically grown blue corn.

"I'm starting to fade," she said. "It's been a busy day."

"I'll say."

"You're welcome to stay over."

But I knew better. I got dressed and she walked me to the door. "You're a sweet man," she said. "I'm glad we did this."

It was cooler out, and I thought I'd take a bus straight down Columbus. But I got itchy standing around waiting for the bus to come, and I started walking, and was halfway home by the time a bus came along. I could have caught it, but I let it go and walked the rest of the way home. Sometimes walking is a good way to get some thinking done, but at other times it's a handy alternative to thinking, and as long as I kept putting one foot in front of the other I didn't have to turn over any rocks and see what was under them.

There were messages at the hotel desk, as I thought there would be. Two calls, Jan and Greg. I looked at my watch and decided it was too late to call either of them. I went upstairs, and when I got out of the shower I picked up the phone and called Greg.

"No luck," he said.

"He'd thrown out Jack's things?"

"No, he bundled them up, just the way he was supposed to. Then just the other day a policeman showed up to collect them. Is that usual?"

Not when they've essentially decided to sign off on the case. "Maybe they've got a lead," I said. "Whoever picked it up would have signed for it. Was it Redmond?"

"It never occurred to me to ask."

"I don't suppose it matters," I said. "Maybe I'll give him a call and see what I can find out."

I rang off, got in bed. Maybe I'd call Redmond, I thought, and maybe I wouldn't. I couldn't see that it made much difference either way.

XXVIII

"T HEY HAD A STORY in the paper the other day," Jim said. "There's this new Chinatown out in Flushing. You take the Shea Stadium train clear to the end of the line. Main Street, Flushing—that's the name of the stop. And there's blocks of Chinese restaurants with different cuisines from the different sections of China. Stuff you wouldn't get here."

"Stir-fried panda," I suggested.

"Including parts of the panda it would never occur to you to eat. So I was thinking we really ought to get out there, just walk into the first restaurant that looks good and see what they serve us."

"Good idea."

He refilled our tea cups. "And then I thought, Hell, who am I kidding? The old established Chinatown's ten minutes away on the A Train, and we never get there, so why would we chase out to Flushing?"

"We're creatures of habit."

"They wrote up this Taiwanese restaurant, not two blocks from the subway stop. It sounded pretty good, I have to say. And yet we'll never get there." He took a bite, chewed, swallowed. "Creatures of habit," he said. "You're in the habit of getting laid on Saturday night, and if one woman disappears you just go find yourself another."

"I didn't think of it that way."

"No, I don't suppose you did. Donna, huh? Fine-looking woman."

"She cut her hair."

"So you said. But you didn't let that stop you, did you?"

We were two of the seven customers at the Lucky Peony, a recent arrival on Eighth Avenue and Fifty-first Street. Until I walked over there to meet Jim, I hadn't left my room all day, and the sesame noodles were my first nourishment since last night's liverwurst sandwich.

And Jim, when he called to pick a time and place for our Sunday dinner, was the first person I spoke to. I didn't say much, but those few words were the only ones that passed my lips.

I never made a conscious decision to spend the day walled off from the world. I kept thinking I'd go out for breakfast in a few minutes, and held on to the thought after I'd changed the meal's name to lunch.

Jan and I generally went to a Sunday morning meeting in SoHo, and I knew I wasn't going to show up there, but there were plenty of other meetings available, all over the city and all through the day, and I thought I'd drop in on one of them. I checked my meeting book, and worked out a plan that would let me fit in a couple of meetings, or even three if I pushed it.

And didn't go to any of them.

Instead I stayed in my room. I had the television set on more often than not, switching back and forth between a football game and a golf tournament, sometimes caught up in what I was watching, sometimes not.

I thought of phone calls I could make, and didn't make them. At one point I remembered the mysterious Mark who'd called a couple of days ago and left a number, which I'd wound up tossing in the wastebasket. I wondered who it was, since I'd determined it wasn't Motorcycle Mark, and I looked in the basket, but it was gone. As one of the hotel's permanent residents, I get weekly maid service — my bed made with clean linen, my bathroom cleaned, my carpet vacuumed, my wastebasket emptied. My room got this treatment every Saturday, so I was a day late as far as Mark's number was concerned, but that was all right, because I'm pretty sure I wouldn't have called him anyway.

My phone rang a couple of times. But the calls came after I'd already spoken with Jim, and there was nobody I wanted to talk to, so I let it ring. If it was important they'd leave messages, and I could collect them on my way to dinner. If I remembered to check.

"Afterward," I said, "I walked all the way home."

"Whistling a happy tune?"

"You know what ran through my mind? Jesus, am I going to have this woman around my neck for the rest of my life?"

"Because how could she possibly let a fine fellow like you get away?"

"Yeah, right."

"Here's what happened," he said. "Just so you know. Donna just got out of a relationship she never should have gotten into in the first place. So she did two things to prove she was done with it. She got her hair cut and she got herself laid. And, to make sure she didn't wind up back where she started, she picked some-body unavailable."

"Because of Jan. But nothing would have happened if Jan hadn't broken our date. That's when Donna got interested."

"Before that she was just grabbing your arm out of friendship."

I had to think about that.

"Look," he said, "she liked you. She wanted to go to bed with you. Then she gave you a sandwich and sent you home."

"She said I could stay."

"'Darling, please stay, and in the morning we'll go out for brunch, and then we'll come back here and make love some more.' Is that how she put it?"

"Not exactly."

"The message you got, and the one she intended to give, was you could stay if you wanted, but she'd just as soon you didn't. Does that sound about right?"

"She was probably thinking, Am I gonna have this guy hang-ing around for the rest of my life?"

"Well, she's an alcoholic, the same way you are. And she just got away from the Pride of Bensonhurst, so yeah, I suspect she was thinking something along those lines. But brighten up, will you? Here's this great-looking woman with a nice apartment, and you're the one she picked to share her canopy bed."

"How'd you know it was a canopy bed?"

"Jesus, who are you, Lieutenant Columbo? You described it."

"Oh."

"And the Oriental rug, and the portrait over the marble fireplace."

"It was a landscape."

"Thanks for clearing that up. She didn't have to pick you, you know. She could have dragged Richard upstairs."

"Richard's gay."

"You think that would have stopped her?"

"Jim—"

"All right, I'll grant that you're a little more available than Richard, and a little more suitable. You're not in love with her, are you?"

"With Donna? No. I like her, but—"

"No fantasies about moving in?"

"No."

"Good, because that's not what she wants either. Donna's got a good job, makes decent money. She works downtown somewhere, doesn't she?"

"She's at an investment bank. I don't know exactly what she does there."

"Whatever it is, it pays well. And the next man she hooks up with, and it's not going to be anytime soon, won't be a guy like Vinnie, a knockaround guy from South Brooklyn who stays sober between drunks. And you know who else he won't be?"

"An unlicensed private eye living in a hotel room."

"There you go. You had a good time, and you didn't have to spend Saturday night alone."

"Right."

"And you came out of it two hundred dollars to the good. What's the matter?"

"Is that what the money was for?"

"No, of course not. The money was so that she wasn't sleeping with you to pay you back for helping her out. Merry Christmas, kiddo."

"Huh?"

"You don't know the joke? Mailman brings the mail to this one house and the wife invites him in, gives him a fresh-baked brownie and a cup of coffee. Next thing he knows she's taking him upstairs to the bedroom. Afterward she hands him a dollar.

"And he says, 'Hey, what's this?' And he tries to hand it back, but she won't take it. 'It's for you,' she says. 'It was my husband's idea.' 'Your husband's idea?' 'Yeah,' she says. 'I asked him what should we do for the mailman for Christmas, and he said, *Fuck him, give him a dollar.* The brownie and coffee were my idea.'"

We went to the meeting at St. Clare's, and afterward I walked him back to his place. On my way home I remembered that I'd walked right past the desk earlier without seeing if any of my callers had left messages. This time I checked, and there was nothing. I went upstairs, picked up the phone, put it down without dialing anybody's number, and went to bed.

XXIX

MONDAY MORNING I called Greg Stillman first thing after breakfast. There was no answer, so I left a message on his machine. I knew better than to call Donna, and I wasn't ready to call Jan. I found the number for Dennis Redmond, and someone else at the precinct answered his phone. I left my name and number.

Redmond and I played phone tag for a day and a half. I was never in my room when he called, and he was never at his desk when I called him back. I went to Fireside for the Monday noon meeting, and to St. Paul's that night. I thought I might run into Donna, but wasn't surprised when I didn't.

Jim wasn't there either, but I found some other people to have coffee with, and it was past eleven when I got home from the Flame. No messages, but Jacob informed me that I'd had a call. "But he didn't leave no name," he said, "nor no number neither."

Nohow, I thought.

I was surprised Greg hadn't returned my call, and decided it wasn't too late to call him. I got the machine again, so either he was out wolfing down strawberry-rhubarb pie or he'd turned in for the night. I hung up without leaving another message and went to bed.

Tuesday afternoon my phone finally rang when I was there to answer it. It was Jan, just calling to say hello. We had a curiously hollow conversation, where what didn't get said was more significant than what did. Neither of us said anything about the past Saturday night, or about the coming one. I didn't say any of the several things I had on my mind, and I don't think she did either.

So it wasn't much of a phone call, but it broke the logjam, because after I got off the phone with her I called Redmond, and this time he was there to answer.

"Sorry," he said. "I've been meaning to get back to you. I did call a couple of times."

"I've been hard to reach myself," I said. "I was just wondering if it was you who picked up Jack Ellery's possessions."

He didn't know what I was talking about. I explained that someone had collected Ellery's belongings from the super, and thought it might be him.

"Jesus," he said. "Why would I do that?"

"That's what I was wondering."

"The super said it was me?"

"I never talked to him," I said. "Gregory Stillman went over there, and he got the impression some police officer had picked up the stuff."

"What stuff? The long-lost loot from the Brinks Job?"

"Well, I don't know," I said. "Stillman thought there might be some notebooks, some AA keepsakes."

"You ever been to his room?"

"Ellery's? No."

"Well, I was, because it was where he was killed. Outside of a razor and a toothbrush and a clock radio, he didn't own a whole hell of a lot. Some old clothes, an extra pair of shoes. Maybe half a dozen books. Some of them were AA books. Is that what you were looking for?"

"I wasn't looking for anything. Stillman —"

"Right, Stillman. There was a brass coin about the size of a half-dollar. Maybe a little larger. Had what I guess is the AA symbol on it. Two *A*s in a circle or a triangle, I forget which."

"Both."

"Huh?"

"Two *A*s in a triangle, with the triangle enclosed in a circle."

"I'm glad you cleared that up for me. Whatever it was, it'd be hard to buy a drink with it."

Some groups give them out for members' anniversaries. There's a Roman numeral on one side, for however many years you're celebrating. I didn't feel Redmond needed to be burdened with this information.

"Anyway," he said, "the poor sonofabitch didn't have much, and I didn't need to see any of it a second time. So whoever picked up his things, it wasn't me. Hang on a second."

I waited, and he returned to report that nobody else knew anything about Ellery's leavings. I said maybe the super had kept them and made up a story. More likely he threw everything out, Redmond said, because there was nothing there to keep. He tossed it, and to avoid getting bawled out he blamed it on the cops.

"Which we ought to be used to," he said. "You know, I was hoping you had something better than a question."

"Like what?"

"I figured maybe your conscience was troubling you and you wanted to tell me how you shot your old childhood pal."

"Why would I do that?"

"I just said. Because your conscience—"

"Why would I shoot him?"

"How do I know? You're the one with the guilty conscience. Maybe he stole a baseball card from you a hundred years ago in the Bronx, and you just realized it was the one that's worth a fortune. I forget who's on it."

"I can't help you there."

"Honus Wagner. So who needs your help? You didn't do it, huh?"

"I'm afraid not."

"Just my luck. Hey, you're not fucking around with the case, are you? Playing detective?"

"No."

"You want to say that a little more convincingly? Never mind. I'd caution you about getting in our way, but the caseload we've got, your pal Ellery's not getting a lot of our time. You run across anything, you know where to bring it."

That was Tuesday. Thursday morning I was reading the paper while I had my breakfast. There was a back-page item I barely registered, a man killed on the street near Gramercy Park, apparently during a mugging. I was several pages past the story when something clicked, and I went back and looked at the victim's name, and right away I knew which Mark it was who'd been trying to call me.

XXX

"Mark Sattenstein," Joe Durkin said. "Killed shortly after midnight within three blocks of his home, death the result of multiple blows to the head. Went out for a couple of drinks at a bar with an Irish name, if you can believe such a place exists. They know him there, not a regular, not a heavy drinker, but he'll come in now and then for a beer. Well, not anymore, he won't. Not the first mugging in that neighborhood, not even the first this month, and it's still early in the month. Wallet gone, watch gone, pockets turned inside out—what's it sound like to you, Matt?"

"Robbery with violence."

"It does sound like robbery, and there's no question about the violence. Which leaves me with two questions. How's this anything other than what it looks like? And, while I'm at it, what's it to you?"

"I knew him."

"Yeah? Old friend?"

No, I thought. That was the other dead guy. I said, "I only met him once. I was looking into a matter for a friend, and I had some questions for Sattenstein. I went to his apartment, talked with him for an hour tops."

"Learn anything?"

"Enough to rule him out."

"Out of what?"

"Out of the picture," I said. "I don't want to go into detail here, but he was one direction I could go, and after I talked to him I realized that would be a dead end."

He looked at me, thought about it. "And this was recent?"

"Within the past couple of weeks."

"And now he's dead, and you figure it can't be a coincidence."

"No," I said, "I figure it's almost certainly a coincidence. But I figure it's worth the price of a hat to rule out the possibility that it's not."

A hat, in police parlance, is twenty-five dollars. A coat is a hundred. I have no idea what a hat actually costs these days, I can't remember the last time I went out and bought one, but argot outlasts its origins. A pound is five dollars, and once upon a time that's what a British pound sterling was worth in American money. I don't suppose you can get much of a hat for five pounds.

And a hat was what I'd be buying Joe Durkin. He was a detective at Midtown North, on West Fifty-fourth, and Gramercy Park was well out of his range, but I didn't know anybody in the precinct where Sattenstein had lived and died, and didn't want to draw attention by making myself known to whoever had caught the case. Easier to ring Joe and get him to make a couple of phone calls.

Which had led to my sitting across a Formica-topped table from him in a coffee shop on Eighth Avenue. He was there because he was doing me a favor, but we both knew it was the sort of favor a person got paid for.

"For the sake of argument," he said, "let's say it wasn't a coincidence, and whoever killed him had a reason. What would that reason be?"

To keep him from telling me something, I thought. Which he might have been ready to do, if I'd had the brains to call him back.

I said, "No idea, Joe."

"None at all?"

"Well, he had a history. I don't know if he's got a yellow sheet, and my guess is he doesn't, but for a period of time he was a receiver."

"Not on the Jets, I don't suppose."

"I don't know if you're familiar with a man named Selig Wolf, but—"

"Jesus, of course I am. A wide receiver if there ever was one."

"Well, Mark's uncle Selig taught him the business."

"Selig was his uncle?"

"His mother's brother. Younger or older, I forget which."

"Woman's got a brother, he would pretty much have to be younger or older."

"He could be a twin."

"One's born first, even with twins. Why are we even having this conversation? Jesus, Selig Wolf. You couldn't want a better teacher."

"So I gather. He followed in his uncle's footsteps for a few years, he got wiped out in a burglary, and the whole mess had the effect of scaring him straight."

"And at the time of his death he was teaching mentally challenged children how to tie their shoes. A tough way to make a living, but a noble calling indeed."

"No, he was working as a bookkeeper for a couple of small firms."

"And cooking the books for them."

"Maybe a little."

"You gotta love this city. You really do. He told you all this in an hour?"

"So? I just told you the whole thing in about ten minutes."

"But that he went and opened up about it." He shrugged. "So maybe you're not bad at what you do. You know, if he never took a bust, odds are there's nobody in the One-Three that knows he was a fencing master. I might feel obliged to pass the word."

"You wouldn't have to say where you heard it."

"A snitch," he said. "A generally reliable source."

"That's me, all right." I passed him the two bills I'd palmed earlier, a five and a twenty. "I appreciate this, Joe. And you could use a new hat."

"Hats I got a whole rack of. What I could use is a coat. Oh, man, the look on your face! Worth the price of admission right there. I'm glad to have the hat, my friend, and glad for the chance to sit down with you for a couple of minutes. Things working out for you?"

"I get by."

"All we can ask," he said. "All anybody can ask."

I was back in my room, running it through my mind, when the phone rang. It was Joe, resuming our conversation as if it had never ended. "This Sattenstein," he said. "Perp might have sized him up as a soft target. On account of he had a bandaged hand."

"It was like that when I saw him."

"You spot a man with a bandaged hand, you're not worried he'll fight back. But how'd he hurt the hand? Maybe he hit somebody. So maybe he's a man with a short fuse, type who'd be apt to take a swing at a guy tries to hold him up."

"With his other hand."

"Whatever. So the perp slams him with whatever he brought along to hit people with. Your traditional blunt instrument."

"It's possible," I said. "You just thought this up?"

"I picked up the phone and passed on the word about the vic's famous uncle Selig. Which was news to all concerned, and my guy there showed his appreciation by mentioning the bandaged hand. A little quid for the old pro quo. I'd say one hand washes the other, but the bandage would get in the way."

So Sattenstein's sitting home and brooding over the woman who decided she was a lesbian, and the walls are closing in on him and he forgot to pick up a six-pack earlier, so if he wants a beer he has to leave the house. And why not walk a few blocks and drink it in the good company a saloon can provide? And who knows, maybe he'll get lucky. You never know.

And there he is, drinking with his left hand because his right hand's still bandaged. And somebody spots him, tags him when he leaves. Hits him too hard.

Why not?

Because I really wanted that to be how it played out. That way it was sheer coincidence. Fate, kismet, karma. Dumb luck. And if it was any of those things, then it wasn't my fault.

I sat in my room and looked up his telephone number and tried to decide if it looked familiar, if it had been written on the message slip I'd crumpled and tossed. If it looked familiar, it wasn't because I'd seen it written out, but because I'd dialed it several times when I was first trying to reach the man.

I dialed it now, and the machine picked up. I listened to a dead man's voice. I hung up, wondering how long it would be before someone unplugged the machine, how long before the telephone company cut off the phone service.

You don't die all at once. Not anymore. These days you die a little at a time.

I don't know how long I sat there, but eventually the thought came to me that I ought to go to a meeting, and I looked at my watch and saw I was too late for any of the noon meetings. It was past two already, and I hadn't been to a meeting or eaten anything since breakfast.

Call your sponsor, a little voice murmured, and I picked up the phone, and when I had the number half dialed I realized I was calling his home number, and he'd be at his shop. I tried his work number and got it wrong, some woman answered, and I apologized and looked up the number, and got a busy signal.

I called Jan. The phone rang twice, and I rang off before she could answer.

I called Greg. The machine picked up, and I rang off. I'd left him enough messages.

But something made me dial the number again, and this time when the machine picked up I let the message play through to the end. After he'd invited me to leave a message after the beep, a mechanical voice cut in to inform me that the message tape was full.

Well, that explained why he hadn't returned my calls. He hadn't returned anybody's calls. Out of town, most likely, and not checking his messages, and —

I rushed out of there. When I got to the street, there was an eastbound cab discharging a passenger in front of the big apartment building across the street. I yelled out, ran across the street, dodged traffic.

"You could get killed like that," the driver said. "What's the big hurry?"

I didn't remember his address. I knew he was on Ninety-ninth between First and Second, and on the uptown side of the street near the middle of the block. There were four houses in a row that looked about the same, and it could have been any of them, but the first one I tried was the second from the right, and I spotted his name on one of the buttons. I pushed it and didn't get a response, but then I hadn't been expecting one.

There was a button at the bottom of the column marked *Sput*, which suggested that the building had a dyslexic superintendent. I rang it, and when nothing happened I rang it again. No response.

I rang a couple of apartments on the third floor, and eventually somebody answered and wanted to know who I was and what I wanted. I remembered the smell of mice. "Exterminator," I said, and the buzzer let me in.

I climbed the stairs. The mouse smell was faint, and I doubt I'd have noticed it if I hadn't remembered our conversation. Mice, cabbage, wet dog with garlic. At the third-floor landing a woman stood in a doorway, frowning at me. If I was an exterminator, why was I empty-handed? Where were my work clothes?

Before she could say anything, I drew out my wallet, flipped it open. I extended a forefinger, pointed upstairs. She shrugged, sighed, returned to her apartment, and I heard the bolt shoot home as she locked her door.

I climbed three more flights of stairs and went to Greg's door. I rang the bell and heard the chimes sound within, and when all was still I knocked on the door. As if that would accomplish anything.

I tried the knob. The door was locked. Well, of course it would be locked. It was too late in the year for him to be at Fire Island, but there were enough other places for a week's vacation, Key West or South Beach or some modest but genteel resort in the Caymans or the Bahamas. And he'd certainly lock up before he left, and what was I doing here anyway? I hadn't returned a telephone call, which may have been from some other Mark and not the one who'd been killed in a street mugging, and to compensate I'd rushed uptown and flimflammed my way into his building, and wasn't it time for me to turn around and go home?

I tried a credit card on the lock. If it wasn't bolted, if the spring lock was all that was keeping me out, I might be able to loid my way in. I spent a couple of minutes establishing that such was not the case. The door was locked, and I couldn't open it, short of kicking it in.

It seemed to me that I could sense something. It seemed to me that I could feel it.

I got down on one knee, lowered my face to floor level. There was a space of perhaps a quarter of an inch beneath the bottom of the door. Enough to show light, if there'd been a light on within the apartment.

I didn't smell mice, or cabbage. Or wet dog with garlic. What I did smell sent me out of the building and down the street, looking for a working pay phone.

XXXI

"Y OU SEE SOMETHING like that," Redmond said, "you want
to cut him down. It's heartless, somehow, leaving him like
that. But you do the humane thing and you catch hell from the
crime lab crew. Just opening a window pisses them off, but that's
just too fucking bad."

He'd opened all the windows, and that was a help. The odor
I'd caught a whiff of in the hallway hit us in the face when the
super opened the door for us, and we walked into a stench that
made me grateful I'd skipped lunch.

Aside from the smell, the living room was as I remembered it,
and in perfect order. The kitchen was immaculate, but for a half-
finished cup of coffee in its matching saucer.

In the bedroom, wearing nothing but a pair of blue-and-
white-striped boxer shorts, Greg Stillman had a black leather
belt looped around his neck, the wide brass buckle mostly hid-
den by his swollen throat. The other end of the belt disappeared

over the top of the closet door, which had been closed to anchor it there. A folding step stool lay on its side, where it would have landed when he kicked it away.

"Nobody would ever do this," Redmond said, "if they had the faintest fucking idea what they'd wind up looking like. Or what they'd smell like."

The head swells, the neck stretches, the face blackens. The bowels and bladder empty themselves. Noxious gases form in the internal organs and find their way out. Flesh rots.

"The poor son of a bitch," Redmond said. "You hate to leave him hanging there. But a fat lot of good it'd do him to cut him down."

The man from the medical examiner's office thought it was a very bad way to kill yourself. "Because you're a long time dying," he said. "And you're conscious. You flop around like a trout on a line, and it's too late to change your mind. Look here, on the door. Scuff marks from kicking. There's pills you can take, you just go to sleep and you don't wake up. And if you have second thoughts after you swallow them, well, you've generally got time to get over to the emergency room and have your stomach pumped."

"Or you eat your gun and at least it's quick."

"Makes a goddam mess, though," the ME told him. "But you're not the one has to clean it up, so what do you care?"

"Me?" Redmond said. "Let's leave me out of it, huh? I'm not about to eat my gun."

He said, "You don't smoke, do you? I quit years ago, but whenever I walk in on something like that, I wish I still smoked and I wish I had a cigar. One about a foot long and an inch thick. Something to smell instead of what we had to smell in there."

We were in the Emerald Star, a Second Avenue bar I'd noticed on my first visit to Greg's apartment. The bartender was a gaunt Hispanic with long sideburns and a pencil-line mustache. Redmond, who'd had whiskey and water when I met him at the Minstrel Boy, said he'd have a double Cutty Sark, neat, no ice.

I thought that sounded like a very sensible choice. But what I ordered was a Coke.

"My first partner," I said, "was addicted to those little Italian cigars that look like pieces of twisted rope. They came in a little cardboard box, five or six to the box. I think the brand was De Nobili, but Mahaffey always called them guinea stinkers."

"Nowadays they'd write him up for uttering an ethnic slur."

"They might, and he wouldn't care. I hated the smell of the things, but when we walked in on something like just now, he'd light one up and he'd give me one, and I'd light it and smoke it."

"And be glad for it, I'll bet."

"It helped," I said.

He picked up his glass, looked through it at the overhead light. I wondered why he did that. I'd done it often enough myself, and never knew why.

"No note," he said.

"No."

"My impression of him was that he'd be the type to leave a note. You knew him better than I did."

"My impression," I said, "was he wasn't the type to kill himself."

"Everybody's the type," he said. "The miracle is there's so many of us who never get around to it."

"Maybe."

"My father killed himself. You know what that means?" I did, but he didn't wait for an answer. "Means my odds aren't good. I forget the numbers, but the sons of suicides are thus and so many times as likely to kill themselves as the rest of the world."

"That doesn't mean you don't have a choice."

"No," he said, and took a drink. "I have a choice. But have I got a choice what choice I make?" He grinned. "Run that little question through your mind a few times, and see where it gets you. So let's run some other questions instead. When's the last time you saw him?"

"I don't remember," I said, "but the last time I spoke to him was Saturday."

"I played his messages. The tape starts on Monday morning. The ME said what, a couple of days?"

"I think so."

"A person could go nuts listening to those messages. You must have heard them, you were standing a few feet away."

"AA friends of his, mostly."

"And some woman describing a piece of jewelry she wanted him to repair. Unbelievable. She goes on and on about it, the size, the materials, this, that, and the other, and then she says how she'll bring it over so he can have a look at it. 'So I don't know why I'm describing it in such detail,' she says. I felt like calling her up, telling her I don't know either."

"I more or less tuned her out."

"I kept waiting for her to say something significant. Then there were the ones telling him they weren't going to drink. Today, they said. Meaning they might drink tomorrow?"

"The idea is, you can't know about tomorrow until it comes. But all you have to deal with is today."

"Makes sense. Why tell him? Or were they just telling themselves?"

"A little of both," I said. "I think they were probably his sponsees."

"What's that, the opposite of a sponsor?"

"They used to call them pigeons," I said, "and some of the

old-timers still do. But the consensus seems to be that the word *pigeon* is demeaning."

"Because a pigeon's a dirty bird that squawks and flies around and shits on your head."

"That must be it."

"No note," he said again. "Other hand, the door was locked. When Rafael—was that his name?"

"I think so."

"When he opened up for us, he turned the key twice, first to draw the bolt, then to snick the catch back. So if somebody helped him on his way, they didn't walk out the door and just pull it shut after them."

"They'd have had to use a key."

"Which they could have done, and how would we know? How can we rule it in or out?"

"There was another lock," I said. "The Fox, the big police lock. Plate in the floor, bar fits into it and braces against the door."

"Keeps the whole world on the other side of the door," he said. "If he really wants to avoid being disturbed, why not engage the police lock? Other hand, he doesn't want to keep people away forever. Just long enough for him to do the deed and be done with it."

With it and everything else.

He said, "Say he did it, because right now I don't see anything that says he didn't. Why would he do it? Aside from he's an alcoholic and he's gay, which are both pretty decent reasons, but can you come up with anything more specific?"

"He blamed himself for Jack Ellery's death."

"How?"

I furnished a very sketchy explanation of the amends process. "Jack was poking around in the past," I said, "and as far as I can tell all that got him was a punch in the nose—"

"Yeah, he'd taken some lumps a week or more prior to his death. That was in the medical report. Tell me something. Why is this the first I'm hearing about any of this? Whose idea was it to withhold evidence, yours or Stillman's?"

"There was no evidence for either of us to withhold. That's what he hired me for, to look for evidence. And turn it over to you if I found anything."

"But you came up empty?"

I'd already said more than I'd wanted to. But a couple of people were dead. Maybe one got mugged and the other killed himself, but maybe not.

"Jack had a list of people he'd harmed," I said. "People to whom he intended to make amends. I went through the list and managed to rule them all out."

"You cleared them."

"Yes."

"The people on his list." He looked off into the distance. "You know, I'm sure your detective powers are fucking legendary, but why didn't you bring me the list and let all the resources of the New York Police Department determine whether or not those suspects ought to be cleared?"

"That's not why I was hired."

"And you didn't want to lose a fee."

"I put in a lot more work than the fee was worth. And if I'd told him to bring it to you, you'd have done one of two things. Either you'd have shined him on and stuck the list in a file—"

"That wouldn't have happened."

"It might. Some bum's AA sponsor, some faggot with an earring, has a list of people the dead guy may have done a bad turn a hundred years ago? Would that keep you up nights?"

"Scudder, you've got no fucking idea what keeps me up nights."

"Fair enough," I said. "But if you took action, what would it be? You'd focus a lot of official attention on people with reasons of their own to stay out of the spotlight."

"If they're clean they've got nothing to worry about."

"Really? You cheat on your taxes?"

"Huh? Where did that come from?"

"Do you?"

"Of course not. My income's all from the City of New York, so I couldn't hide anything if I wanted to. And I file on the short form. It's all a hundred percent straightforward."

"So you'd have nothing to worry about in that area."

"Absolutely not. If you'd like to pick a better example, one that might apply to me—"

"Which is to say that it wouldn't bother you much if you got a notice from the IRS that they were doing a line audit of your returns for the past three years."

"They'd have no reason. I just told you—"

"Strictly random," I said, "and just the luck of the draw. Make you happy?"

"All right," he said at length. "I get the point."

"These were men," I said, "who got on the list for one reason only. Somewhere along the way, Jack fucked them over. He burned one in a drug deal, he set one up for a burglary, he beat up the owner in the course of a store holdup, and he went to bed with another guy's wife."

"Nice guy we're talking about."

"He was turning into a nice guy," I said, "or at least he was trying to. I don't know that it would have worked, I'm not sure to what extent anybody's capable of changing, but I'd be hard put to argue that he was wasting his time."

"On paper," he said, "you've got a guy who looked for all the world like a total rat bastard. And yet there were an awful lot of people who showed up for his funeral, and they weren't there just to make sure he was dead."

"The only thing missing," Redmond said, "is the note. And the fact of the matter is, you can kill yourself in this world without writing one. It's not an absolute requirement."

Once, back when I still had a gold shield and a wife and a house on Long Island, I sat up late one night in my living room with the business end of a gun in my mouth. I can still remember the metallic taste of it. It seems to me I never had any real intention of going through with it, but I did have my thumb on the trigger, and it wouldn't have taken much pressure to send a round through the roof of my mouth.

And they wouldn't have found a note. I'd never even thought about writing out a note.

"Aside from that," he said, "everything looks right. He had the petechial hemorrhages in the eyes, showing strangulation as cause of death. Chair was right where it ought to be if he stood on it and kicked it over. Place was neat as a pin otherwise, showing no evidence of a struggle, no sign that there was ever another person in the room."

"Maybe the autopsy will show something."

"Like blunt force trauma to the head? They'll look for that, of course. Because somebody could have knocked him out and then hoisted him up there, though it's not the easiest thing in the world. Plus the killer would have had to strip him to his shorts, because Stillman would have been dressed when he let the guy into his place." He frowned. "And why fucking bother? Say you're the guy, you want to kill Stillman, want to make it look like suicide. You get behind him, you conk him over the head, and he's out cold."

"So?"

"You're gonna take the time to undress him? And risk that he'll come to while you're doing it? Why not just string him up and be done with it?"

"You'd need the belt," I said.

"So? You take it and put it to use. You figure his pants'd fall off without it?"

"A lot of people undress before they kill themselves."

"Or just stay undressed, if he was sitting around his apartment in his shorts. But do you go to the trouble of undressing a guy to make it look more like suicide? I don't know, I suppose you could, but it sounds like more trouble than it's worth."

"Maybe."

"Most things," he said, "are more trouble than they're worth. And maybe that's all it was. Stillman got up, had his morning coffee, watered his plants, and took a long look at his life. And decided it was more trouble than it was worth."

XXXII

THAT NIGHT I thought of going to Sober Today, Greg's regular Thursday night meeting on Second Avenue. As if by going there I might slip into an alternate universe, one in which he was still alive. We'd chat on the break, and after the meeting we'd go out for coffee. Maybe we'd see what kind of pie they had at Theresa's. And we'd talk about High-Low Jack, and the perils of the Ninth Step, and whatever else came to mind.

I didn't go to that meeting, or any other. I thought I might go over to St. Paul's, but didn't, and then I thought I might catch some of the St. Paul's crowd at the Flame. But I stayed in my room.

I sat at the window, and at one point I realized I was looking down at the liquor store across the street. It got to be ten o'clock, and I stayed where I was, and sometime between ten and ten thirty they turned off the lights. They would have closed at ten, but if someone showed up while they were still in the store, someone they'd known for years, they'd open the door and sell him what he needed. But once the lights were off, once the neon sign no longer glowed with promise, then they were well and truly shut for the night.

Of course the bars were still open. The bars would be open for hours yet, some of them until the legal closing hour of four a.m. And there were after-hours joints, any number of them, if you knew where to go. The Morrissey Brothers were out of business, but that didn't mean a man with a thirst couldn't find someone to sell him a drink after hours.

Now and then I glanced at the phone. I thought of calling Greg's number, and I thought of calling Mark Sattenstein's number, but those were just passing thoughts and I didn't feel the need to make the calls. I also thought of other calls I might make, to living people — Jim Faber, for example, or Jan Keane. But I never picked up the phone.

If it rang, would I answer it? It seemed to me that I might, but it seemed just as possible that I might not. I envisioned myself sitting there while the telephone rang and rang and rang. Wondering who it might be, and yet unwilling to find out.

At twenty minutes of twelve I thought of the midnight meeting. All I had to do was go downstairs and flag a cab. I'd get there in plenty of time. They drew a raffish crowd, with active drunks apt to put in an appearance, and it wasn't unheard-of for a punch or a chair to be thrown, but there was plenty of sobriety in the room all the same, and there had been times when it had helped me get through a bad night.

And maybe Buddha would be there. Maybe he'd explain to me that it was my dissatisfaction with what is that was the cause of all my unhappiness.

Right. I stayed where I was.

XXXIII

I HAD TO FORCE myself to go out and eat breakfast. I'd skipped
dinner, and couldn't remember if I'd had lunch. It seemed to
me that I hadn't.

Don't get too hungry, angry, lonely, or tired. The acronym is
HALT, and it's standard advice for beginners, and remains
applicable no matter how long you've been sober. Ignore it and
your mind begins working against you, and the next thing you
know you've got a glass in your hand.

I'd been all those things the previous night, hungry and angry
and lonely and tired, but I'd managed to get through the night
in spite of myself. I had a plate of bacon and eggs with toast and
home fries, and once I got the first bite down my appetite
returned, and I cleaned my plate and drank three cups of coffee.
I'd bought the *Times* on the way to the Morning Star, and someone had read and abandoned the *Daily News,* and I read each
paper carefully, looking for stories of violent death. There were

plenty of them, there always are, but for a change none of the newly dead were people I knew.

Back in my room, I looked up phone numbers and made calls. I rang Dukacs & Son, and recognized the proprietor's voice when he answered. But I made sure: "Mr. Dukacs?"

"Yes?"

I broke the connection, called Crosby Hart at his office. He picked up the phone and said, "Hal Hart."

"Wrong number," I said, and rang off.

I made a third call to Scooter Williams. The phone rang and rang, and I wondered if a quick trip down to Ludlow Street would be overreacting. Then he picked up. He was out of breath, and something made me ask if he was all right.

"Yeah, I'm fine," he said. "I just got out of the shower, I had to run to the phone. Uh, who is this?"

I gave my name.

He said, "Matthew Scudder. Matthew Scudder. Oh, right! Jack's friend."

"Right," I said, figuring that was close enough.

"Yeah, I remember. I was gonna call you, man."

"Oh?"

"Can't remember why. It came to me, you know, and then it went away. Something you asked me, but don't ask me what it was. Oh, wow. You asked me but don't ask me?"

"You can't remember."

"Hey, if it came to me once it'll come to me again. Like swallows to Capistrano, you know? You want to give me your number again? You gave it to me, but I don't know what I did with it."

I gave it to him again. He said, "Matthew Scudder. Okay, got it. Hey, you know what? You're Scudder and I'm Scooter."

"And to think some people doubt the existence of God."

"Huh? Oh, right. Years since anybody called me that, though. Ages. Hey, it'll come to me and I'll call you."

"That's great," I said, and finally managed to hang up.

So they were alive, all three of them.

I got to the noon meeting at Fireside. There was a message in my box when I got back. *Red Man,* it said, and there was a number. It took me a minute, but I figured out that it was Dennis Redmond, and made the call from my room.

"I figured Monday for the autopsy results," he said, "but either they've got a light load over there or Stillman jumped the queue. No sign of blunt force trauma to the head. Or to any other part of him, as far as that goes."

"So it looks like he did it himself."

"It always did," he said. "Of course somebody could have drugged him and strung him up. But that didn't happen either. No drugs in his system, no blood alcohol."

So he'd died sober.

"In fact," he said, "all the physical evidence supports a verdict of suicide. Strangulation's the cause of death. There ought to be a law."

"Against suicide? I think there already is."

"Against belts," he said. "Where do they get off making them strong enough to support a man's weight? You might as well be putting a loaded gun in the hands of a child."

"How else are people going to keep their pants up?"

"What the hell's wrong with suspenders? Or you could do like they do with fishing line. A certain amount of pressure and it snaps, gives the fish a sporting chance. Why not do the same with belts? A weight of more than a hundred pounds and it breaks. Think of the lives that would be saved."

"And what about children?"

"Never thought of it," he said. "But you're right, it'd just trigger an epidemic of juvenile suicide. I guess there's only one answer."

"And that would be?"

"Warning labels. Works with cigarettes. Matt, I just thought you'd want to know. Your friend killed himself. Though I don't suppose it makes you happy to hear that."

"No," I said. "How could it? But at least it saves me having to figure out what to do next."

I was watching television when the phone rang. ESPN was showing a Gaelic football game, or a match, whatever they call it, and I sat there while a lot of young men in shorts and long-sleeved jerseys showed enormous energy doing something entirely incomprehensible. There was running and passing and kicking involved, and the score kept changing, in what struck me as a wholly arbitrary way.

I hit the Mute button and picked up the phone, and it was Jan. She said, "I think we should talk."

XXXIV

TIFFANY'S IS THE FAMOUS Fifth Avenue jewelry store, and if I'd told a friend I was off to meet my girlfriend at Tiffany's, he'd probably assume we'd be shopping for rings. But Tiffany's is also the name of a coffee shop on Sheridan Square, open twenty-four hours a day, and Jan had picked it as a meeting place because it was midway between her neighborhood and mine.

I took my time walking to the subway, but even so I had to wait for her, and she showed up with a companion, a sharp-featured woman in her fifties with unconvincingly black hair. They came to my booth, each carrying a shopping bag, and Jan introduced the woman as Mary Elizabeth. We nodded at each other, and I motioned for them to sit down, and Jan looked at Mary Elizabeth, who shook her head.

"We won't stay," Jan said. She put her shopping bag on the table, and Mary Elizabeth placed hers alongside it. "I think this is everything," Jan said.

I nodded, lost in thought, and then when nobody moved or said anything I remembered my assigned role in the proceedings. I reached into my pocket and took out a ring of keys. I put them on the table, and they just sat there for a beat, and then Jan reached for them, picked them up, weighed them in her hand, put them in her purse.

She turned to go, and Mary Elizabeth turned with her, and then Jan turned back to face me again. All in a rush she said, "I really hate this, and what I hate most of all is the timing. Right before your anniversary."

"In a couple of days."

"Tuesday, isn't it?"

"I guess so."

"I was going to wait until afterward," she said, "but I thought maybe that would be worse, and—"

"Let it go," I said.

"I just—"

"Let it go."

She looked on the point of tears. Mary Elizabeth said, "Jan," and she turned and walked after her, to the door and out.

I stayed where I was. Two shopping bags shared the top of my table with the cup of coffee I'd ordered but so far hadn't touched. One shopping bag was from a department store, the other from a company that sold art supplies. Each was a little more than half full, and Jan could have managed both of them herself. Mary Elizabeth, I decided, was there for moral support.

I went to St. Paul's for the evening meeting. Afterward I followed the crowd to the Flame and sat there until everybody went home. I walked down Ninth to Fifty-seventh, then walked on past my hotel and all the way across town to Lexington Avenue.

I turned on Lexington and walked down to Thirtieth Street and got there just in time to help set up chairs for the midnight meeting.

There were a few familiar faces in the room but nobody I really knew. They didn't have a speaker, and the chairperson asked me if I had ninety days clean and sober. I said I'd spoken recently, and didn't feel up to it. She found somebody else. They can always find somebody.

I sat there for an hour and drank a couple of cups of bad coffee and ate a few cookies. I didn't pay much attention to the speaker and didn't raise my hand during the discussion. At the end I thought about finding someone to go out for coffee with, and decided the hell with it. I walked up to Forty-second Street and caught a cab the rest of the way home.

My two shopping bags were as I'd left them, unpacked, standing side by side on the floor next to the bed. I went to bed, and they were still there the next morning. When I came back from breakfast, the maid had serviced my room, making my bed with clean sheets, emptying my wastebasket. And the shopping bags remained right where I'd left them.

I picked up the phone, called Jim. "I've got two shopping bags on my floor," I said, "and I can't seem to figure out what to do with them."

"Empty shopping bags?"

"About half full." He waited, and I said, "Clothes of mine. That I'd left at Jan's place."

"What I like about you," he said, "is you always come right to the point."

So I talked and he listened, and I waited for him to ask me why I'd waited the better part of a day before telling him what was going on, but he never said a word about my silence. He waited until I'd run out of words, and then he said, "You knew it was coming."

"I suppose so."

"That make it easier?"

"Not especially."

"No, I didn't think so. How do you feel?"

"Devastated."

"And?"

"Relieved."

"That sounds about right."

I thought for a moment. Then I said, "I keep thinking that I made this happen."

"By going to bed with Donna."

"Right."

"You realize, of course, that just because you keep thinking it doesn't change the fact that it doesn't make any sense."

"It doesn't?"

"Think about it, Matt."

"She didn't know about Donna."

"No."

"She didn't even pick it up subliminally, because we haven't spent any time together since then. We've barely even talked on the phone."

"Right."

"I'm just looking for a way for it to be my fault."

"Uh-huh."

"I went to the midnight meeting last night."

"Probably didn't hurt you."

"Probably not. I think I'll spend most of the weekend in meetings."

"Not a bad idea."

"SoHo meets tonight. I think I'll go somewhere else."

"Good thinking."

"Jim? I'm not going to drink."

"Neither am I," he said. "Isn't that great?"

I went to meetings throughout the weekend, but I was in my room Saturday afternoon just long enough to get a phone call.

It was Joe Durkin. "I don't even know if this is worth passing on," he said, "but you were brooding about that mugging in Gramercy, and I thought you'd like to know it was just what it looked like. A mugger who didn't know his own strength."

"They got the guy?"

"In the act," he said. "Well, not in the act of hitting your guy. Saperstein?"

"Sattenstein."

"Close enough. He wasn't the first person mugged in that part of town, just the first who died from it, so they used a decoy from Street Crimes, put him in plain clothes, poured some booze on him, and had him walk around looking like he was half in the bag."

"I don't know why I never got assignments like that."

"It must have been a treat," he said, "to see the look on the skell's face when the perfect victim showed him a badge and a gun. What I hear, they're about to clear ten or a dozen cases. Guy's confessing to everything they've got."

"Including Sattenstein?"

"'Oh, the poor man who was killed? No, that one I didn't do.' But he'll cop to it too, by the time he gets to court. His lawyer'll see to that. Get everything listed in the plea agreement so there's nothing left to come back at you later on."

Sometimes things were just what they appeared to be.

Gregory Stillman hanged himself, Mark Sattenstein got killed by a mugger.

I got out of there and headed off to another meeting.

Sunday afternoon I went to a meeting in a synagogue on Seventy-sixth Street a few doors west of Broadway. I'd never been there before, and when I walked in my first impulse was to turn around and walk out again, because Donna was there. I stayed, and we were cordial to each other, and she thanked me again for helping her out the previous Saturday, and I said I'd been happy to help, and it was as if we'd never been to bed together.

I met Jim for our usual if-it's-Sunday-this-must-be-Shanghai dinner, and we didn't talk about Jan or Donna or the state of my sobriety. Instead he did almost all of the talking, telling stories from his own drinking days, and back before his first drink, back in his childhood. I got caught up in what he had to say, and it wasn't until later that I realized he'd purposely avoided discussing what was going on in my life these days. I couldn't decide whether he was giving me a break or just trying to spare himself, but whatever it was, I was grateful.

We went to St. Clare's, and then I walked him home and went home myself. Jacob was behind the desk, looking confused. I asked him what was the matter.

"Your brother called," he said.

"My brother?"

"Or maybe it was your cousin."

"My cousin," I said. I was an only child. I had a couple of cousins, but we'd long since lost touch with one another. I couldn't think of one who was likely to call.

"It was a man," he said. "Have to be, if it was your brother, wouldn't it?"

"What exactly did he say?"

"Says he calling Mr. Scudder. I ask would he like to leave his name. Scudder, he says. Yessir, I know it's Mr. Scudder you calling, but what would your name be? So he say it again, Scudder, and I'm feeling like them two guys."

"Which two guys?"

"You know. Them two guys."

"Abbott and Costello."

"Yeah, them two. So I say, lemme see now, you're also Mr. Scudder. And he say, I am *the* Scudder."

"'I am *the* Scudder.'"

"Yeah, just like that. So I say, then you and Mr. Scudder be brothers. And he say how all men be brothers, and at this point it's getting way too weird for me."

"Gee, I can't imagine why."

"Say what?"

"Nothing. He leave a number?"

"Say you have it."

"I have his number."

"What he say."

"All men are brothers, and he's the Scudder, and I have his number."

He nodded. "I tried to get it right," he said, "but man like that don't make it easy."

"You did fine," I told him.

XXXV

I RODE UP in the elevator, feeling pleased with myself. I'd managed to figure out who my caller had to be, and that was the first detecting I'd done in longer than I cared to remember.

I looked up his number, dialed it, and when he answered I said, "If you're ever in the neighborhood, stop in and apologize to my desk clerk. You had the poor guy caught up in an Abbott and Costello routine."

The silence stretched until I started wondering if my detection had gone awry. Then he said, "Who's this, man?"

"Scudder."

"Oh, wow," he said. "When I called, you know, I thought that'd be you answering your phone. But you're at some kind of hotel."

"Well, it's not the Waldorf."

"And this cat I was talking to, he's the desk clerk?"

"That's right. His name is Jacob."

"Jacob," he said. "Jay. Cub. Great name, man. You don't meet many Jacobs."

"I guess not."

"Though you probably meet this particular one just about every day. I was goofing with him, you know? On account of the man's got a little bit of an accent. He from the Indies?"

"Somewhere down there."

"Yeah, well, I asked for you, and he repeated your name, like to take the message? Except the vowel sound came out more *oo* than *uh*. Like Scooder, you know?"

"Sure."

"So he asks my name, and I may have been, you know, the least bit high at the time."

"Hard to believe."

"Under the righteous influence of a benevolent herb, if you can dig it. And I thought, Right, I'm the Scooter calling for Mr. Scooder. And, well, you can see how we sort of went around in circles from there."

"I figured it was something like that."

"Abbott and Costello," he said. " 'Who's on first?' Them the cats you mean?"

"The very gentlemen."

"Can't keep 'em straight, though. Abbott and Costello. Which one had the mustache?"

"Neither one."

"Neither one? You sure about that?"

"Pretty sure," I said. "Uh, Scooter —"

"You're wondering why I called."

"I guess I am."

"High-Low Jack," he said. "You still there?"

"I'm here."

"Because you didn't say anything for a minute there. That was what you asked me when you were over here, right? After we talked about Lucille?"

"Right."

"You wanted to know about his name. What it meant, where it came from. Right?"

"Right."

"Well, there's that thing from the card game. High, Low, Jack, and the Game. But why call him that? There's Smiling Jack, there's One-Eyed Jack, there's Toledo Jack. Why High-Low Jack for Jack Ellery?"

Sooner or later he'd get to it.

"Mood swing," he said.

"Mood swing?"

"Very changeable guy. He's up, he's down. He's laid-back, he's jumpy as a cat. He'll hug you or he'll slug you. Hey!"

"Hey?"

"Rhymes," he said. "Hug you, slug you. Anyway, High-Low Jack. Now, wasn't for the card game, wouldn't have stuck. Like if his name was Ted, you wouldn't call him High-Low Ted, because it wouldn't mean anything. Or say his name was Johnny instead of Jack, which it could have been, they're both short forms of John, right? High-Low Johnny? I don't think so."

"High-Low Jack," I said.

"Right. Mood swing. Up one minute, down the next."

Well, that was at least slightly interesting. Maybe it even made sense. One thing it didn't do was shed any light on the question of who killed him, or why.

"He like that as a little kid?"

"How's that?"

"You knew him when you were kids, right? Was he like that then, up one minute and down the next?"

"Not that I remember."

"Maybe he was manic-depressive," Scooter said. "I don't know, everybody's got good days and bad days, don't they? Shrinks want to hang a label on everybody."

I was beginning to tire of the conversation. The bottom line seemed to be that Jack was a moody guy, and I didn't see that leading me anywhere. Whatever moods the man had had, one could only assume they ended at the grave.

"The world's a heartless place," I said, and Scooter said he couldn't agree with me more. I had that right, he assured me.

"High-Low Jack," he said. "I don't know why I didn't think of it the first time you asked. Seems so obvious now."

"Now that you think what a moody fellow he was."

"Yeah, that's a fact. One minute he's cool as a cucumber, next minute he's hot as a pistol. Wow!"

"Wow?"

"Just thinking, man. It came to me just like that."

"What did?"

"Expressions, man. How you can turn 'em around and have fun with 'em. Like you could say cool as a pistol, you know?"

"I guess you could."

"Or hot as a cucumber. Oh, man, can you dig it? 'That chick is hot as a cucumber.' I mean, wow."

"Wow."

"Just switching things around, you know? Or think how everybody always says they searched every little nook and cranny. Turn it around — every little cranny and nook. Makes just as much sense that way, and yet you never hear it."

"Remarkable."

"You said it, man. Why does it always have to be *lo and behold*? From now on I'm gonna make a point of saying *behold and lo!* instead. Can you dig it?"

"Right," I said.

"Right as a whip. Smart as rain."

"Uh—"

"Even Jack. High-Low Steven."

I was hanging up when the last phrase came through. I brought the receiver back to my ear. "Say that again," I said.

"What?"

"What you just said. About Jack."

"Oh, just more switching, man. Like you say High-Low Jack and Even Steven, and I switched 'em around."

"Oh, just expressions."

"Right, having to do with Jack and his buddy."

"His buddy."

"Yeah, Steve."

"Steve."

"You're like an echo, man. Scooder and Scooter, and there's another echo right there."

"Tell me about Steve," I said.

He couldn't tell me much.

Jack had this running buddy, and if Jack was a creature of changeable temperament, Steve was just the opposite, always steady, always calm and cool. Hence Even Steven, as opposed to High-Low Jack.

He didn't even know how close the two had been, or what common interest might have bound them in friendship. It was the coincidence of their names that linked them as much as anything else.

"Like with Jack," he said, "and calling him High-Low Jack, because there's already the expression from the card game. But you wouldn't call him High-Low Ted."

"So you said."

"And the same with Steve. If it doesn't rhyme, you don't pin the label on him. Even Steven, but not, like, Even Ted."

"Steady Teddy," I suggested.

"Oh, wow!"

That sent him zooming off on a tangent, but it wasn't too hard to get him back on course. He didn't know Steve's last name, and didn't know that it was a matter of memory, as he had the sense that he'd never known Steve's last name. Lucille, who'd very likely been to bed with Steve, probably hadn't known his last name, either, and might or might not remember him, and anyway it was all academic, since Lucille had long since vanished somewhere out west.

And if it hadn't been for Jack, nobody'd call his buddy Even Steven. The two names seemed to go together. It was funny with names, he said.

"Like I had a Vespa for about ten minutes," he said. "Little motor scooter? And that was enough, and to some people I've been Scooter Williams ever since. I mean, people who never even knew me when I had the bike."

"Like Jacob."

"Jacob," he said. "Oh, *your* Jacob! Scooter and Scooder!"

"Right."

"Yeah," he said. "Like Jacob. Funny, isn't it?"

I agreed that it was. And, he wondered, was this helpful, any of it? About Jack's name and where it came from, and Even Steven?

I said we'd have to see.

I called Poogan's, and Danny Boy came to the phone. "One quick question," I said. "Even Steven."

"That's not a question, Matthew."

"You're right," I said. "It's not. Does the name Even Steven —"

"Mean anything to me?"

"That's the question."

"Not out of context. Is there a context?"

I told him what I knew.

"An old pal of Jack Ellery's," he said. "High-Low Jack and Even Steven. You know, the fact that a man's unflappable, that he doesn't have to take Librium to keep from bouncing off walls, that's not the kind of trait that makes him instantly identifiable."

"I know."

"What it is, it's the absence of a trait. It's sort of like 'Oh, you know who I mean. He's the guy who hasn't got a wooden leg.'"

"Well, if you happen to hear anything."

"We'll see," he said. "I gather you're still on that case."

"Sort of."

"Well, if the client's still footing the bill —"

"My client's dead."

"Oh."

"He killed himself."

"Oh."

"Hanged himself with his belt. I liked him too."

Danny Boy didn't say anything for a long moment, and I'd already said more than I'd intended. Eventually he said he'd let me know if he came up with anything, and I told him not to worry if he didn't, and that's where we left it.

XXXVI

IN THE MORNING I made a couple of phone calls before I went out for breakfast, then worked the phones some more after I'd eaten and read the paper. I had a name to try on people—Even Steven—and I bounced it off everybody I could think of, including Bill Lonergan in Woodside and Vann Steffens in Jersey City. Could anybody come up with a fellow named Steve who'd hung out with Jack Ellery? Did anybody get any kind of a hit off the name Even Steven? I kept busy, but I wasn't getting anywhere.

And why was I even bothering? I didn't have a case, and my client was dead. He'd hanged himself. The only way someone else could have strung him up was by knocking him out first, and that hadn't happened.

Unless—

Unless he had a visitor, a calm and credible fellow with a good cover story. Someone who might even pass for a cop, someone who might have turned up at Jack Ellery's rooming house and convinced the fellow in charge to hand over whatever remained of Ellery's belongings.

Someone who inspired confidence. Someone who could get behind Greg Stillman and get him in a choke hold, cutting off the flow of blood to the brain, inducing unconsciousness. Not choking him enough to strangle him, just enough to put him under, just enough to render him helpless while he staged the suicide. Stripped to his shorts, the belt around his neck, its end secured by the closet door.

And then what? Drop him and let him hang? Or wait until he began to come out of it, and then let him go, so you could watch him thrash around, kicking at the closed door, struggling for breath, for life.

The choke hold might leave marks, some form of physical evidence. But the belt would cover up all of that.

Even Steven.

The super at Jack's rooming house was named Ferdie Pardo. Short for Ferdinand, I suppose. He wore a dark blue work shirt with the sleeves rolled up. He had a pack of Kools in his shirt pocket and a pencil behind his ear, and he looked like a man who didn't expect the day to turn out well.

"There was a guy showed up maybe a week ago," he said. "Asking the same question. What did I do with Ellery's stuff?"

"And what did you tell him?"

"Same thing I'm telling you. Guy showed up and I gave it to him."

"He sign for it?"

He shook his head. "There was nothing," he said. "Just crap, you know? Imagine you live your whole life and when you're gone you leave some old clothes and a couple of books."

"That's all?"

"Pair of shoes, a notebook, some papers. I didn't think any-body was gonna come for it. I had it down in the basement, all packed up in this duffel bag, and I have to say the duffel bag was worth more than everything inside it put together. And it was a worn-out old duffel bag that wasn't worth anything much to begin with."

"So you didn't think a signature was required."

"Another week," he said, "and I'd of put it out for the garbage pickup, and I wouldn't make them sign for it, either. He was a cop, he had some reason to collect it, so I gave it to him."

"You say he was a cop."

He frowned. "He wasn't a cop?"

"I'm the one asking."

"Well, now I'm asking you." Maybe so, but he didn't wait for an answer. "I *think* he said he was a cop. He definitely gave that impression."

"Did he show ID?"

"Like a badge?" He frowned. "I had any sense, I'd just say yes, absolutely, showed me a badge, showed me his ID, Patrol-man Joe Blow, Detective Joe Blow, whatever."

"But as luck would have it you're an honest man."

"Shit," he said. "What I am, I'm a man who thinks of things a couple of seconds too late. What I think he did, and even so I can't swear to it, is he took out his wallet and flashed it at me. Like, I'm a cop and I can't be bothered wasting my time showing some asshole like you my ID. Like that."

"But the impression you got was police."

"Yeah. He looked like a cop."

"Can you describe him?"

"Jesus," he said. "I wish you'd ask me to describe the other one that showed up. Skinny fag with an earring. That'd be easier. *He* sure as shit didn't look like a cop."

One more flattering obituary notice for Greg. I said, "Take a shot at describing the cop, why don't you."

"Oh, so he's a cop after all? Okay, fuck it. About your height and weight."

"How old?"

"I don't know. What are you?"

"Forty-five."

"Yeah, that sounds about right."

"So he's about forty-five."

"Well, forty, fifty, somewhere in there. Split the difference and you got forty-five."

"Maybe it was me," I suggested.

"Huh?"

"My age, my height, my weight—"

"Maybe he was a little heavier," he said grudgingly. "Sort of a blocky-type body, thicker through the middle."

"What about his face?"

"What about it?"

"Can you describe it?"

"It was a face, you know? Two eyes, a nose, a mouth—"

"Oh, a face."

"Huh?"

"If you saw him again, would you know him?"

"Sure, but what are the odds? What are there, a couple of million people in New York? When am I gonna see him again?"

"How was he dressed?"

"He was dressed okay."

Jesus. "You recall what he was wearing?"

"A suit. Suit and tie."

"Like a cop might wear."

"Yeah, I guess. And glasses. He was wearing glasses."

"And he took Ellery's duffel bag and left."

"Right."

"Never told you his name, that you remember, and I don't suppose he gave you a business card."

"No, nothing like that. Why give me a business card? What business am I gonna give him? Call him up, tell him the shitter in Room Four-oh-nine won't flush? Let him know one of my deadbeats moved out in the middle of the night, and if he comes real quick he can have the room?"

"And everything Ellery left," I said, "was in the duffel bag."

"Except for the suit they buried him in."

They didn't bury him, they cremated him, but that was more than my new friend needed to know.

"And you rented his room."

"The man's dead," he said, "and I cleaned all his crap outta there, and he's not coming back, so what do you think I did with it? There's a guy in there right now."

"Even as we speak?"

"Huh?"

"Is the new tenant home?"

"He's not a new tenant," he said. "He moved to Ellery's room because it's a little bigger than the one he was in. He's been living here, oh, maybe three years at this point."

"What I was asking—"

"And no, he's not home. This hour he's at OTB, two blocks down on Second Avenue. That's where you'll find him, all day every day."

"Good," I said. "You can show me his room."

"Huh? I told you, it's rented. Somebody's already living there."

"And he's welcome to it," I said. "I just want a few minutes to look around."

"Hey, I can't let you do that."

I took out my wallet.

"What, you're gonna show me ID? I still can't let you in there no matter how many badges you show me."

"I can do better than that," I said.

Pardo thought he should be in the room with me while I searched it. I told him he'd be better positioned in the hall, in case the current tenant made a sudden reappearance.

"I told you," he said. "He's gone for the day. Long as those betting windows are open, he's there."

"Even so."

"I don't know," he said. "I should be here to keep an eye, you know?"

"Because I might be running an elaborate scam," I said, "where I go around paying fifty dollars to gain access to rooms of people who don't own anything."

He wasn't happy, but he went out into the hall and I closed the door, and used the hook-and-eye gadget to keep him out. Then I got to work looking for anything Jack might have tucked away where it wouldn't be easy to find.

A piece of carpeting covered most of the floor. It was a bound remnant, and it hadn't been tacked down, so it was easy enough to roll it up after I'd moved a couple of pieces of furniture. And it was almost as easy to replace everything after I'd established that the carpet hadn't been hiding anything.

The next place I looked was the dresser, a dark wood chest of drawers, its top scarred by neglected cigarettes. I took out each drawer in turn, stacking its contents on the floor, turning over the empty drawer to check its bottom, then putting everything back. One drawer, the wood warped with age, didn't want to come out, but I coaxed it, and had no more luck with it than with the one before it, but the next drawer, just one up from the bottom, was the charm. There was a 9×12 manila envelope Scotch-taped to its underside. An envelope just like it had held Jack's Eighth Step.

I picked at the tape, freed the envelope. One wing of the metal clasp broke while I was opening it. If the contents turned out to be the new tenant's can't-miss formula for picking winners, I'd be hard put to leave it as I found it. But I wasn't really worried on that score.

The envelope held three sheets of unlined notebook paper, covered in what I was able to recognize as Jack's careful handwriting. There was a newspaper clipping as well, and I took a look at it before I read what Jack had written.

It was from the *Post,* and it ran to the better part of a full page. I read it all the way through, although I could have stopped after the first paragraph.

I remembered the case.

When I'd finished the clipping I read the first paragraph of what Jack had written, then decided the rest could wait. I put the dresser drawer back, then returned everything to the envelope, fastened it with what remained of the clasp, and tucked the envelope inside my shirt. I can't say it improved the fit of that garment, but with the shirt buttoned over it there wasn't much chance anyone would take notice. And I could leave Jack's old room as empty-handed as I'd entered it.

I let myself out. Pardo was a few steps down the hall.

"Nothing," I told him.

"What did I tell you? These people had anything, they'd live somewhere else."

XXXVII

I WALKED DOWNTOWN, looking for someplace to have a cup of coffee while I read what Jack had written. I wound up at Theresa's. I skirted the counter, where Frankie Dukacs was giving his full attention to a bowl of soup, and took a booth where all he'd see of me was the back of my head.

I didn't want a meal, but I remembered the last time I'd been here and ordered a piece of pie with my coffee. They didn't have strawberry-rhubarb, but they had pecan, and I decided that would do just fine.

The newspaper clipping told of a man and woman who'd been shot dead in what the *Post* called a "Bohemian love nest" on Jane Street. It was Bohemian because it was not only in the Village, but in a back house, a onetime carriage house located to the rear of the Federal-period town house that fronted on the street. And it was a love nest because the two victims were nude, and in bed, and the man was married to somebody else.

He was a big player in the financial world. His name was G. Decker Raines, with the *G* standing for Gordon, and his name got in the papers a lot in connection with corporate takeovers and leveraged buyouts. Her name was Marcy Cantwell, and she'd come to New York to be an actress. What she'd become instead was a waitress, but she'd taken some classes and had a turn in some showcase and workshop productions.

One night she waited on Raines's table, and caught his eye, and he was back the next evening all by himself. He was still there at closing time, and walked her back to where she was staying at the Evangeline House, a residence for young women on West Thirteenth Street. Male guests weren't allowed upstairs, but they were able to sit together in the parlor.

A week later she was living in the Jane Street back house, and she wasn't waiting tables anymore.

A few months later she was dead, and so was he.

I didn't get all of this from the clipping, or from Jack's account of the incident. I read through everything a couple of times, then got myself down to the microfilm room at the library, where I read everything the *Times* had. The story had stayed alive a long time. It couldn't really miss. She was a beauty and he was a rich guy, and his wife was socially prominent and his kids went to private schools, and best of all the case never got solved. That meant it might be just what it looked like, a home invasion that turned violent, but it might be something else—a contract killing arranged by a business rival of Raines's, or something spawned by jealousy, either the wife's or that of a prior boyfriend of Marcy's. She'd had a couple, including a bartender with a history of violence toward women, and the cops knocked on a lot of doors and asked a lot of questions, but they never caught a break.

Or maybe I should say *we* and not *they,* because I was still with the NYPD when it happened, and in fact still attached to the Sixth Precinct. Our house caught the case, but I was never assigned to it, and we didn't have it long before all the publicity led the Major Case Squad to take it away from us.

A while ago, this was. Before the bullet that killed Estrellita Rivera swept me along in its wake, out of my job and marriage and into a room at the Northwestern. Before Jack Ellery got tagged for something else, and went away for it, and came out and got sober. A full dozen years ago, and more than enough time for the case to go very cold. There were cold cases where you knew who did it, even though you couldn't do anything about it. And there were cases where you didn't know a thing, and this was one of those.

But I knew. Jack did it. Jack and Steve.

"I'm writing this out separately," Jack's account started out. "This is part of my Fourth Step, and I'll discuss this in my Fourth Step and talk about it with G. when I do my Fifth Step. But there is someone else involved, so I am going to write this out now just for myself. And of course for my Higher Power, who might be reading over my shoulder, or listening to my thoughts."

Then there was some speculation on the nature of that Higher Power, or God. It was interesting enough, but nothing special, and really just Jack thinking some thoughts of his own on paper.

After a couple of paragraphs of that, he got back to the matter at hand. He told how an acquaintance, whom he neither named nor identified, had pointed out Marcy Cantwell as a former actress-waitress who now had plenty of time for auditions and acting classes, because she'd found a sugar daddy with a fat wallet. And how he'd shared this information with a friend. "I will call him S.," he added, and that's what he called him for the rest of the document, never revealing any personal information about him, never describing or identifying him.

He didn't say how they got the keys, only that they'd had access to the locked passage leading back to the carriage house and to the house itself. It was early evening when they let themselves in, and they burst into the bedroom before either of the two lovers was aware of their presence.

"I had a gun in my hand," he wrote, *"and when the man went for a gun, I shot him without thinking. He was naked and was grabbing for his pants to cover himself. I don't know why I thought he was going for a gun. I shot him in the chest and he fell back and I said we have to do something, we have to call somebody. And then S. took the gun from me. He told me to shut up. He told me I had to calm down. He said she'd seen our faces, she could identify us. She was crying and begging, and trying to cover herself with her hands, and I was like No, you can't do this, and he was ice-cold the way he always was and he just shot her between the breasts and she fell back next to the man. I don't know if she was alive or dead. And E.S. took the gun and put it back in my hand, and wrapped his own hand around mine, and said, Come on, you have to do this. And I had my finger on the trigger and his finger was over mine, and together we shot her in the forehead. And he took the gun and shot the man one more time, also in the head, to make sure."*

And that was that.

He'd changed it when he recounted it to his sponsor. Shifted the scene from the Village to the Upper West Side, recast the personnel, changing a money guy and his playmate to a drug dealer and his Spanish girlfriend. The most vivid image of all, S. pressing the gun into his hands and making him shoot the girl, somehow never made the final cut.

Some of it had likely been designed to render the event less identifiable, and it had certainly worked; I'd been unable to find a case that fit the account I got from Greg. Beyond that, I had to believe he'd tailored the story to lessen its impact on his sponsor. Jack had wanted to be honest, but he hadn't been capable of one hundred percent honesty right off the bat. He had to work his way up to it.

It was getting dark out when I left the library. I'd lost all track of the time, and when I checked my watch I saw that it was past five. It wasn't fully dark, but the sun was down, and a gray day was drawing to a close. Every day the sun disappeared a little earlier than the day before. There was nothing out of the ordinary about that, it happened every year, but there were times when I felt there was a sadness attached to it, that the poor old year was dying a day at a time.

One more day and I'd be a year sober.

I hadn't even thought of it, not on this particular day, not until this moment, standing on the library steps between the two stone lions, weighed down by the encroaching darkness and by the greater and deeper darkness of what I'd been reading. Gordon Decker Raines, Marcia Anne Cantwell, John Joseph Ellery — all dead. And one man, S. or Steve or Even Steven, who'd put bullets in all three of them. And I was alive and sober, and in another day I'd have a year.

I knew I ought to go to a meeting. I'd been too busy to go at noon, but it's a rare time of day when Manhattan doesn't have a meeting on offer somewhere, and there were several in and around midtown in the hours between five and seven, designed to catch the office worker on his way home. I'd been to one called Happy Hour a couple of times, and there was Commuters Special, near Penn Station, and another around the corner from Grand Central. I was at Forty-second and Fifth, just a few blocks west of Grand Central, and there might be another even closer, but I didn't have my meeting book with me. It's always in my back pocket, but I'd evidently not transferred it to the pair of pants I had put on this morning, and I didn't know where the meetings were or exactly what time they started.

I decided I could go home and shower and shave and maybe even go so far as to eat something. And I could put away the manila envelope, which now held some notes I'd made at the library, along with the clipping and Jack's account of the twelve-year-old killing on Jane Street. And I'd be able to show up at my regular meeting at St. Paul's, and I could raise my hand and announce that tomorrow would be my anniversary.

Or I could wait until tomorrow, and announce it then.

Either way, people would applaud. They'd clap for me, as if I'd done something remarkable. And maybe I had.

But not yet I hadn't. The announcement could wait, I decided, until the year was complete.

I was tired, and was all set to hail a cab until I remembered that it was the heart of the rush hour, and the traffic would be impossible. I didn't want to sit in an unmoving taxi while the lights changed and changed again, but neither was I ready to face the sardine-can crush of the rush-hour subway.

It had rained a little earlier. It felt as though it might rain some more. But maybe it would hold off, at least for as long as it took me to walk home.

I was four or five blocks from my hotel when the rain started. I was just passing a chain drugstore when I felt the first drops, and I thought about stopping for an umbrella, and decided it wasn't coming down hard enough to justify spending the three or four dollars. I already had four or five of them in my room, and if I bought another I'd have five or six, and I never remembered to take one unless it was already pouring when I left my room.

I walked another block or two and the rain slackened, and I was congratulating myself on my good judgment when the skies opened up. I ducked into a shoe repair shop, and the only umbrellas he had cost ten bucks. I bought one, and by the time I got outside and opened it, the rain had stopped altogether, and not another drop fell all the rest of the way home.

There are days when that sort of thing gets a laugh out of me, or at least a chuckle, but this wasn't one of those days. I wanted to smash something, perhaps the umbrella, perhaps the man who sold it to me. But I didn't. I was, after all, a model of sobriety, one day away from my anniversary, and I reminded myself of this as I carried my umbrella into the hotel.

No messages. I went upstairs, walked down the hall to my room. I had my key out, and it seems to me that I felt something, had some sense of foreboding. And maybe I did, maybe I picked up a vibration, maybe without identifying it I caught some scent coming under the door or through the keyhole.

And maybe not. The memory tends to fill in the blanks, furnishing what seems fitting whether or not it ever happened. Maybe I sensed something and maybe I didn't, but either way I stuck my key in the lock and opened my door.

XXXVIII

A T FIRST I didn't recognize the smell. It was strong, it hit me in the face the minute I had the door open, and I'm sure it was as unmistakable in its own way as the stench that had permeated Greg Stillman's apartment. I thought, That's an awful smell, that's unhealthy to breathe, I'd better open a window and clear the place. So I recognized the nature of it, but I couldn't say what it was.

And then in an instant I could. It was booze, it was ethyl alcohol, it was more specifically bourbon.

The whole room reeked of it. Was it really there? Was my mind doing this, conjuring up a smell in response to the stress of my work and the anxiety that precedes an AA anniversary? It was as if the cleaning woman had broken a bottle in my room, but I didn't keep whiskey in my room, so there was no bottle for her or anyone else to break. And it was Monday, and Saturday was the day she cleaned my room, and she'd have no reason to be there, and neither would anyone else, and I'd left the room locked, and it had been locked just now because I'd needed to turn my key to let myself in, and God, God in Heaven, what was going on?

Then I looked over at my desk. My chair was drawn up next to it, turned just enough toward the door so that it seemed to be inviting me to sit down. And on the desk there was a glass tumbler of the sort they used to call an old-fashioned glass, not because there was anything old-fashioned about it, but because it had been designed to hold that cocktail called an old-fashioned.

Did anybody order old-fashioneds anymore? Had I ever had one myself? It seemed to me that I had, that I must have. It seemed to me that, with just a little effort, I could remember what it tasted like.

I did not own a glass like this. I owned a couple of water tumblers. One had a sort of bell shape to it, of the type in which drugstores sold Coca-Cola when drugstores still had soda fountains. The other wasn't strictly speaking a glass at all, in that it was made out of plastic, so that it wouldn't shatter when I dropped it on the bathroom floor.

I couldn't take my eyes off the glass. I'd had glasses of that size and shape when I lived with Anita and the boys in Syosset. Like every proper suburbanite, I'd had a fully equipped bar in the den, with all the glasses one might be called upon to provide for one's guests. And, while nobody had ever asked me to mix up a batch of old-fashioneds, that was the glass of choice for serving a drink on the rocks. This wasn't one of the glasses from that set, which I could only presume were still in the finished basement of the Syosset house, but it was that type.

Yet I could swear I recognized the glass. It was just the sort in which Jimmy Armstrong served drinks on the rocks.

Or a double bourbon, straight up, no ice, if that was your pleasure.

This glass, this glass on my desk, was filled to within perhaps a half inch of its brim with a clear amber liquid. I was able to identify it as a bourbon called Maker's Mark. There may be gifted human beings who could have made that identification on the basis of the color and aroma alone, but I am not one of them. I did not recognize the brand so much as I deduced it, and I based my deduction on the presence of the bottle of Maker's Mark bourbon that stood on my desk just a few inches from the glass.

I couldn't move. I couldn't look anywhere but where I was looking—at the desk, at the glass and the bottle.

Thoughts rushing at me, one after the other:

It was a hallucination. There was no bottle, no glass, no smell of whiskey.

It was a dream. I'd come home, I'd lain down for a nap, and now I was having an impossibly vivid drunk dream.

It was my sobriety that was the illusion, the hallucination. I'd been chipping around for months, having a drink here and a drink there, telling myself and everyone I knew that I didn't drink anymore. But it was all a lie, a 364-day lie, and the proof lay before me, because I'd poured a drink before I left my room that morning and there it was, waiting for me on my return.

I blinked, and it was still there. I forced myself to look away, and then looked back, and it was still there. I felt myself drawn toward it. I wanted to approach it, not to pick it up, God no, not to touch it, but to somehow make it go away. I had to make it go away. I couldn't let it stay there.

I don't know how long I stood there, neither approaching the desk nor walking away from it. Then finally I wrenched myself away, yanked the door open, slammed it shut, locked the whiskey away behind it. I rushed down the hall, didn't even ring for the elevator. I dashed down the stairs and out into the street.

XXXIX

D URING MY DRINKING DAYS, there were worse things than hangovers. Blackouts were worse — coming to and realizing there were vast holes in one's memory, hours when some other part of oneself was running things, steering the car and grinding the gears. Seizures were worse, and waking up in a hospital bed in restraints. And, more subtly, the day-by-day erosion of one's whole life, that surely was worse than a hangover.

Hangovers were bad enough, however, and some of them were worse than others. But what I remember most vividly in that regard is not so much any particular hangover as the way one of them ended.

I was in my hotel room, and I felt terrible, and knew that the only thing that would ease my pain was a drink. And of course there was nothing in my room to drink. If there had been, I'd have drunk it the night before.

So I got myself dressed and downstairs and around the corner, and it must have been around eleven because Armstrong's was open but the lunch crowd wasn't there yet. In fact the place was empty, or the closest thing to it, and Billie Keegan was behind the stick, and he took one look at me and knew not to say a word. Instead he set a glass on the top of the bar, and filled it about halfway full, so that I wouldn't spill it if my hands happened to shake a little.

I stood there while he poured, and I took a breath, and I felt better. I hadn't had a chance to get the alcohol to my lips yet, let alone into my bloodstream, but its simple physical proximity made all the difference. It was there, and I was going to be able to drink it, and it would help me feel better again — and because I knew this I felt better already.

I thought of this when, finally, I heard Jim Faber's voice.

First I had to find a phone that worked. Then I had to dial his number, and wait while it rang, and when his wife answered I had to ask to speak to Jim. She said, "He's not here, Matt. He's got a rush job keeping him at the shop. Do you need the number?"

"I have it," I said. "And I've got plenty of quarters too."

I don't know what she might have made of that, because I broke the connection before I could find out. I spent one of those abundant quarters, and waited while it rang, and then he answered. And right away I felt better.

"I don't think you had a hallucination," he said. "I know that sort of thing can happen, but that's not what this sounds like to me. I think you've got a real glass of bourbon on your desk, and a real bottle keeping it company. You said Maker's Mark?"

"That's right."

"Well, if you're determined to hallucinate, you might as well go straight to the top shelf. I only had it a couple of times myself, but it seems to me that Maker's Mark was pretty decent sippin' whiskey."

"I used to know a woman who liked it."

"You don't suppose—"

"She's dead," I said. "She died a long time ago."

Carolyn, from the Caroline. Another name for my Eighth Step list, I thought, if I stayed sober long enough to write one.

"You didn't pour it for yourself, Matt, and you're not in the middle of a drunk dream either. You went out this morning, and that was waiting for you when you got back. You know what happened."

"I left the door locked."

"So?"

"It wouldn't be that hard to swipe a key from behind the desk. Or to open the door without one."

"And?"

"And somebody came into my room," I said, "and brought a bottle with him."

"And a glass from Armstrong's."

"It could have been from anyplace. Half the bars in the city have that kind of rocks glass."

"So he brought a bottle and a glass."

"And set the stage," I said. "Poured a drink. Left the bottle there, with the cap off."

"Just the one glass. Inconsiderate bastard, wasn't he? Suppose you had company?"

I said, "Jim, he wanted me to drink."

"But you didn't."

"No."

"You didn't even want to, did you?"

I thought about it. "No," I said, "I didn't. But at the same time

I couldn't take my eyes off it. I felt like a bird hypnotized by a snake."

"Stands to reason."

"I found the thought of drinking it terrifying. As if it might jump off the desk and pour itself down my throat. As if it had that power."

"Uh-huh."

"It was magnetic," I said. "I didn't want it, but I was drawn to it anyway."

"You're an alcoholic," he said.

"Well, we knew that."

"Yeah, and we just got some more evidence, in case we entertained the slightest doubt."

"I wanted to pour it down the sink," I said.

"Better than keeping it around."

"But I was afraid to go near it. I didn't want to take a step in that direction, let alone pick it up."

"You were right."

"I was? Isn't it crazy, giving the shit that kind of power?"

"It's already got the power."

"I guess."

"The way you give it more power," he said, "is by picking it up and drinking it. And the first step in picking it up and drinking it is picking it up at all."

"So I left it there."

"And locked the door on it. What time is it? Shit."

"What's the matter?"

"This isn't something for you to do all by yourself," he said. "I'd go with you after the meeting, assuming I can wrap this up in time to go to the meeting, but I don't like the idea of letting it sit there for the next few hours. Or letting you sit somewhere between now and meeting time, locked out of your room and with no place to go. I'd come over now, but—"

"No, you've got work to do."

"It would be really inconvenient to leave now. You've got phone numbers, right? People in the program, people who live nearby?"

"Sure."

"And you've got quarters."

"And subway tokens," I said, "though I can't see how one of those will come in handy right now."

"You never know. You're where? Down the block from your hotel?"

"Five blocks away. It took me that long to find a working phone without somebody already using it."

"Make some calls. Get somebody to keep you company, and call me as soon as you pour out the booze. Will you do that?"

"Sure."

"Call me from your room. And if you can't find somebody, don't go back to your room alone."

"I won't."

"Call me instead. And we'll figure out something. Matt?"

"What?"

"Didn't I tell you? Sometimes things get a little crazy right before a person's anniversary."

There were a couple of phone numbers I didn't have to look up. Two of them were Jim's, of course, at home and at his place of business, and another was Jan's. I'd already spoken to Jim and I wasn't about to call Jan.

I'd have called her if I had to. When I was just starting to string sober days together, before we'd begun to become a couple, she'd made me promise to call her before I picked up a drink.

In the world we shared, sobriety trumped everything, so even if we had ceased keeping company, either of us could call the other in order to stay sober.

But not now. There were plenty of other people I could call, and they were a lot closer than Lispenard Street.

I was limited, though, to the ones whose numbers were in my wallet. Now and then someone will hand me a card, or a slip of paper, and I'll find room for it in my wallet until I get a chance to copy it into my book. I have a little memo book, itself about the size of a business card, that I use for AA phone numbers, and that's where they wind up. I keep the book in my room, next to the phone, so that it's handy if I want to call someone. I almost never do, the only AA calls I make with any frequency are to Jim, but it's good to have the book, if only because I can periodically copy down new phone numbers and clear out my wallet.

The point of this is that I now needed to call someone, and I had plenty of phone numbers, but they were all in the book. If I wanted to have someone with me when I returned to my room, I was largely limited to whatever numbers were still in my wallet. There were a few of those, and the first one I came to was Motorcycle Mark. I caught him on his way out the door, and he said that was no problem, he didn't have anything to do that wouldn't keep. Where should he meet me?

I said I'd meet him at my hotel, and by the time I'd walked the four or five blocks he was already there, with his bike parked out front. On our way through the lobby he said he'd noticed the hotel hundreds of times, and often wondered what it was like inside. It seemed all right, he said, and I agreed that it wasn't bad.

The door to my room was locked, as I'd left it, and as I was fitting the key in the lock I had this sudden image of finding the room not as I remembered it but as I'd left it that morning, with no bottle and no glass and no smell of whiskey. And Mark, in his boots and leather jacket and with his helmet under his arm, would nod his head knowingly and talk gently to me in that tone you use with ambulatory psychotics. Calming me down, talking me off the ledge.

The image was so vivid it made me reluctant to open the door. But I did, of course, and it was all still there, the uncapped bottle of Maker's Mark, the glass filled almost to the brim, the chair positioned to welcome me, and the raw smell of bourbon suffusing the room.

"Fucking Jesus," Mark said.

"That's what I walked in on."

"Man, the smell! It's like a fucking distillery. That's not from one drink sitting in a glass."

"It's strong, isn't it?"

He moved past me, walked over to the bed. "Come here, Matt. Look."

That was what made the smell so strong. My pillow and mattress were soaked. My visitor had upended a bottle of bourbon over my bed.

I turned from it, went to the desk. The open bottle had no more than a couple of ounces missing, less than the glass contained. So he'd come to my room with a glass and two bottles, poured a drink, emptied a bottle on my bed, and left me plenty of bourbon to get good and drunk on.

"Unbelievable, man. Who could pull some shit like this?"

"Steve," I said.

"You know the guy?"

"Just his name."

He shook his head, and we both stood there for a moment, taking it all in. Then he said, "First things first, Matt. The bottle and the glass."

"Right."

"You want me to—"

"No, let me do it," I said, and picked up the glass and carried it into the bathroom. I held the thing at arm's length, as if it were a snake that might whip its head around and bite me, and I upended it over the sink and ran water to wash its contents down the drain. I held the glass under the tap and rinsed it out, and then I dropped it in the wastebasket. It was a perfectly good drinking glass, and perfectly safe now that I'd rinsed the residue of bourbon out of it, but what did I need with it?

I went back for the bottle, and emptied it into the sink, and let the tap water speed its passage through the plumbing. I rinsed out the bottle, too, and Mark handed me the cap, and I held that under the running water before I screwed it back onto the bottle. Then I put the thing in the wastebasket, with the glass.

"That's better," he said. "Be hard to drink it now. You'd have to go down into the sewer after it, and the alligators'd beat you to it."

"A load off my mind," I said.

"Next we got to do something about that bed. No way you can sleep on it."

"No."

"There a porter or somebody who can get it out of here?"

"Not at this hour."

We stood there thinking about it. Then Mark said, "You know, that mattress is done. You can't fix a mattress like that. It'll stink of alcohol forever."

"I know."

"The pillow too. Total loss."

"Right."

He walked over to the window, opened it as wide as it would open. "Good it's a single bed," he said. "Never work with a double."

"You think?"

"What else, man?"

I let him take charge. He was a good fifteen years younger than I, and I'd been sober a little longer, but he seemed to know what to do and that was more than I could say for myself. We stripped off the bed linen, and Mark had me help him lug the bare mattress over to the window. When we had it balanced half in and half out, he sent me downstairs to make sure no one was underneath the thing when he shoved it out.

I walked past Jacob and out onto the pavement. I looked up, and there was my mattress, hanging out of my window. An older man wearing a suit and a tie had just emerged from McGovern's, and I waited while he walked toward me with the careful gait of a man who's drunk and knows it. He looked up to see what was holding my attention, decided it was nothing he had to be concerned about, and walked on by. The sidewalk was clear now, and I called out to Mark, and my mattress came sailing down at me and landed at my feet.

I got hold of it, dragged it over to the curb. I went inside and asked Jacob which rooms were vacant. There was a single on my floor, at the rear of the building. He gave me the key.

The room had been serviced since the last guest had departed. It was a little smaller than mine, but had the same iron bedstead, and the same size mattress. Mark and I took the mattress, linen and all, and carried it the length of the hall to my room, and placed it on my empty frame.

"Like it's been there forever," Mark said. "Just one thing missing."

I fetched the pillow from the vacant room, and set it on my bed. We took my pillow and my sheets, balled them up, and put them in the service pantry. There was a big trash can there, and it got the contents of my wastebasket, the empty bottle and the glass. I locked the vacant room, and we stopped downstairs at the desk to return the key.

"It's a funny thing," I told Jacob, "but there's no mattress on the bed in that room."

"There ain't?"

"No," I said, "but I'm sure the porter can rustle up a spare from the storeroom first thing in the morning." A couple of bills moved from my hand to his. "For his trouble," I said. "And for yours."

"Don't see no problem there," he said.

Outside, Mark looked at my old mattress and nodded his approval. "I always wondered what it would be like to throw one of those out a window."

"And?"

"One minute it was there," he said, "and then it wasn't. It was sort of satisfying, actually. Made more of a noise landing than I thought it would."

"Nobody on the street seemed to notice."

"Well, New York," he said. "That dude at the desk. Jacob? He was pretty cool about the whole thing. He high on something?"

"He has a fondness for cough syrup," I said.

"Well, shit," Mark said. "Who doesn't?"

XL

THERE WAS TIME for a quick bite before the meeting, and Mark suggested a deli on Broadway. "We'll take the bike," he said.

It was eight or ten blocks away, and we got there in a hurry. When we were seated and had ordered our pastrami sandwiches, I excused myself and made a phone call.

Jim was still at the shop. "I was supposed to call as soon as I got rid of the booze," I told him, "and it slipped my mind completely." I brought him up to date, and he asked me how I felt now. "A lot better," I said.

He said he might be late for the meeting, but that he'd see me there. I went back to the table and told Mark I'd never been on a motorcycle before. "You're kidding," he said. "Never?"

"Not that I remember," I said, "and I think it's something I'd remember. Even in a blackout, that's the sort of thing that would cut through the fog."

"You should get one, man. Seriously."

The pastrami was good, the french fries well-done. I liked the place, and wondered how come I'd never happened on it before. It wasn't that far from my hotel, and I had to have walked past it dozens of times over the years.

Mark told me parts of his story while we ate. There was a lot of heroin in it, and a lot of hectic trips back and forth across the country. He'd spent a lot of time in Oakland and San Francisco, and sometimes he missed it. "I'll hear California calling," he said, "but I'll hear a needle calling, and it's the same voice, you know? So I figure for now I'll stay right where I'm at."

A couple of times over the years I've had dreams in which I was capable of flight. I soared over the rooftops, banking and turning effortlessly, reveling in the simple delight of it all. After our meal I got a second ride on the back of Mark's Harley, from the deli to St. Paul's, and it had an unreal quality that brought those flying dreams to mind. I had slipped into a zone of unreality when I opened my hotel room door the first time, and in this new world mattresses sailed out of windows and motorcycles tore through the night.

Then we walked into the meeting at St. Paul's and the world came back into focus.

Jim wasn't there. I got a cup of coffee and took a seat, and an exchange speaker from Bay Ridge told a story that started at age four, when he circled the living room the morning after a party and polished off the dregs of everybody's drinks. "Right away," he said, "I knew what my life was going to be about."

I raised my hand during the discussion and said I'd had a difficult day, and one that had included a challenge to my sobriety. But I'd stayed sober, and what especially pleased me was that I'd actually gone so far as to ask for help, which was by no means characteristic behavior on my part. I'd received the help I needed, made a friend in the process, and capped the experience with an adventure. Just a little adventure, I said, but that was about as much excitement as I could stand. And, I added, if I just managed to go to bed sober, when I woke up the next morning I'd have a year.

That got some applause. Several people congratulated me during the break, including Jim, who must have come in toward the end of the qualification. Afterward the two of us followed the crowd to the Flame, but instead of joining the big table we took a small one by ourselves. He ordered a full meal—he'd come straight to the meeting from the shop—and I had a cup of coffee.

"You didn't go into detail," he said.

"It was a little more drama than I wanted to share. Not that it wouldn't have made a good story. We wound up throwing the mattress out the window."

"That must have been fun."

"I didn't get to do it. I went downstairs to make sure it didn't land on anybody. I figured I'll have enough names on my Eighth Step list as it is."

"Good thinking."

"Actually," I said, "Mark did all the thinking. He took complete charge and showed real executive ability. Though I worked out how to replace the mattress."

"You swiped one from an empty room."

"I reassigned it," I said. "But Jesus, Jim, when I opened the door..."

He let me talk my way through it. When I was done he frowned and said, "It wasn't a practical joke, was it?"

"It was serious as a heart attack," I said. "You couldn't file charges, but what it was is attempted murder."

"He figured you'd pick up a drink and it would kill you. And it would have, though it might have taken a couple of years."

"He knew I was getting close," I said. "And he didn't want anybody getting close. He killed Jack Ellery because he was convinced he'd wind up in the spotlight as a direct result of Jack's process of making amends. He killed Mark Sattenstein to keep him quiet, and he killed Greg Stillman to close down my investigation. He didn't have to do all that, I'd done all I'd signed on to do, but every time he stirred the pot something new floated up and got me into it all over again. So the only way Steve was going to get rid of me was to kill me."

"You know his name?"

"His first name. They called him Even Steven, as a counterpart to High-Low Jack. Because Jack had mood swings and Steven didn't, evidently. He was cool as a pistol."

"Isn't it —"

"Hot as a pistol, cool as a cucumber. A fellow who knew them both hit on the idea of inverting clichés, and it only took him twenty-five years of daily marijuana use to come up with it."

"Cannabis, friend to man."

"If he could get me to drink," I said, "I probably wouldn't be able to pursue the investigation any further, and even if I did I'd lack credibility. I'd be another raving drunk with paranoid delusions, and the cops see plenty of those. And if I went on a decent bender, there was a good chance it'd kill me outright, and at the very least it would make me an easy victim. Things happen to people when they're drunk. They fall down flights of stairs or off subway platforms, they lurch off curbs in front of buses. He'd made Sattenstein's death look like a mugging and Stillman's like a suicide, and he could find a way to kill me and make it look like something else."

"And now?"

"He'll look for another way."

"And what will you do?"

"Try to get him," I said, "before he gets me."

He thought about it. "You know," he said, "sometimes I'll sit around the shop all day, and then at the last minute a job comes in and it has to be done in a rush. I wind up missing dinner with my wife and the first half of my meeting."

"And that's what happened tonight."

"It is," he said, "and it invariably annoys the bejesus out of me. But nobody pours top-shelf bourbon for me, and nobody's trying to kill me, so maybe I haven't got all that much to complain about."

When we left the Flame he said, "You know, you're always going out of your way to walk me home. Tomorrow's your anniversary, and I think it's time I walked you home for a change."

And when we reached the Northwestern he said, "All these months and I've never had a look at your room."

"You want to see it?"

"Long as I'm here."

I said, "Jim, I'm all right."

"I know that."

"Mark and I left the room in good shape. There was still a faint odor of bourbon, but we left the window open, so it'll be gone by now."

"Probably true."

"And he wouldn't have come back. He tried something and it didn't work, so he'll try something else."

"Stands to reason."

"But you still want to come up."

"Why not?"

We went upstairs, and I opened my door to a room that was

just as I'd left it, if a good deal colder. I closed the window. Jim looked around the room, then walked over to the window himself. "Nice view," he said.

"It's something to look out at," I said, "when I'm in the mood to look out at something."

"A man couldn't ask for more. It seems to suit you."

"I think so."

"And when you wake up tomorrow," he said, "you'll have a year."

"Sometimes that sounds like a lot," I said, "and sometimes it doesn't."

"You know what else you'll have tomorrow? One more day to get through. And sometimes *that's* a lot."

"I know."

"And it's all a day at a time, and there's no need to think in long-range terms, but if you keep it up you might wind up with long-term sobriety. You know how to make sure you achieve that elusive distinction?"

"How?"

"Don't drink," he said, "and don't die."

I told him I'd see what I could do.

When he left I decided I needed more than a shower. I drew a hot bath and soaked in it until the water wasn't hot anymore. It took the tension out of my muscles and the back of my neck, but what it didn't do was make me sleepy. I lay in bed with the lights out, and of course the new mattress felt unfamiliar, and so did the pillow. There was nothing really wrong with either of them, and it was clear to me that they weren't keeping me awake. It was my mind that was keeping me awake.

I got up and turned the light on. Jim had once suggested I read the chapter on Step Seven in *Twelve Steps and Twelve*

Traditions as a cure for insomnia. "It'll stop a charging rhino in his tracks," he said. "Years ago I'd read the first chapter of *Swann's Way,* which is as far as I ever got with Monsieur Proust. Put me out every time. But the Seventh Step is almost as good."

I read the first couple of paragraphs, then put the book back on the shelf and hauled out Jack Ellery's account of the double homicide on Jane Street. I read it through and set it aside and thought about it, and decided I wasn't any closer to sleep than I'd been before, and that it felt out of the question, at least for the time being.

I thought about Motorcycle Mark, and how there'd been more to him than I would have suspected. People surprise you that way, especially the sober ones. It had been sheerest happenstance that led me to call him: a phone call from someone else had led me to ask if he'd called, and he'd responded by asking for my number and giving me his, and I'd taken it from him more out of politeness than anything else. And, because I didn't have my phone book with me, and because I still had his number in my wallet, he'd been the one I'd called. And I couldn't have made a better choice.

Funny how it works.

I decided I ought to have his number in my book, and that the task of copying it, along with the other cards and slips of paper in my wallet, was just the right sort of task for my current state of mind. I sorted everything, put a batch of receipts in the cigar box where I stow them when I remember, and found a fine-point pen to copy Mark's number and the others I'd accumulated since I last forced myself to perform this particular task.

Halfway through, something brought me up short. I stared at the card in my hand, copied the number into my book, stared at the card some more, and returned it to my wallet.

I picked up Jack's confession, read it through one more time, and noticed something I'd missed the first time through. "I will call him S.," he wrote of his partner, and so he did, S. for Steve. And then when he described the killing itself, he called the man E.S. For Even Steven, obviously.

Maker's Mark, I thought. There was Mark Sattenstein, and there was Motorcycle Mark, and now there was Maker's Mark.

Why had he picked that brand?

It wasn't a very popular bourbon. I couldn't remember the last time I'd seen it advertised — but then I tried not to pay much attention to liquor ads these days. It was expensive, but less so than Dickel or Wild Turkey, and it didn't have their reputation. Nor was it a brand I ordered often.

At bars I didn't always specify the brand. I might just order bourbon, or I might look at the bottles on the back bar and name whatever label caught my eye. Old Crow, Old Forester, Jim Beam. Jack Daniel's. There were bourbons I'd try because I liked the sound of their name, or the look of the bottle they came in. And when I went across the street for a bottle I generally came back with Early Times or Ancient Age, or maybe J. W. Dant — something modestly priced and serviceable, smooth enough to go down easy, strong enough to do the job.

It was Carolyn Cheatham who had a fondness for Maker's Mark. She was Tommy Tillary's girlfriend, and one night she turned up at Armstrong's without him. She lived nearby on Fifty-seventh Street, just a few doors west of Ninth Avenue, in an Art Deco building with a sunken living room and high ceilings, and that night the two of us began consoling each other and wound up sharing her bed, along with a fifth of Maker's Mark.

She killed herself in that apartment, shot herself with a gun Tommy had given her. She called me first, and I got there too late, but in plenty of time to commit a felony of my own, and so arranged things that Tommy Tillary, who'd gotten away with killing his wife, wound up going to prison for killing his girlfriend.

I thought about all of this, and while I was thinking I was getting dressed — undershorts, shirt, pants, socks, shoes. I grabbed a jacket and went out of my room and down to the street. I turned right and walked to the corner and turned right again.

I got as far as the Pioneer — or Piomeer, as you prefer. The dingy little market was still open, and so of course was the gin-mill next door to it. I could go in and belly up to the bar, and the fellow standing behind it would probably be able to answer the question I'd come to ask him.

And who could say what else I might ask? Whatever it was, he'd have the answer.

XLI

But i turned around and went home instead. It was late enough for the newsstand at the corner of Eighth and Fifty-seventh to have the early edition of the *Times,* but when I got to my hotel I let my feet do the smart thing for a change and take me inside. I went upstairs and got undressed again and pulled the chair over to the window and sat for a little while looking at nothing in particular.

I'd headed for Armstrong's because I had a question to ask. And I'd turned back because I'd just spent a day that had put me physically closer to a drink than I'd been in the past year, and I was one day away from the one-year anniversary of my last drink. I didn't want a drink now, I didn't feel like drinking, but enough had sunk in during the previous 364 days to make me realize just how vulnerable I was and just how dangerous that room was for me now.

Oh, I could have called someone, some sober friend to keep

284 • LAWRENCE BLOCK

me company while I asked my question. But I didn't have to do that either. I could just go home and get to bed. My question would still be there in the morning.

I didn't know if I'd be able to sleep. I got in bed, turned off the light, stretched out on the unfamiliar mattress, settled my head on the unfamiliar pillow.

The next thing I knew it was morning.

The first thing I did after breakfast was call Dennis Redmond. I got him at the station house, and he was on his way out when I reached him. I told him I was pretty sure I had something. He said, "On Ellery? Because it's gonna take a lot to make Stillman look like anything but suicide."

"Try G. Decker Raines," I said. "And Marcy Cantwell."

"Now why are those names familiar?"

"A few years back," I said. "A double homicide on Jane Street in the West Village. A Bohemian love nest, according to the *Post*, and—"

"I remember the case. Still unsolved to this day, if I'm not mistaken. Why? You're saying you know who did it? Well, who was it?"

"Jack Ellery."

"You're shitting me."

"He confessed to it. In writing."

"And you've seen this confession."

"I have it in hand."

He thought about it. He said, "I don't suppose he did it all by his lonesome."

"He had a partner."

"And Ellery got religion, or whatever you want to call it, and the partner was afraid he'd talk. Hell, I've got to get out of here. You remember that place I met you before? The Minstrel Boy?

Say two this afternoon? And Matt? Bring that confession, will you?"

I hung up and the phone rang almost immediately. It was Jan, calling to wish me a happy anniversary. It was a curious conversation, because the things we weren't saying drowned out the things we said. She said how happy she was for me, and how hard I'd worked for that year, and I told her how grateful I was for the unwavering support she'd given me from the very beginning, and when she was off the line I wanted to call her right back. But what would I say to her?

I had a couple of other calls to make, but the phone rang right away and this time it was Jim. He asked me gruffly if I was still sober, and I said that I was, miraculously enough, and he said damn right it was a miracle, and I should never forget that. And he congratulated me, and told me the first year was the hardest. "Except for all the ones that come after it," he said.

"After you left last night," I said, "I had trouble falling asleep."

"So you took three Seconal and washed them down with a pint of vodka."

"I put my clothes on and walked over to Armstrong's."

"Seriously?"

"I had a question I wanted to ask the bartender."

"And?"

"I decided it would keep, and that probably wasn't a good place for me to be. The point is, I'm going over there now, on the chance that the day-shift barman will be able to answer my question. And if he can't I'll be dropping by again this evening."

"You could call around, find someone to keep you company."

I said I'd think about it.

*　　　*　　　*

286 · LAWRENCE BLOCK

Armstrong's generally opened around eleven, and it was twenty or thirty minutes past that by the time I got there. I'd put in some time on the phone and managed a quick visit to the squad room at Midtown North. What I didn't do was call someone to back me up when I went around the corner, so I was by myself when I walked into a room that smelled not unpleasantly of beer and tobacco smoke.

Two tables were occupied, and there was a fellow at the end of the bar, nursing a beer while he worked his way through the *Daily News*. Lucian was behind the stick, assembling a Bloody Mary, and he paused in midpour at my approach. He was surprised to see me, and trying to hide it.

"It looks beautiful," I said of his handiwork, "but it's not what I'm here for. I just stopped by to ask you a question."

"Go right ahead, Matt. If I don't know the answer I'll make something up."

"I was just wondering if anybody came around recently asking questions about me."

"Questions. I don't think so. What kind of questions?"

"What I used to drink."

"Why would anybody ask that? But you know, there was an old friend of yours in here the other day."

"Oh?"

"He sat here, had a couple. Paid for his drink when he got it, waved away the change. 'That's good, have one yourself.' So, you know, guy's like that, you fill the glass a little fuller on his next round."

"Sure."

"Same story the second time around. 'That's good, have something for yourself.' And he says how this is a nice place, and an old buddy of his used to come here."

"And he mentioned me by name."

He nodded. By now he'd finished putting the Bloody Mary together and strained it into a stemmed glass. I'd assumed it was for a customer, but he took a sip of it himself. "Long night," he explained. "Got to get the heart started."

"Sound policy."

He took another sip. "The impression I got," he said, "was you were cops together."

"He was a cop?"

"Used to be, would be my guess."

"I don't suppose you got his name."

"No, and I don't think he got mine either. We never got that far."

"What did he look like?"

He frowned. "You know," he said, "I didn't pay a whole lot of attention. Middle-aged, not fat, not skinny. Sort of average. He was drinking Scotch, I remember that much, and I think it was Johnnie Red, but I couldn't swear to it."

"And he talked about me."

"Just did I ever see you, and did you ever get here now that you weren't drinking anymore, and how you used to be a bourbon drinker."

"He remembered that."

"But what he couldn't remember," he said, "was what your favorite bourbon used to be."

"Ah. What did you tell him?"

"I don't think you had a favorite. But he wanted an answer. Say it was a special occasion. What was that bourbon you would order then? Like he used to know, and he wanted his memory refreshed."

"What did you tell him?"

"I don't know if I ever poured it for you," he said, "and what difference did it make what you used to drink, since you're not drinking it now? But he had to have an answer, Mr. Have Something for Yourself, and I remember somebody else was going on about how one particular brand of poison was the best in the world, and I think it was Turkey, but it might have been Evan Williams, and you named another bourbon and said it was as good as either of them. You remember the conversation?"

I shook my head.

"No reason why you should. This was years ago. But it stuck in my mind, and a day or two later I had a taste of it myself, and I decided you were right. Can you guess the label?"

"You tell me."

For answer he reached and drew down the bottle from the top shelf. Maker's Mark.

And he hesitated for a second or two, it couldn't have been any longer than that, and then he replaced the bottle on the shelf.

"So that's what I told him," he said. "You know the guy, Matt?"

"I had an idea who it was," I said, "and your description nailed it down."

"Yeah, I'm hopeless at describing people. He was wearing glasses, if that helps. Was it okay what I told him?"

"Sure."

He hesitated, then said, "You know, it's funny. Just now, when I had the bottle in my hand, I had the feeling you were going to ask me to pour you one."

"Really."

"Just for a second. How long has it been?"

"Just about a year."

"No kidding? That long?"

"A year today, as a matter of fact."

"No shit. Jesus, you know what I almost said? 'That calls for a drink.' But I guess it doesn't, does it?"

*   *   *

I caught the noon meeting at Fireside. I got the usual round of applause at the beginning when I announced my anniversary.

I sat there drinking coffee and listening to somebody's drinking story, and I remembered that moment when Lucian had brandished the long-necked bottle of bourbon. *Oh, what the hell,* said a voice in my head. *Let's see if it tastes as good as I remember.*

XLII

THE FIRST TIME I'd met him at the Minstrel Boy I got there first, and I played John McCormack's version of the bar's theme song while I waited for him. This time I was a few minutes early, and I played the flip side of the record:

> *She was lovely and fair as the rose of the summer*
> *Yet 'twas not her beauty alone that won me.*
> *Oh no, 'twas the truth in her eyes ever dawning*
> *That made me love Mary, the Rose of Tralee...*

Redmond came in during the final chorus, stopped at the bar for a drink, came over and sat down. He was respectfully silent until the record ended. "Hell of a voice," he said. "How long you figure he's been dead?"

"No idea."

"I know he was long gone before I ever heard of him. My mother had all his records. Well, a bunch of them, anyway. Seventy-eights, in an album. I can picture it on a shelf in our living room. Don't ask me what became of them, but he's still here on the jukebox, and the voice is still as clear as a bell, all these years later."

He took a drink, put the glass on the table. I had a Coke in front of me, and no great urge to drink any of it. He said, "Well, what have you got?"

"Hell of a document," he said. He rolled Jack's confession into a scroll, tapped it against the top of his now-empty glass. He'd read it through twice, and we'd talked for a while, and now he'd read it through again. "I suppose we could establish that he's the one who wrote it. There must be samples of his handwriting around for comparison purposes. Of course there's always going to be an expert witness for the defense swearing up and down it couldn't possibly be his handwriting, because look at the little loops on the Ds. And that's assuming you could get the document admitted as evidence, which is no sure thing. You found it in his room?"

"Taped to the bottom of a drawer."

"Where we'd have spotted it if we'd had any reason to look for it, but we didn't. How'd you know to look?"

"Stillman went to collect Jack's effects from the super. But somebody'd already been there."

"You thought it was me."

"I thought it might be."

"And it could have been me," he said, "if we'd given the case a higher priority. But I'd already looked at everything in the room, and there wasn't much."

"No."

"So it wasn't me," he said, "or my partner, or anybody else with a badge. It was whoever killed him, looking to see if there'd been anything in the room that he'd missed."

"Right."

"And was there?"

"I think there was a copy of Jack's Fourth Step."

"Which you said he'd talked over with Stillman."

"And that was when he told Stillman he'd killed someone," I said, "but without saying who or when. It seemed likely to me that he'd written out a more detailed version for his own benefit, and that's what I went to his room hoping to find."

"It would have been better," he said, "if *I* had found it."

"Well, you didn't know to look for it, and—"

"If you'd come to me," he said, "and we'd gone over there together, and made the discovery, that would have been better. But instead we've got you bribing the super to look the other way, and being on premises where you've got no legal right to be, and bringing back something you say you found in a particular place at a particular time. Which I don't for a moment doubt you did, but I don't get to decide what's admissible and what isn't."

"I know."

"So from an evidentiary standpoint—"

"I know."

"Not that it would prove anything anyway, beyond the fact that the dead man who wrote it claims he and a partner killed a couple of people. He doesn't even name the partner."

"No."

"Even Steven. So it's some guy named Steve."

"I had a friend check a couple of files full of aliases and nicknames. He couldn't come up with anything."

"It might be on a list somewhere," he said, "but that's right up there with saying the cash or the dope or the stolen jewelry is in an evidence locker somewhere. That doesn't mean anybody's ever going to see it again. Even Steven." He shook his head. "But you know who he is."

He studied the business card. "Says he's your friend in Jersey City."

"Half of that's true."

"The Jersey City part?"

"I spoke to a journalist who knows him. He hangs around the courthouse, does favors, arranges things."

"Lot of guys like that," Redmond said. "Hardly an endangered species on that side of the river. Vann, it says. How'd that turn into Steve?"

"His mother named him Evander," I said, "and he knocked that down to one syllable, and put a second *N* on it to make it clear that it was his first name."

"Could be Dutch otherwise. Van Steffens."

"I can't be sure of this," I said, "but I think it dropped down to two syllables before one of them disappeared. From Evander to Evan."

"Evan Steffens." He nodded slowly. "Which doesn't have far to go to become Even Steven."

"When Jack wrote about it," I said, "he started out by saying he'd call his partner S. And he did, just using the single initial all the way through. Toward the end, though, he referred to him as E.S."

"Which could stand for Even Steven."

"But who uses initials for a nickname? Once I thought of that—"

"Yeah, I can see how you got there. Okay, let me get another drink, because the one is barely a memory at this point. And then you can lay the whole thing out for me."

* * *

By the time I was done his second drink was mostly gone. I'd switched from Coke to coffee, and my cup was empty, too.

"Ellery gets sober," Redmond said, "and he wants to get right with God. What's he gonna do, turn himself in for the Love Nest Murders?"

"Not necessarily. He hasn't even gotten specific with his sponsor. But he wants to find some way to make amends for what he did that night."

"How does Steffens find out?"

"They're both in a world where word gets around," I said. " 'Hey, you hear about High-Low Jack? He's going up to all the assholes he gave a screwing to years ago, looking to make things up to them.' Or he could have gone to Steffens himself. 'I just wanted to tell you that something may come out about what we did on Jane Street, but you've got nothing to worry about, because I'll be sure to keep your name out of it.' "

"If I'm Steffens, I don't know that I find that tremendously reassuring."

"No, of course not. If Jack ever tells anybody with a badge what he did, how long before they get the rest out of him?"

"Or even if he doesn't, Matt. If it lands on my desk, first thing I do is look at his known associates. Maybe Steffens's name comes up, maybe it doesn't, but if you're Steffens, how can you know it won't?"

"One way to make sure."

"And it would have worked if it hadn't been for Stillman. Down-and-out ex-con living in a furnished room — you know how those get solved. Someone gets drunk and talks too much. Steffens never talked about Jane Street, so why should he talk about High-Low Jack?"

"He wouldn't."

"No, he'd have gotten away with it, and I'm not happy about

it, but the fact is a lot of people get away with a lot of murders. Including the ones that don't make it into the book as murders, which I guess is the case with Gregory Stillman. But the other one came first, didn't it? Sattenstein?"

"And that's a murder," I said, "but it'll wind up on somebody else's tab."

"The guy they grabbed for the other muggings. But you say he claims Sattenstein wasn't his work. Well, they've got him cold on the others, and by the time he gets out of prison he'll be too old to mug anybody, so it hardly matters. As far as the cops downtown are concerned, he did Sattenstein along with the others, and that case is closed."

"Sattenstein called me," I said. "The last thing I'd asked him was where the name High-Low Jack came from, and he didn't know."

"And then he remembered?"

"I'll never know, because I didn't get back to him in time. My guess is he didn't, but he thought of someone who'd know."

"Steffens."

"Sattenstein was a fence," I said. "If he knew Jack, he probably knew some of the people he worked with. 'Hey, where'd Jack get that nickname? I figured you'd know, seeing as how they used to call you Even Steven.'"

"Not too hard for Steffens to set up a meeting in Sattenstein's neighborhood. Not too hard to get into Stillman's place either. 'Hello, Gregory? I'm a police officer investigating the murder of a friend of yours. I collected some belongings of his from his super, and there are a couple of articles here that I'd like to turn over to you.' Or 'He had this notebook, and there's something he wrote that I'd like to discuss with you.' Stillman would have let him in."

"No question."

"And then a choke hold? That would work, and it wouldn't

show up, not after the poor bastard spent a few hours hanging with a belt around his neck. And then to top everything off the son of a bitch tried to buy you a drink."

"Shows you the depths a person can sink to," I said, "once he starts off with a simple act of murder."

"Maker's Mark, you said?"

"He probably bought it at the liquor store right across the street from my hotel. If he did, there was probably a little gummed tag stuck to the back of the bottle, the store's address and phone number. They used to put one of those on every bottle they sold, to remind you where you got it in the hope that you'd come back for more."

"You didn't look for a tag."

"No. I poured it out without looking at it, and I dumped it and the glass in the wastebasket, and it all went in the big trash can next to the service elevator. The porter empties it a couple of times a day. I'm sure it's gone by now."

"It doesn't matter."

"No. What would it prove? That somebody bought a bottle of bourbon across the street? He probably bought two bottles, one to leave for me and the other to pour over my bed, and I wonder how often the place across the street sells two bottles of Maker's Mark to anybody. They'll remember him, but so what? He's over twenty-one. He can buy all the booze he wants."

"Ellery's super met him," Redmond said. "When he passed himself off as a cop. That's a crime, but it's a hard case to make if all he did was flip his wallet open and let the man draw his own conclusions." He gave me a look. "A lot of people do that."

"He didn't flash his leather at Armstrong's," I said, "but the day bartender had the impression he was a cop, or used to be. He went there to ask him what I liked to drink. But that's not a crime either."

"No. Here you've got a guy who's shaping up as a one-man crime wave. He killed two people years ago in the Village, and the one man who could put him on that one is dead. Dead because our boy shot him, but we've got no evidence and no witnesses for that one, or for the two men he killed to cover up the Ellery killing. As far as I can see, we can't prove he did a thing."

"He committed an act of vandalism," I said, "by dowsing a perfectly good mattress with a perfectly good bottle of whiskey."

"A misdemeanor," he said, "and he had to commit unlawful entry in order to accomplish it, which might up the ante to a low-grade felony. I'd have to take a run at the penal code, but I don't think I'm going to, because even there we've got no evidence."

"I know."

"It's annoying," he said, "because I'd like nothing better than to get this son of a bitch. I'd like to get him for Ellery, just on general principles, and I'd like even more to get him for Stillman, who struck me as a pretty decent guy."

"He was."

"And one who'd still have a pulse, if he'd had the sense to leave well enough alone. But yeah, I'd like to get Steffens for Stillman. And I can't tell you what a treat it would be to nail him for the man and woman in the Village. A case that was that hot and then went bitter cold for so long — Jesus, wouldn't it be satisfying to close that one?"

"As far as I can tell," I said, "he never got arrested for anything."

"He hasn't got a sheet? Hard to believe. He was running with Ellery, so he must have been pulling some of the same crap, but he never got tagged with it." He tapped the table with Ellery's scrolled confession. "If this is the way it went down, and there's no reason for Ellery to embroider it —"

"No, it figures to be straight."

"Then Steffens's ice-cold reaction was to kill the woman. And to force Ellery to fire one of the shots. Does that sound to you like the act of a man who never did this before?"

"Probably not his first kill."

"And we know it wasn't his last. But how many do you figure he ran up in between? It's how he solves problems. How many problems you figure he encountered over the years?"

That hung in the air. You couldn't answer it and it wouldn't go away. I said, "Do you see any way at all? To get him for anything?"

He thought about it. "No," he said. "No, I don't. And neither do you, and you couldn't have expected more. So why are we here, Matt? Why did you call me?"

"I figure he's not done."

"Not done killing? He'll never be done, if that's how he solves his problems. But you'd think he'd be out of problems for the time being. Who's left?"

"Well," I said, "there's always me."

XLIII

I GOT TO my regular meeting at St. Paul's that night, and it was good that I did, as I'd signed up a while back to speak for my anniversary. I sat down thinking I'd tell my story, the way I usually did, but I wound up starting with that last drink, the one I took but didn't take, the one I ordered and left on the bar. And I went on from there, and spent close to half an hour talking about the past year, my first year of sobriety.

It doesn't really matter what you say. One morning I'd gone to a meeting called Bookshop at Noon, on West Thirtieth Street. They introduced the speaker and he said his name and that he was an alcoholic, and then he just looked at the twenty or thirty of us who were waiting for him to say something. He smiled and said, "It's your meeting," and opened it up for discussion.

Nobody criticized him for shirking his duty, and in fact a couple of people complimented him on keeping it simple. Later I reported the incident to Jim, and we considered the possibilities—that he'd told his story so often recently that he couldn't face repeating himself, that he was a drama queen looking to do something memorable, or that he'd had a slip within the past three months and thus felt unqualified to lead a meeting, but wasn't ready to own up to it in public. We conjured up a few more scenarios, all of them plausible enough, and concluded that it didn't matter. The meeting had gone on, and it had done me no harm. I was still sober, wasn't I?

And I was still sober now, when the meeting began and when it ended.

"It's hard to know what to do," Dennis Redmond had said earlier. "There's not going to be any evidence, hard or soft. I'll go through the files, see if they ever even looked at him or Ellery in connection with Jane Street. Though I can't see what difference it would make. You know what you could do?"

"What?"

"What's he drink? Not Maker's Mark."

"Scotch. Johnnie Walker, I think it was. Why?"

"Get the brand right," he said, "and send him a bottle a day for the next year or two. As long as it takes."

"As long as what takes?"

"As long as it takes for him to become an alcoholic. Then he can join that club of yours, and he can climb up those famous steps, and when he writes out his confession we can fall on him like a ton of bricks."

"How'll we know?"

"You can be his rabbi, except that's not what you call it."

"His sponsor."

"Right on the tip of my tongue. His sponsor. You can be his sponsor, and you can rat him out. But a sponsor wouldn't do that, would he?"

"It's not part of the job description."

"I was afraid of that. Well, in that case I'm out of ideas. Of course we could put a wire on you, but that wouldn't work, would it?"

"He'd never say anything we could use."

"No, and even if he did it might not be admissible. You know he'll lawyer up the minute he gets pulled in for anything, and if he's hooked into the Jersey City machine he'll know what lawyer to call. Well, he got away with two murders for what, a dozen years? He's about to get away with two or three more. Can you live with that?"

"I guess I'll have to."

"And so will I. When you're on the job a few years you find out you can live with almost anything." His eyes narrowed. "But you resigned, didn't you? Had a gold shield and gave it back. So I guess you found something you couldn't live with."

"But it wasn't the job," I said. "I'd have told you it was at the time. That's what I thought. There's an element in a lot of stories you hear in AA, it's called a geographical solution. Guy moves to California because New York is the problem. Then he moves to Alaska because California's the problem. But he's the problem himself, and wherever he goes, there he is."

"So you were the problem." He thought about it. "Well, now you're Even Steven's problem, aren't you? And we know how he solves his problems, and geography hasn't got a lot to do with it. How are we gonna keep you alive?"

"I've been wondering that myself."

"I can't even offer you police protection at this stage, and that'd be a joke anyway, wouldn't it? We assign some cops to guard you, and they do, and nothing happens, and we reassign them, and you're right where you are now, because he's smart and he's patient. He can wait as long as he needs to. You have a gun?"

302 • LAWRENCE BLOCK

"No."

"If you had, you know, an unregistered weapon——"

"I don't."

"Well, if you should happen to get your hands on one, it might not be a bad idea to carry it. As a matter of fact..."

His voice trailed off. I looked at him, raised my eyebrows in anticipation.

"I want to keep this hypothetical, not that anybody but the two of us is gonna hear it. If someone's out to kill me, and I know it, and I also know there's not a damn thing I can do about it, well, then there's one thing I *can* do about it. If you get my drift."

"I'd thought of that myself."

"One thing you ought to know," he said, looking off to the side, "is if something happened to our friend, and if they were looking at you in connection with it, I wouldn't have any recollection of this conversation. In fact I wouldn't remember any of the conversations we had." His eyes met mine. "Just something for you to think about," he said.

I didn't have a gun, registered or not. Acquiring one didn't strike me as the most challenging task in the world, and I thought about it, but it wasn't something I wanted to do.

After the meeting, after an hour at the Flame, after some private time with Jim, I was back in my room with my thoughts for company. He was out there somewhere, and if his thoughts weren't of me, well, in a day or a week or a month they would be.

I was a problem for him. And I knew what solution he'd look for. When your only tool is a hammer, they say, then every problem looks like a nail.

I lay there in the darkness and wondered if I was afraid. I decided I was, but not of dying, not exactly. If I'd died a year ago, if I'd died drunk, that would have been as awful an ending as my life could have had. But I'd stayed sober for a year, and if I didn't feel like celebrating, that didn't mean I didn't cherish the accomplishment. And if I died now, well, nobody could take that away from me. Cold comfort, I suppose, but better than no comfort at all.

What I was afraid of, I realized, was that there was something I could do about this, and that I wouldn't be able to figure it out.

When I woke up the sun was shining and someone was playing the radio in the room next to mine. I couldn't make out the words, but the announcer's enthusiasm came through all the same. I showered and shaved and got dressed, and somewhere along the way my neighbor turned off his radio. The sun was still shining. I decided it wasn't a bad day, and that I knew how to spend it.

I wanted breakfast, but first I found Vann Steffens's card and dialed his number. I was surprised when he answered; I'd expected to get a machine and leave a message. He said hello, and I said, "You probably know who this is."

"I might."

"You bought me a drink the other day," I said, "and I never got the chance to thank you for it."

"I seem to recognize the voice," he said, "but I can't say I've got any idea what you're talking about."

"I don't always know myself. I think we should talk face-to-face."

"Oh?"

"To clear the air."

"Never a bad idea. Breathing's easier when the air's clear. And you probably think I got that from a fortune cookie, but I'm proud to say I made it up myself."

"I'm impressed."

"Which is not to say Confucius wouldn't have said it if he'd thought of it first. You want to meet? Where and when?"

We met at three in the afternoon in the Museum of Natural History. I got there early and waited beside the fossilized skeleton of a dinosaur, and he showed up right on time, wearing a suit and tie and carrying a topcoat over his arm. His glasses were steamed up, and he handed me the coat to hold while he cleaned the lenses with his pocket handkerchief.

The coat would have felt heavier, I decided, if there'd been a gun in the pocket. But I hadn't expected him to come armed. He'd suspect a trap, and if he brought a gun he might have to explain it to somebody.

He put his glasses on, blinked at me through them, and took his coat back. "Thanks," he said. He walked over to the nearest dinosaur and said, "Hi there, buddy. All these years and you haven't changed a bit."

"An old friend?"

"My daughter loved these guys," he said. "Don't ask me why. I'd bring her here every other Sunday to see the dinosaurs and the other divorced daddies. But that was a while ago."

"I guess she outgrew them."

"She would have," he said, "but her mother took her along to the Caribbean for a winter break. There's this island called Saba. You know it?"

I didn't.

"You get there by taking a small plane from another island. I forget which one. Saba's this volcanic island, so basically it's a mountain with a beach at the base of it, and every once in a while one of the small planes that go there crashes into the side of the mountain."

Was there something for me to say to that? I couldn't think what it might be.

"The divorce hadn't become final yet," he said, "so officially I'm a widower. With a dead kid too, but I don't think there's a word for that. And if you look at it a certain way it's heartbreaking, but you don't want to get all choked up about it. Because it was just about time for her to be getting too old for dinosaurs, and what was stretching ahead of us was a fucking lifetime of not having much of anything to say to each other. So she was spared that, and so was I."

"That's an interesting way to look at it."

"Is it? If you're wearing a wire, you can transcribe that touching little story and show it to the shrinks. God knows what they'll make of it."

"I'm not wearing a wire."

"No? Maybe you are and maybe you aren't, and if you were younger and better-looking I'd pat you down. If you were a girl, that is. Nothing queer about old Vann."

"That's reassuring."

"But what good would it do me? What would it prove? The cloak-and-dagger boys keep coming out with newer and better gadgets. Ballpoint pens with microphones in them, and just the other day I heard about a recording device the size of an aspirin tablet. You swallow it, and along with all the intestinal gurgles it picks up any conversation within a twenty-yard radius. Of course you wind up having to pick through your own crap, but those clowns are doing that metaphorically anyway, aren't they? Come on, let's get out of here. We can't really talk here, and they don't allow you to smoke. Like it's gonna bother the bronto-fucking-saurus."

XLIV

He lit up as soon as we were out the door. We crossed Central Park West and walked a few hundred yards into the park. Steffens considered three benches and rejected them all for unspecified reasons. Then he found one he liked and wiped the seat with the handkerchief he'd used earlier to clean his glasses. He sat down, and I sat beside him without bothering to wipe the seat.

"It's your meeting," he said. "Let's hear what you've got to say. I'm just gonna sit here and take it all in."

I took three sheets of paper from my jacket pocket, unfolded them, handed them to him.

I'd reached the age where reading was more comfortable with glasses, especially if the print was small or the light dim. Steffens was the opposite, he wore glasses all day long and took them off to read. He'd removed them when I handed him Jack's confession, and when he was done he didn't put them on again right away. Instead he sat looking off into the distance.

There were trees across the way, their leaves mostly gone now. *Bare ruined choirs,* a poet had written, but I couldn't remember his name or anything else from the poem.

He said, "This is a Xerox copy."

"That's right."

"There an original?"

"In a safe place. And there's another photocopy."

"In another safe place, I'll bet."

Bare ruined choirs, where late the sweet bird sang. That was the whole line, but what came before or after it, and who was it who'd written it?

I noticed that he'd put his glasses back on. For a moment I thought he was going to return Jack's account, but instead he folded the papers and put them in his pocket, then got a fresh cigarette going.

Bare ruined choirs. Was it *bird* or *birds?* It made sense either way. And was *sweet* right?

"You have to wonder," he said, "how much of it is true."

"Hard to say."

"Hard? Try impossible. The writing's good, though. I'd have to say that. The choice of words, I mean. The phrasing. The narrative flow. I'm not talking about the penmanship."

"I didn't think you were."

"Because outside of the nuns, who gives a rat's ass about penmanship? It has a flow to it. It's easy to follow. But you have to ask yourself, where does memory leave off and imagination take over?"

"That's always hard to know."

Birds, I decided. It had to be. If a single swallow didn't make a summer, then it certainly took more than one bird for a choir.

"This fellow he calls S. Does he even exist? He could be a figment of the writer's imagination."

"Could be."

"Suppose S stands for *self*? It's his own self that decides the woman has to die, because she's a witness. The whole thing with S. wrapping his hands around the writer's hands, that's a perfect example of a psychotic break. The guy becomes two people at once, and the bad part makes the good part do something he's ashamed of."

Bare ruined choirs. Was it Keats? I'd have to look it up in *Bartlett's Familiar Quotations.* Two minutes with *Bartlett's* and I'd know the poet and the poem, and then I'd spend another two hours skipping around, reading no end of other fragments that I'd half remember on other occasions.

Jan had a copy of *Bartlett's,* and sometimes I'd turn to it when she was busy in the kitchen, or fitting in a little work on the current sculpture-in-progress.

Maybe I'd go to the Strand and pick up a copy of my own. That was probably simpler than searching for another girlfriend who already had the book on her shelf.

"But if there is an S.," he said, "he doesn't strike me as a guy with a whole lot to worry about. It might be different if the writer was around to back up what he wrote, but the document all by itself, well, I don't see it as enough to put a man in jail, do you?"

"No," I said. "But that's if the document's all by itself, and it isn't."

"Oh?"

"There's what you might call an interpretation. A few pages identifying Mr. S. and telling us what else he's been up to since those days."

"Written by somebody else."

I nodded.

"Handwritten? Copies made?"

"The penmanship's not as nice as in the specimen you saw," I said. "But as you said, who cares about penmanship?"

"Only the nuns."

"Right."

"And damn few of them. Still, you say the penmanship's not so hot, and the content has to be mostly conjecture. If the writer could prove it, he wouldn't have to go through all this crap."

"And S. would be in a cell in the Tombs."

"Assuming there's an S."

"Right."

He lit another cigarette, smoked for a few minutes, blew the smoke at the trees across the way. Maybe he had the same line rattling around in his head. *Bare ruined choirs.* Maybe he knew the rest of the poem, and the name of the poet. Who knows what's going on in somebody else's head?

"What do you want, Matt?"

"To go on living."

"So? Who's gonna stop you?"

"S. might try."

"And if he did, those two documents, similar in theme but differing in penmanship, would find their way to parties who might take an official interest. Does that sound about right?"

"It does."

"But if nothing happens to you—"

"Then nothing happens with the documents, and S. gets to go on living his life."

"It's not a bad life."

"Neither is mine."

"That's all fine," he said, "but nobody lives forever."

"I've heard that."

"I'm not wishing it on you, God knows, but you could die of natural causes."

"I hope to, eventually."

"And if that should happen—"

"It'd be exactly the same as if somebody shot me in the mouth and the forehead," I said. "The two documents would get delivered. But the odds are you'd have nothing to worry about by then."

"How do you figure that?"

"Well, you're three years older than I am. You're carrying more weight, and how much do you smoke? Three packs a day?"

He'd just taken a cigarette from his pack, and he put it back. "I've been thinking about cutting down."

"Ever try cutting down in the past?"

"Maybe a couple of times."

"Have much luck with it?"

He returned the pack to his pocket. "You never know," he said. "What's your point exactly?"

"You're overweight and you smoke. You drink, too."

"Not that much."

"A lot more than I do. What's my point? My point is you'll probably die before I do, in which case you've got nothing to worry about. And if you wind up outliving me, well, that'll be time enough to worry about some charges that nobody could make stand up in court anyway."

"Jesus," he said, and frowned. "What happens if you start drinking again?"

"It would be better for both of us," I said, "if I don't. So the next time you get the urge to pick up a bottle or two of Maker's Mark, make sure you drink it yourself."

"I knew that fucking bourbon was a bad idea. I got carried

away with the beauty of it all. You know, you walk in, there's the glass, there's the bottle. I figured it would have an impact."

"Well, you were right about that."

"What effect did it have? Were you tempted?"

"You have any fear of heights?"

"Heights? What the hell has that got to do with anything?"

"I just wondered."

"I don't mind airplanes. I'm closed in, I've got nothing to worry about. But, like, being out on a ledge, or near a cliff—"

"That's different?"

"Very."

"I'm the same way. You know what the fear is? That I'll want to jump. I don't want to jump, but I'm afraid I'll suddenly get the urge."

He took this in, nodded.

"I didn't want to drink. But it was there, and I was afraid that I would want to. That I'd be struck by an impulse I couldn't resist."

"But you weren't."

"No."

"As I said, the minute I got out of there and thought about it I knew it was a bad idea. But we're both here, aren't we? We both survived. You know, the Mexicans have a word for it."

"Oh?"

"For our situation. But I don't know how you say it in English. The fucking Mexicans would call it *un standoff.*"

He took out his pack of cigarettes, shook one loose, put it between his lips. "Fuck cutting down," he said. "Why would I want to do that?"

When I told Jim about it he took it all in and thought it over and said, "Then it's over."

"It looks that way."

"You don't have to worry about this fellow anymore? You've left him with no reason to kill you?"

"And every reason not to."

"So it all works out."

"I suppose it does," I said, "if you overlook the fact that the son of a bitch killed five of his fellow citizens and gets away with it."

"If anybody ever gets away with anything."

"I don't think his conscience will be troubling him. I don't think he has one. But I suppose there's always karma."

"So they say." He reached for the teapot, refilled both our cups. "Jasmine," he said. "The first sip's a nice surprise, and by the third cup you wish they'd just give you the usual green tea. Matt, whatever keeps this guy at a distance looks good to me. I just hope you're satisfied with how it turned out."

"Satisfied," I said. "I'd like it better if he went away for it. Or if he made a move and got killed trying. But I guess I'm satisfied. And that reminds me."

"Oh?"

"I've been thinking about it," I said, "and I think the Buddha's full of crap. It is our dissatisfaction with what is that separates us from the beasts of the field."

"And when did this revelation come to you?"

"While I was shaving."

"You nicked yourself and —"

"No, that's just it. I didn't nick myself. Because the razor's this new twin-blade number that shaves you closer and smoother. It's like some sort of tag team, one blade holds the whisker down while the other cuts it."

"You sound like a commercial."

"And I have to say it was better than the last razor I had, and that was better than the one before. And I thought about watching my father shave. He used a safety razor, though it must have been a fairly primitive one. But *his* father would have used a straight razor. And why do you suppose the razors keep getting better every couple of years? And the cars, and all the other little conveniences of modern life?"

"I'm sure you'll tell me."

"Dissatisfaction," I said. "Every once in a while somebody throws his razor down in the middle of a shave and says there's got to be a better way. And he looks for it and finds it."

"So dissatisfaction turns out to be the mother of invention. And here I always thought it was necessity."

I shook my head. "Nobody *needs* a double-bladed razor. Nobody *needs* to go sixty miles an hour in a car, or fly through the air in a plane."

"There's probably something wrong with your reasoning," he said, "but I'm not dissatisfied enough to figure out what it is. But the next time I run into the Buddha, I'll set him straight."

"Well, if you're looking for him," I said, "you'll generally find him at the midnight meeting at the Moravian church."

Early One Morning...

"A Mexican standoff," Mick Ballou said. "I've often wondered why they call it that. Have you any idea?"

"No."

"If Kristin were here," he said, "she'd take out her iPhone and consult her Google and provide a full explanation in the wink of an eye. The world is a strange place and growing stranger by the day. There was no Google twenty-five years ago, and no iPhones either. But men have always told stories, and that was a good one. Did he ever make trouble again?"

"Steffens? As far as I know, he stayed on his side of the river. There was a state or federal task force that took on the courthouse gang in Hudson County, and a batch of Jersey City politicians went to jail, but I didn't see his name in the papers. Then sometime after that, it must have been a dozen years ago, I got an unsigned card one Christmas. Santa Claus looking down at a plate of milk and cookies and *taking a belt from a hip flask. It had a Jersey postmark, and I had the feeling it might have been from him."*

"Is he still alive?"

I shook my head. "He's been gone, oh, getting on for ten years now. A one-car accident on the Garden State. Three o'clock in the morning, and he hit a bridge abutment head-on at something like seventy miles an hour. No skid marks, so he never tried to stop. And he went through the windshield, so he couldn't have been wearing a seat belt."

"Suicide, do you suppose?"

"Be hard to rule it out. He'd had emphysema for a couple of years, and had recently been diagnosed with lung cancer. He would have had a gun around the house, and he certainly knew how to use it, but maybe he just went for a ride and made his move on the spur of the moment. Put the gas pedal down, take a hard left, and let the cops clean up after you."

Somewhere along the way he'd returned his bottle to the back bar and came back with a liter of Evian water. And there we sat, two old men up past our bedtime, talking and drinking water.

"You think 'twill come out even," he said. "With the ends trimmed, and tied in a bow. The murderer found out, and dealt with in a satisfying manner."

"Like a television program."

"Even there," he said, "they'll surprise you now and again. The villain goes free. But your man was found out, wasn't he? Do you suppose he had occasion to kill anyone else? In Jersey City?"

"No way to know."

"And who's to say we're not better off in our ignorance? What dark things did he do in the years after he killed the man and woman in the Village? He moved across the river and found a new life in politics, but did he have a use for the gun in that new life?"

"We'll never know," I said, "but when the time came to pick it up he remembered how to use it."

He drank some water. "All those years," he said. "Where do they go?"

"Might as well ask where they come from."

"But we never question that, do we? Tomorrow's always there, just over the horizon. Until the tomorrows run out. The people you spoke about, some of them are gone."

"Yes."

"Jim Faber. Shot dead, wasn't he?"

"By a man who mistook him for me."

"Oh, that was a bad time. There were a lot killed in this very room around that time."

"There were."

"Did you blame yourself for his death?"

"Probably. What helped was his voice in my head, telling me to cut the crap."

"Ah. The woman, the one who cut her auburn hair. Did the two of you ever get together again?"

"Twice, maybe three times. After Jan and I were finally done with each other, and before I reconnected with Elaine. Donna and I would get to talking, and there'd be a current in the air, and we'd wind up in her canopy bed for an hour or two. Then she got married and moved away, and I think I heard that she got divorced."

"And Jan is gone."

"Yes."

"I remember she wanted you to get her a gun. Did she ever use it?"

"No," I said. "She let the cancer run its course. But she found it a comfort to have the gun, in case she decided to take that way out."

"You were the one she turned to. But you'd long since broken things off."

"She brought me my clothes," I said, "and I gave her back my set of keys, but it turned out we weren't quite done with each other. That took a while longer. We really cared for each other, so we kept trying to make it work, until it was just too obvious that it wouldn't."

"Ah."

"Who else? I got together with Dennis Redmond now and then, for a meal or a cup of coffee. I called him a couple of times when I had a case I thought he might be able to help me with. But then we lost track of each other. I figure he must be retired by now."

"Like the other one."

"Joe Durkin. We became close over the years, but he was on the job and I wasn't, and that puts a limit on just how close you can get. He's working security for a Wall Street firm now, and between that and his city pension he's doing okay."

"But you don't see much of him."

"Not too much, no. That bar Redmond liked, the Minstrel Boy? Last time I looked it was gone."

"Places come and go."

"They do, and the leaves fall from the trees. Bare ruined choirs — that was Shakespeare's line, from one of the sonnets."

"Ah."

"I don't know where I got the idea it was Keats. Jimmy Armstrong's dead. He lost his lease and moved a block west, and then he died, and somebody else took over and changed the name. The new place had a dish I liked, an Irish breakfast they served at all hours, but then they changed the menu, so that's gone too. Theresa's is gone, in case you were hoping for a piece of strawberry-rhubarb pie. Same with Dukacs and Son. There's a chain drugstore filling the space where both of them used to be, Duane Reade or CVC, I forget which. I don't know what became of Frankie Dukacs, whether he died or just lost his lease."

"He moved to Nova Scotia," he suggested, "and became a vegetarian."

"*I suppose it could happen. After Billie Keegan quit tending bar for Jimmy, he moved to California and started making candles. And Motorcycle Mark married a Gujarati girl from Jackson Heights and moved somewhere upstate. Putnam County, I think it was, and the two of them are running a day-care center. He stayed sober, he shows up at St. Paul's every couple of months. He's still got the Harley, but these days his regular ride is an SUV.*"

"*And the other one with the bike?*"

"*The other — oh, Scooter Williams? Last I heard, he was still living on Ludlow Street and enjoying the sixties. It's become a very desirable neighborhood now, believe it or not. Piper MacLeish got out of prison a couple of years ago. They let him out early, sent him home to die. No idea if Crosby Hart is alive or dead, but Google could probably find him, after it tells us why they call it a Mexican standoff. What else? Tiffany's has been gone for years. The coffee shop on Sheridan Square, not the jewelry store. That'll be doing just fine as long as there are Japanese tourists to shop there.*"

"*And the Museum of Natural History? Where you met with himself? It's still in business, is it not?*"

"*Last I checked. Why?*"

"*Because,*" he said, "*there ought to be a place for a couple of old dinosaurs.*" And he picked up his glass. There was nothing in it but water, but all the same he held it aloft and gazed through it at the light.

ABOUT THE AUTHOR

Lawrence Block published his first novel in 1958 and has been chronicling the adventures of Matthew Scudder since 1975. He has been designated a Grand Master by the Mystery Writers of America, and has received Lifetime Achievement awards from the Crime Writers' Association (UK), the Private Eye Writers of America, and the Short Mystery Fiction Society. He has won the Nero, Philip Marlowe, Societe 813, and Anthony awards, and is a multiple recipient of the Edgar, the Shamus, and the Japanese Maltese Falcon awards. He and his wife, Lynne, are devout New Yorkers and relentless world travelers.

...AND HIS NEXT NOVEL

In February 2013 Mulholland Books will publish *Hit Me*, Lawrence Block's next book in the Keller series. Following is an excerpt from the novel's opening pages.

T HE YOUNG MAN, who would have looked owlish even without the round eyeglasses, unfolded a piece of paper and laid
it on the counter in front of Keller. "The certificate of expertiza-
tion for Obock J1," he said. "Signed by Bloch and Mueller."

He might have been a Red Sox fan invoking Ted Williams,
and Keller could understand why. Herbert Bloch and Edwin
Mueller were legendary philatelists, and their assertion that this
particular stamp was indeed a genuine copy of Obock's first
postage-due stamp, designated J1 in the Scott catalog, was
enough to allay all doubt.

Keller examined the stamp, first with his unaided eye, then
through the magnifier he took from his breast pocket. There was
a photograph of the stamp on the certificate, and he studied that
as well, with and without magnification. Bloch and Mueller had
sworn to its legitimacy in 1960, so the certificate itself was almost
half a century old, and might well be collectible in and of itself.

Still, even experts were sometimes careless, and occasionally mistaken. And now and then someone switched in a ringer for an expertized stamp. So Keller reached for another tool, this one in the inside pocket of his jacket. It was a flat metal oblong, designed to enable the user to compute the number of perforations per inch on the top or side of a stamp. Obock J1 was imperforate, which rendered the question moot, but the perforation gauge doubled as a miniruler, marked out in inches along one edge and millimeters along the other, and Keller used it to check the size of the stamp's overprint.

That overprint, hand-stamped on a postage-due stamp initially issued for the French Colonies as a whole, had the name of the place—Obock—in black capitals. On the original stamp, the overprint measured 12½ millimeters by 3¾ millimeters. On the reprint, a copy of which reposed in Keller's own collection, each dimension of the overprint was half a millimeter smaller.

And so Keller measured the overprint on this stamp, and found himself in agreement with Mr. Bloch and Mr. Mueller. This was the straight goods, the genuine article. All he had to do to go home with it was outbid any other interested collectors. And he could do that, too, and without straining his budget or dipping into his capital.

But first he'd have to kill somebody.

The Dallas-based firm of Whistler & Welles conducted auctions of collectibles throughout the year. At various times they sold coins, books, autographs, and sports memorabilia, but the partners had started out as stamp dealers, and philatelic holdings remained the largest component of their business. Their annual Spring Equinox sale, held each year in the Hotel Lombardy on the third weekend in March, was one Keller had wanted to attend for years. Something had always prevented him from going. He'd marked up copies of their catalogs over the years, sent in unsuccessful mail bids on a few occasions, and one year had a hotel room reserved and a flight booked before something or other came up and forced him to cancel.

He'd lived in New York when Whistler & Welles put him on their mailing list. Nowadays he lived in New Orleans, and the name on their mailing list was one he'd borrowed from a local tombstone. He was Nicholas Edwards now, and that was the name on his passport, and on all the cards in his wallet. He lived in a big old house in the Lower Garden District, and he had a wife and a baby daughter, and he was a partner in a construction firm specializing in purchasing and rehabilitating distressed properties.

A year earlier, he'd looked with longing at the Whistler & Welles catalog. Dallas was a lot closer to New Orleans than to New York, but he and Donny Wallings were putting in twelve-hour days and seven-day weeks, just trying to keep up with everything they had going on.

But that was a year ago, before the collapse of the subprime mortgage market and everything that followed on its heels. Credit dried up, houses stopped selling, and they'd gone from more business than they could handle to no business to speak of.

So he could afford the time. A couple of days in Dallas? Sure, why not? He could even take his time and drive to Dallas and back.

And there were plenty of stamps on offer that he'd be eager to add to his collection, with Obock J1 at the very top of his wish list.

Now, though, he couldn't afford it.

The Lombardy, an independent locally owned older hotel trying to survive in a world of modern chains, was starting to show its age. The carpet in Keller's room, while not yet threadbare, was due for replacement. A sofa in the lobby was worn on the arms, and the wood paneling in one of the elevators needed touching up. None of this bothered Keller, who found the hotel's faded glory somehow reassuring. What better venue for men of a certain age to compete for little pieces of paper that had done their duty carrying the mail long before any of them were born?

Whistler & Welles had booked a large conference room on the mezzanine for their three-day sale, which would begin promptly at nine Friday morning. New Orleans and Dallas were a little over five hundred miles apart, and Keller drove most of the way Wednesday, stopping for the night at a Red Roof Inn at a handy exit from the interstate. He checked into his room at the Lombardy a little after noon, and by one o'clock he was signing Nicholas Edwards on the bidder register and walking over to the long table where they were showing the auction lots.

By two thirty he'd had a look at all the lots that interested him, and had made cryptic notes in his auction catalog. Every sales lot was illustrated with a color photograph, so he didn't absolutely have to see them up close and personal, but sometimes you got something that way that you couldn't get from a photo in a catalog. Some stamps reached out to you while others put you off, and it probably didn't make any real sense, but the whole hobby was wacky enough to begin with. I mean, spending a fortune on little pieces of colored paper? Picking them up with tongs, putting them in plastic mounts, and securing them in albums? Why, for heaven's sake?

Keller had long since come to terms with the essential absurdity of the pastime, and didn't let it bother him. He was a stamp collector, he derived enormous satisfaction from the pursuit, and that was all he needed to know. If you thought about it, just about everything human beings did was pointless and ridiculous. Golf? Skiing? Sex?

Upstairs in his room, Keller reviewed the notes he'd made. There were stamps he'd initially considered and now decided to pass on, others he might buy if the price was right, and a few where he'd be bidding competitively. And there was Obock J1. It was rare, it didn't come up that often, and this particular specimen was a nice one, with four full margins. Imperforate stamps had to be cut apart, and sometimes a careless clerk snipped off a bit of the stamp in the process. That didn't keep a letter from reaching its designated recipient, but it made the stamp considerably less desirable to a collector.

According to the Scott catalog, Obock J1 was worth $7,000. In their catalog, Whistler & Welles had estimated the lot conservatively at $6,500. The actual price, Keller knew, would depend on the bidders, those in the room and those participating by mail or phone, or via the Internet, and the hammer price wouldn't tell the whole story; to that you'd have to add a 15 percent bidder's premium and whatever sales tax the state of Texas saw fit to pile on. Keller, who wanted the stamp more than ever now that he'd had a look at it, figured he might have to bid $12,000 to get it, and the check he'd write out would be uncomfortably close to $15,000.

Would he go that high?

Well, that's why they had auctions, and why bidders showed up in person. You sat in your chair, and you'd decided in advance just how high you'd go and when you'd drop out, and then they got to the lot you were waiting for and you discovered how you really felt. Maybe you did exactly what you planned on doing, but maybe not. Maybe you found out your enthusiasm wasn't as great as you'd thought, and wound up dropping out of the bidding early on. Or maybe you found yourself hanging in far beyond your predetermined limit, spending considerably more than your maximum.

No way to guess how it would be this time. It was Thursday, and tomorrow's morning and afternoon sessions would both be devoted to U.S. issues, and thus of no interest to Keller. He wouldn't need to be in the auction room until Saturday morning, and the French Colonial issues, including Obock J1, wouldn't come up until early Saturday afternoon.

He went downstairs, walked outside. It was cool, but not unpleasantly so. Football weather, you'd call it, if the calendar didn't insist that it was March. Cool, crisp—a perfect October day.

He walked a couple of blocks to another hotel, where there was a queue of waiting cabs. He went to the first one in line, settled into the backseat, and told the driver to take him to the airport.

He'd been working on his stamps when the phone rang. He was alone in the house, Julia had left to pick up Jenny at day care, and he almost let the machine answer it because calls were almost invariably for Julia. But there was always a chance it was Donny, so he went and picked it up half a ring ahead of the machine, and it turned out to be Dot.

Not that she bothered to identify herself. Without preamble she said, "Remember that cell phone you had?" And she broke the connection before he could respond.

He remembered the phone, an untraceable prepaid one, and even remembered where he'd left it, in his sock drawer. The battery had long since run down, and while it was charging Julia and Jenny came home, so it was a good half hour before he was back in his den with the phone.

For years he'd lived in New York, a few blocks from the United Nations, and Dot had lived north of the city in White Plains, in a big old house with a wraparound porch. That house was gone now, burned to the ground, and the same wind that had blown him to New Orleans had picked up Dot and deposited her in Sedona, Arizona. Her name was Wilma Corder now, even as his was Nicholas Edwards, and she had a new life of her own. Back in the day she had arranged the contract killings he had performed, but that was then and this was now.

Even so, he closed the door before he made the call.

"I'll just plunge right in," she said. "I'm back in business."

"And the business is—"

"Holding its own. Not booming, but a long way from flatlining, which seems to be what everybody else's business is doing."

"What I meant—"

"I know what you meant. You want to know what business I'm in, but do you have to ask? Same old."

"Oh."

"You're surprised? You're not the only one. See, there's this thing I joined, Athena International."

"It sounds like an insurance company."

"It does? It's what they call a service club, like Rotary or Kiwanis. Except it's exclusively for women."

"Can't women join Rotary?"

"Of course, because it would be sexist to keep them out. But men can't join Athena."

"That doesn't seem fair."

"Keller, if it bothers you, you can put on a dress and a wig and I'll drag you along to a meeting. If you're still awake at the end of it I'll buy you a pair of high heels."

"But you enjoy it."

"The hell I do. I must have been brain-dead when I joined.

We do things like pick up trash once a month around Bell Rock, and I approve of that, since I've got a view of the damned thing from my bedroom window, and it looks better without the beer bottles and gum wrappers. I'm not crazy about walking around in the hot sun hunting for other people's garbage, but I go once in a while. And we raise money to give some deserving girl a scholarship to college, and if I'm not out there running a table at the bake sale, or God forbid baking something, at least I'll write out a check. But I mostly pass on the monthly meetings. I've never been a meeting person. Endless talking, and then the damn song."

"What song?"

"The Athenian song, and no, I'm not about to sing it for you. But that's how we close the meeting. We all stand in a circle and cross our arms over our chests and clasp hands and sing this Mickey Mouse song."

"Minnie Mouse," he suggested.

"I stand corrected. The thing is, most of the members have careers of one sort or another, and we don't just pick up garbage. We network, which means we take in each other's laundry."

"Huh?"

"Beth's a travel agent, Alison's a Realtor, Lindsay does Tupperware parties."

"So you've been buying Tupperware," he suggested. "And houses."

"No houses. But when I went to Hawaii for a week I let Beth make the booking," she said, "and one of our members is a lawyer, and when I need a lawyer she's the one I go to. And of course I bought the Tupperware. You go to the party, you buy the Tupperware."

"And drink the Kool-Aid. I'm sorry, go on."

"Anyway," she said, "there they all were with their careers, and there I was, with all the money I needed, and it couldn't help me from feeling time was passing me by."

"That's what time does."

"I know. But I couldn't shake the feeling that I ought to be doing something. But what? Volunteer at a hospital? Help out at a soup kitchen?"

"Doesn't sound like you."

"So I picked up the phone," she said, "and made a few calls."

"How'd that go? I mean, officially, aren't you dead?"

"As a doornail," she agreed. "Shot in the head and burned up in a fire. You google Dorothea Harbison and that's what you'll find out. But the people who would call me to arrange a booking, they never heard of Dorothea Harbison. A few of them knew me as Dot, but most of them didn't even have that much. I was a phone number, and a voice on the phone, and a mail drop where they sent payments. And that was as much as anybody needed to know."

"And how much did you know about them?"

"My customers? Next to nothing. But I did have a couple of phone numbers."

And one day she drove to Flagstaff and rented a private mail-box at a franchise operation on South Milton Road, a block from the Embassy Suites Hotel. On her way home she picked up a prepaid and presumably untraceable phone, and over the next few days she made a couple of calls. "I wondered what happened to you," the first man said. "I tried your number, but it was disconnected."

"I got married," she told him, "and don't bother congratulating me, because it didn't work out."

"That was quick."

"For you, maybe. You weren't there. Long and short, I'm here for you when you need me. Let me give you the number."

She had other numbers, too, of men who'd done what Keller used to do. Not all of those numbers worked anymore, but she was able to reestablish a contact or two, and one fellow said he could really use the work. Then she sat back and waited for something to happen, not entirely sure she wanted her new phone to ring, but it did, and within the week.

"And here's something interesting, Keller. The call was from someone I hadn't called myself, someone I hadn't even worked with before. One of my old clients passed the word, and here was this guy calling me out of the blue, with a piece of work to be done in the great state of Georgia. So I called the guy who'd told me how he needed work, and he couldn't believe I was getting back to him so quick. And I sat back and got paid."

Like old times, Keller suggested, and she agreed. "I'm still me," she said. "I'm a rich lady, and I look better than I used to. I moved to Sedona and the pounds started to drop off right away. The place is crawling with energy vortexes, except I think the plural is vortices."

"What are they?"

"Beats me, Keller. I think it's something like an intersection, except the streets are imaginary. Anyway, some of the women I know are fat as pigs, and they've got the same vortices I do. I belong to a gym, can you believe it?"

"You told me."

"And I've got a personal trainer. Did I tell you that, too? His name is Scott, and I sometimes get the feeling he'd like to get a little more personal, but I'm probably wrong about that. It's not as though I turned into whistle bait, and what would he want with a woman old enough to use a term like that? Whistle bait, for God's sake."

"I guess people don't say that anymore."

"They don't whistle much, either. Look, this is a mistake, isn't it? I shouldn't have called."

"Well."

"For God's sake, you've got your life to live. You've got a beautiful wife and an amazing daughter and you're the Rehab King of New Orleans real estate. So why don't you just wish me luck in my new venture and hang up, and I'll leave you alone."

Keller limited himself to monosyllables en route to the airport, and gave the driver a tip neither large nor small enough to be memorable. He walked through the door for departing flights, took an escalator one flight down, and a bubbly girl at the Hertz counter found his reservation right away. He showed her a driver's license and a credit card, both in the same name, and one that was neither J. P. Keller nor Nicholas Edwards. They were good enough to get him the keys to a green Subaru hatchback, and in due course he was behind the wheel and on his way.

The house he was looking for was on Caruth Boulevard, in the University Park section. He'd located it online and printed out a map, and he found it now with no trouble, one of a whole block of upscale Spanish-style homes on substantial landscaped lots not far from the Southern Methodist campus. Sculpted stucco walls, a red tile roof, an attached three-car garage. You'd think a family could be very happy in a house like that, Keller thought, but in the present instance you'd be wrong, because the place was home to Charles and Portia Walmsley, and neither of them could be happy until the other was dead.

Keller slowed down as he passed the house, then circled the block for another look at it. Was anyone at home? As far as he could see, there was no way to tell. Charles Walmsley had moved out a few weeks earlier, and Portia shared the house with the

Salvadoran housekeeper. Keller hadn't learned the housekeeper's name, or that of the man who was a frequent overnight guest of Mrs. Walmsley, but he'd been told that the man drove a Lexus SUV. Keller didn't see it in the driveway, but he couldn't be sure it wasn't in the garage.

"The man drives an SUV," Dot had said, "and he once played football for TCU. I know what an SUV is, but—"

"Texas Christian University," Keller supplied. "In Fort Worth."

"I thought that might be it. Do they have something to do with horny frogs?"

"Horned frogs. That's their football team, the horned frogs. They're archrivals of SMU."

"That would be Southern Methodist."

"Right. They're the Mustangs."

"Frogs and Mustangs. How do you know all this crap, Keller? Don't tell me it's on a stamp. Never mind, it's not important. What's important is that something permanent happens to Mrs. Walmsley. And it would be good if something happened to the boyfriend, too."

"It would?"

"He'll pay a bonus."

"A bonus? What kind of a bonus?"

"Unspecified, which makes it tricky to know what to expect, let alone collect it. And he'll double the bonus if they nail the boyfriend for the wife's murder, but when you double an unspecified number, what have you got? Two times what?"

Keller drove past the Walmsley house a second time, and didn't learn anything new in the process. He consulted his map, figured out his route, and left the Subaru in a parking garage three blocks from the Lombardy.

In his room, he picked up the phone to call Julia, then remembered what hotels charged you for phone calls. Charles Walmsley was paying top dollar, bonus or no, but making a call from a hotel room was like burning the money in the street. He used his cell phone instead, first making sure that it was the iPhone Julia had given him for his birthday and not the prepaid one he used only for calls to Dot.

The hotel room was okay, he told her. And he'd had a good look at the stamps he was interested in, and that was always helpful. And she put Jenny on, and he cooed to his daughter and she babbled at him. He told her he loved her, and when Julia came back on the phone he told her the same.

Portia Walmsley didn't have any children. Her husband did, from a previous marriage, but they lived with their mother across the Red River in Oklahoma. So there wouldn't be any kids to worry about in the house on Caruth Boulevard.

As far as the Salvadoran maid was concerned, Dot had told him the client didn't care one way or the other. He wasn't paying a bonus for her, that was for sure. He'd pointed out that she was an illegal immigrant, and Keller wondered what that had to do with anything.

That first night, he hadn't called Dot back right away. First he and Julia had tucked Jenny in for the night—or for as much of it as the child would sleep through. Then the two of them sat over coffee in the kitchen, and he mentioned that Donny had called earlier, not because some work had come in but on the chance that he might want to go fishing.

"But you didn't want to go?"

He shook his head. "Neither did Donny, not really. He just wanted to pick up the phone."

"It's hard for him, isn't it?"

"He's not used to sitting around."

"Neither are you, these days. But I guess it must be like old times for you. You know, with lots of time off between jobs."

"Stamp collecting helped take up the slack."

"And I guess it still does," she said, "and that way there's no fish to clean."

He went upstairs and sat down with his stamps for a few minutes, then made the call. "So you're back in business," he said. "And you didn't call me, and then you did."

"And I guess it was a mistake," she said, "and I apologize. But how could I be in the business and not let you know about it? That didn't seem right."

"No."

"And it's not like you're a recovering alcoholic and I'm opening wine bottles in front of you. You're a grown-up. If you're not interested you'll tell me so and that's the end of it. Keller? You still there?"

"I'm here."

"So you are," she said. "And yet you haven't told me you're not interested."

One of his stamp albums was open on the table in front of him, and he looked at a page of Italian stamps overprinted for use in the Aegean Islands. There were a few stamps missing, and while they weren't at all expensive they'd proved difficult to find.

"Keller?"

"Business dried up," he said. "There's no financing. We can't buy houses and we can't sell them, and nobody's hiring us to repair them, either, because there's no money around."

"Well, I'm not surprised. It's the same everywhere. Still, you've got enough money to see you through, haven't you?"

"We're all right," he said. "But I've gotten used to living on what I earn, and now I'm dipping into capital. I'm not about to run through it, there's no danger of that, but still..."

"I know what you mean. Keller, I've got something if you want it. I had a guy lined up for it and I just learned he's in the hospital, he flipped his car and they had to yank him out of there with the Jaws of Death."

"Isn't it the Jaws of Life?"

"Whatever. His own jaw is about the only part of him that didn't get broken. I guess he'll live, and he may even walk again, but there's no way he can get it all together by the end of the month and spare my client the agony of divorce."

"And the heartbreak of community property."

"Something like that. It has to happen before the first of April, and either I find somebody who can take care of it or I have to send back the money. You probably remember how much I like doing that."

"Vividly."

"Once I have it in hand," she said, "I think of it as my money, and I hate like the devil to part with it. So what do you think? Can you get away for a few days in the next couple of weeks?"

"My calendar's wide open," he said. "All I've got is a stamp auction I was thinking about going to. That's the weekend after next, if I go at all."

"Where is it?"

"Dallas."

There was a thoughtful silence. "Keller," she said at length, "call me crazy, but I see the hand of Providence at work here."

MULHOLLAND BOOKS

You won't be able to put down these Mulholland books.